To my mother, who taught me how to be a hero.
And to the ones who taught me how to cherish myself.
I love all of you.

THE

GIFTED

Prologue

Here, I have been, surpassing twenty eons, waiting and waiting for even the smallest glimmer to call to me.

Yet, nothing changes.

The darkness twists in all directions, sinking its talons into my flesh as I idle upon this frail cliffside, this piece of me that will shatter at the mere drop of a pebble.

I'm . . . I'm so cold.

Fangs like ice drag along my veins, slicing through the surface to let the blood leak. Numb from head to toe. Not even a moment to collect myself, to carry my mind to that safe space,

because the safe space is here,

in this domain of emptiness that flaunts the noose,

that taunts me with the promise of ascension.

But you can't help the things you long for.

So, in the end, I merely suffer, the fragments of my happiness withering away. And as I gaze ahead, as I look deep into that abyss before me, I'm reminded that this is the only path, the only foundation which my reality will keep its integrity.

They assure me so, those grotesque hands peeking through the blackness below. They remind me of my place in this broken, wondrous world.

Worthless.

Alone.

Waste of space.

Sometimes, I become just a little brave. I study the space above me, confident that a beacon of brilliance will erupt and carry me forth.

The more I look, however, the denser the shadows breathe, until I come to believe that I've gone blind.

No,

it's just me here,

wallowing in this nightmare of no end, this fiction that evil itself would not dare describe.

It's just me here,

clawing at these merciless manacles.

Always,

it'll just be me here.

* * *

Darkness—that was what furnished the ruined hallway.

Only a single source of light could be admired: the glow of the moon, shining daintily through the gaping hole in the ceiling. Chunks of debris, large and tiny, littered the cracked tiled floor while injured lockers stood on the sides, their bodies marred by jagged indentations. Some even had scarlet liquid splattered against their faces as particles of dust fluttered amidst the silent air like lightless fireflies.

Yet, despite the damages no mere man could accomplish, the area knew nothing of desolation, housing a single character nestled between two lockers. His back against the wall, he wrapped his arms tightly around his knees.

A young boy, he was, appearing to be six to seven years old. His frame thin, he had cuts and scratches decorating his coffee-colored skin, pairing oddly well with the buzzcut atop his head; black like ink, much like his rich yet hollow irises. To shield them, a pair of rectangular glasses rested upon the ridge of his nose, the frames shaded like the wings of a crow. His clothing consisted of a red tank top, basketball shorts, ankle socks, and red sneakers.

His expression hinted that he had just witnessed a genocide.

He let loose a sigh, hugging his knees closer to his chest.

"Every time," he whispered.

Suddenly, featherweight footsteps arose at the hallway's end, and it took only seconds for the eyes of a little girl to emerge, peering around the corner.

She studied the area, becoming satisfied only when her sights fell upon the little boy.

The little girl then smiled.

"There he is."

She stepped into view to amble towards her target.

Much like he of the wounds, this girl's body leaned towards miniature, her muscles nonexistent and her height even lesser. Ergo, she could be seen as another first grader. She had smooth, light skin and silky, raven-like hair that plummeted to her shoulders, matching well with the breathtaking blue that flooded her irises, purer than any ocean. Her outfit consisted of a black blouse with white polka dots, white ankle socks, and dark tap-dance shoes. A silver necklace looped around her neck, complete with a pink, heart-shaped gem hanging from the center.

The girl paused once she reached the boy.

"Jeremy?" she asked, looking down at him. "Are you okay?"

No answer.

The girl leaned forward to lay her hand on his shoulder.

"It's okay," she said. "I know you didn't mean to."

"It's not okay," the boy argued. "I'm a monster."

The girl's voice softened. "You're not a monster. You're the bestest friend I've ever had, and my best friend is nowhere near a monster."

At last, the fractured boy found the courage to lift his head, revealing the tears dribbling down his cheeks.

"I'm . . . your best friend?" he asked.

The girl's smile grew brighter. "Of course! I wouldn't say it if it wasn't true. I mean, you're so awesome!"

The boy simply stared at his companion, unable to let any syllables flow free.

She continued. "Come on, Jeremy, don't think that you're a monster, because you're not. You're my cool and awesome best friend, so be happy!"

Sure enough, a smile slowly began to form on the boy's face. However, just before it could fully form, his lips straightened once more.

He darted his eyes back down to his knees.

"I'm a monster," he whispered, "no matter what anyone says. What you're saying, it isn't true; that's not me. No one would care if I was gone. I could leave tomorrow morning and not a single person would notice. I could die right now and—"

Suddenly, the girl lunged forward, sticking herself closely to her companion.

The broken one let out a soft gasp as he felt the warmth of her embrace.

"Just stop, okay?" the girl begged softly, shutting her eyes. "If you keep talking like that, I'm going to get sad too."

The boy gave no reply, his sights never abandoning the floor.

"You're very special to me, Jeremy," the girl said. "I don't know what I'd do without you. You're like the red to my heart—you make it full." She tightened her hold. "If you left, I'd notice in a second! No, a nanosecond! I'd notice so quick, you'd think I was crazy!"

"Like how I'm crazy . . ." the boy whispered.

"You're not crazy! You're just different. Think of it like a video game: you're an original character. You know, the one with all the awesome powers and stuff."

"Original?"

"Mm-hm! You're an original character, and that's what I love the most about you. That's why I love having you as a best friend."

The girl's words pierced through the boy like a sword.

He scrunched his face weakly as his body began to tremble, his tears flooding down his face to splash onto his pants.

"Avella . . ." he uttered weakly. "Please . . . help me . . ."

"I'm always here to help," the girl assured. "You just have to let me know what's up."

Like a child accepting his mother's love, the little boy tenderly returned his friend's embrace.

"Avella," he choked, "I'm so sorry."

"It's okay. It's okay. I got you."

The boy sniffed messily, stirring his mucus. "Avella . . ."

What followed—stillness, as the two children struggled to find comfort in their vibrating souls.

But the bliss would not keep alive.

Before long, a fresh sound erupted into the space, one that shook chills into the boy's blood.

A hiss.

A resonant hiss, slithering devilishly from wall to wall, burrowing into the boy's eardrums like an insect.

His eyes widened.

His teeth chattered.

Hesitant, he fired his sights towards the end of the hall, and what he discovered drowned his bones in overwhelming terror, much so that he soon began to hyperventilate.

"Hey," the girl said, noticing the distress, "what's wrong?"

The boy gave no answer, his focus never straying from the source of pure horrors.

His monster.

A grotesque creature, one that prowled on all fours. Pasty, white flesh composed the body, stained with dried, crusty blood that sprinkled off with each step taken. The claws on its hands and feet surpassed the sharpness of fine knives, whereas its head possessed no definite face. Just a lipless mouth packed with shark-like teeth. Droplets of crimson spilled down its chin, splattering messily onto the floor below.

"Jeremy?" the girl asked.

As the creature drew closer, it unhinged its jaw.

Splat! Splat! Splat!

"No . . ." the boy begged. "Please . . ."

"*Alone . . .*" the creature hissed. "*You're so alone . . .*"

Panicked, the boy shoved away his friend.

"Huh?" the girl muttered, confused. She stared at the disturbed little boy. "Jeremy, what's wrong?"

"*Worthless . . .*" the creature whispered. "*You're so worthless . . .*"

"No!" The boy shut his eyes and covered his ears. "No! No! No!"

The girl grabbed his shoulders. "Jeremy, it's okay! You're okay!"

At her touch, he reopened his vision. But the nightmare never vanished, proven by the beast that persisted onward.

"*Useless . . .*" it whispered. "*Why are you so useless?*"

The boy's pupils quivered like mad, his breaths all but controllable.

I have to get away, he decided. *I have to get away.*

Swift as lightning, the boy sprang to his feet, and using all his might, he bolted for the other end of the hallway, away from the whisperer of Hell.

"Jeremy!" the girl cried, watching her friend flee. She chased after him, although she wouldn't make it far, stumbling upon a chunk of ceiling and tumbling clumsily onto the ground.

"Ow," she whimpered.

She tilted her head to where the boy had sprinted, but alas, his presence had already melted away.

"Jeremy . . ."

Curious, she turned her attention to her backside;
yet, all she could see
was nothing.

The little boy raced at top speed, dodging the rubble
that dare barricade his path. His heart throbbed uncontrollably
as tears spurted from his eyes.

"Coward . . . Such a coward . . ."

He took a series of turns, weaving through the endless
maze of ruined scenery until, eventually, he came across a
heavenly sight: a pair of large, metallic, red doors.

In that moment, a glimmer of hope fluttered upon his
person, and straining every muscle he owned, he pushed past
his limits, reaching the crimson obstacles and, ultimately,
charging his body through to swing them open.

Crisp air whiffed into his nostrils as the scenery around
him flickered into that of an eerie forest. Now, rather than
kicking away rubble, he had to dodge bulky towers of oak. The
frigid wind crawled into his chest as he gasped for air, invoking
the sensation of blades poking at his lungs.

"Worthless . . . You are so worthless . . ."

Those sinister syllables echoed through the vacant
valley of the little boy's mind.

"No!" he cried. "Stop it! Just stop it!"

But the voices would not obey.

"Waste . . . You're such a waste . . ."

"End your life . . ."

"You're so alone . . ."

With each passing second, the whispers grew and grew,
suffocating the boy's thoughts, stripping him of any sense of
being. It was like a disease, poisoning his character from top to
bottom, from inside to out.

"Ahhh!" he screamed. *"Make it stop!"*

Suddenly, the boy stumbled over a thick root, forcing
him to collapse clumsily to the damp, cool grass.

"Ow . . ." he whimpered as he rose to his knees. He had escaped the maze of towering wood but now found himself on the outskirts of a wide, circular plain, the trees acting as the boundaries.

"Foolish . . . You are so foolish . . ."

"Please . . ." the boy whispered. "Just get out of my head." He covered his ears. "Just leave me alone." He soon began to weep, his face scrunched. "I don't want this anymore . . . I can't do this anymore . . ."

Then, the ease,

for just as the voices could carve themselves into his brain matter, they vanished, as if the laws of reality had beaten them into submission.

"Huh?" the boy muttered.

He let go of his ears, half-expecting the whispers to return full force; however, all he could find was the loving caress of the zephyr.

"Why did it just . . .?"

He looked around until his vision stumbled upon the possible answer: an extensive beam of light, shining down from the heavens towards the center of the plain. As it drew closer, the base widened, and the substance which composed it—the glimmering particles hued like the Northern Lights—intensified. At first glance, one would consider this a path to the very heart of the universe.

The little boy merely gazed with moist cheeks.

He then watched as the ray of light roared in illumination, urging him to squint his eyes for protection. A little later and the likely source appeared: a humanoid figure, drifting calmly down the pillar of luminance. Their feet soon kissed the grass, their entire person ready to view.

A man.

A divine-like man, with skin as white as an angel's wings and eyes brimming with a pulsating royal purple. On his head stood a white mohawk, although the boy could barely see it due to the man's mountainous, muscular frame. He wore the outfit of an unfastened, white, short-sleeved coat whose bottom skimmed the blades of grass, a red undershirt, dark pants, and brown combat boots. A black strap ran diagonally across his chest, with various vials and tools tucked into the pockets. On his back, he brandished a silver-bladed broadsword with a hilt of red and black.

The man smiled at the boy as he approached.

"Hello, there," he said. A gentle voice.

From the little one, no response. Only a gape.

"What's your name?" the man asked kindly.

"J-Jeremy . . ." the boy answered, timid.

The newcomer quickly noticed the distraught the child had barreled through.

"Have you been crying?" he asked.

The boy lowered his head and gave the shameful mumble, "Mm-hm . . ."

"Oh my. How come?"

"The monsters . . . They keep . . . whispering to me, telling me things."

"Monsters?"

The boy nodded. "The voices, they won't stop, no matter how much I ask . . . They just . . . keep going."

"And how long have you been able to hear these 'voices?'" the man asked.

As their eyes met once again, the boy held nothing back in his sorrowful confession.

"Ever since I could think."

The man took his focus to the crimson lines stretching across the boy's skin.

"And those injuries?" he asked.

"They're real," the little boy explained. "The monsters—they're real. No one can see them, but I can."

The man knelt down to be at eye level with the boy, and as the human looked back with a mixture of fear and awe, the heavenly visitor couldn't help but curve his lips.

"I can feel it," he said softly. "I knew you were promising the moment I discovered you. I can sense the powerful light dwelling within you; there's no doubt about that. Even with all these shadows shrouding your heart, there's still enough illumination to light a handful of galaxies. Once you dispose of all this darkness, you'll most definitely have enough light. I'm sure of it." His eyes brightened. "You're well worthy of becoming my successor."

The boy could not understand a single word this man spoke, but judging by his tone, he could tell that he was serious.

"Listen, Jeremy," the man said, "how would you like to get rid of those voices in your head?"

"Get rid . . . of the voices . . . ?" the boy asked.

The mere concept was a myth in itself.

The man nodded, enthusiastic.

Hopelessness, however, gripped the child's legs, keeping him from marching towards that delicious hope.

"It's not possible," he admitted, defeated.

"Oh, yes, it is," the man assured. "It'll take some time, but there is a way."

"Really?" The little boy's gaze begged for the truth.

"Yes, but you're going to have to keep a secret. Can you do that?"

"A secret?"

"Yes. I'm going to give you something, but you have to promise to me that you won't tell a living soul about it. You can't tell your mother, or your father, or even your best friend Avella."

"You know Avella?"

"Oh, yes. I also know how close you two are. But you have to swear to me that you won't tell her about the gift I'm about to give you. Can you do that?"

The boy pondered upon the scenario. "This gift . . . Can it really get rid of the voices?"

"Of course. But it will only work if you keep it a secret. Are you able to do that?"

The boy envisioned it—that promised land where the shadows kept out of sight, where the lilies swayed and sang upon the sight of his genuine smile.

A dream, possible to morph into a golden reality.

"Yes," he uttered.

"Are you sure?" the man asked. "If you tell, then the voices will only get worse."

The little boy offered his pinky. "You have my word. Pinky promise."

The man stared dumbly at first, but only for a short while, until his lips curved sweetly.

He gladly joined pinkies.

"Sounds like a plan."

A jovial atmosphere clicked around the pair, as if two halves of the rainbow had joined forces, crafting a more vibrant galaxy.

It didn't take long, however, for the man to return to business. After releasing the boy's pinky, he reached into his back pocket, and after shuffling his fingers, he fished out a peculiar object and held it before the little one:

a tiny, cube-shaped container composed entirely of glass, designed to hold a ring; only this case housed an even greater collection of matter—a glowing, triangular gem. Roaring with sapphire, it gave off a low ring, and with a trio of minute orbs rotating around it, the item basked in the appearance of an atom.

The gem's glimmer bounced off the boy's dumbstruck stare.

The man offered the case. "Here you go."

The child held out his hands, and the man dropped the case in his palms.

"What is this?" the boy asked.

"Sorry, but I can't tell you," the man said. "I do promise, however, that it will make the monsters go away."

"When?"

"In time. You just have to be patient. Understood?"

The answer: a nod of the head.

"All right." The visitor rose back to his feet. "I must get going."

He went to retreat to the beam of light, turning back to the boy only when he had reached.

"Remember," he said, "you have to keep that a secret. Okay?"

"You have my word, Mister," the boy promised. "By the way, what's your name?"

The visitor smiled shyly. "Sorry, but I can't tell you that either. Not yet, anyways."

"Then how can I thank you?"

The heavenly stranger grinned. "When you're ready, I'll come back. Then, I can answer all of your questions."

"Once I'm ready?" the boy mumbled to himself.

"Goodbye, Jeremy," the man said. "Stay strong. Until we meet again."

He smiled and waved as he floated back up to the unending night sky.

The little boy gazed with awe as the visitor ascended. Once his gift-giver had vanished, however, the child tilted his head back down to catch another glimpse of his new gift.

The Usual

Nine years later . . .

Beep! Beep! Beep!

The cry of the alarm, zipping through the air, tearing apart the serenity I had been savoring since the stars gifted their hello.

Give me a break . . .

But the mechanical devil refused to listen, drilling into my ears its high-pitched squeals.

So, despite the loving embrace of Lady Fatigue, I parted my eyelids, finding myself gazing up at my whited-out ceiling. Near one wall, the rays of the sun begged to be let in, halted only by the bouncer known as the blinds. Other than that source, the dimness of my bedroom made itself apparent, as if weakened shadows thrived in the corners.

A zombie in his wake, I pushed my blanket off my person, subjecting myself to the cool air of the A/C.

But the sacrifice was worth it, especially as I slammed my hand on the alarm clock nearby, finally silencing the little gremlin.

Beyond that, I sunk back right into my mattress, my body refusing to inch a single muscle.

Tired . . .

The alarm clock, whilst forced to surrender its vocals, still begged to ruin my morning, its face grinning with the blurry digital characters **7:02**.

Looks like I don't have much of a choice.

I searched far and wide within, finding the will to, at last, drag myself out of bed. (Fair warning: the mattress and blanket gave no mercy in whispering their sweet nothings.)

Warmth swirled into my toes as I curled them against the softened carpet. As I stretched, the bones of my neck popped, right as my muscles became less tense.

Let's get this started.

Dressed in nothing but a T-shirt and boxer briefs (anime-style, of course), I carried myself to the bathroom across the hall. There, I commenced the morning routine: brushing my teeth and washing my face, clearing my eyes of the usual bits of gunk. In that time, I studied my reflection. Thin frame but not scrawny. Tall. Skin shaded like coffee, with irises darker than the purest of inks. Atop my head, short curls of hair spread across, as dark as a crow's beak. Thin, dry cracks marred my lips, adding to my ideal expression—the *"I don't want to live on this planet."*

Afterwards, I headed back to my room, where I got dressed. My closet showcased an array of options, but I opted to dress in my favorite outfit: a red pullover hoodie, tan cargo shorts, and black ankle socks. I had already checked outside, and judging by the dullness invading the skies, I made the call.

It's gonna be cold.

Last but not least, I grabbed the dark, rectangular glasses resting near my phone on the windowsill. And as I plopped them upon the ridge of my nose, my vision enhanced to crystal clear.

I grabbed my phone and checked the screen.

No notifications.

Just the time.

7:25.

I'm gonna be late.

I shoved my phone into my pocket, then headed for the exit, grabbing my backpack and the lanyard that hung on the wall. A silver key glinted from one end.

As I departed from my bedroom, I shut the door behind me. I then scurried down the lightless hallway, approaching the inevitable fork in the road.

To the left, my living room, complete with every teenage boy's luxuries—a flatscreen TV and video game console, alongside a lengthy, comfy couch.

To the right, a pocket-sized kitchen, the floor ripe with white tiles that held up a tiny, circular table and a barren countertop, save a microwave. Towards the back wall, a door with a metal knob faced me, calling for my arrival.

I accepted the challenge, bringing myself to the obstacle. And after twisting the knob and gently pulling, I quickly felt the blast of morning air flutter into my home, kissing gently the whole of my cheeks. Goosebumps erupted across my skin like landmines, and with each inhale, my nostrils grew a bit numb, my lungs cuddling just a little closer to one another. With each exhale came thin clouds of fog.

I marched onward, abandoning the comfort of my apartment, and after shutting and locking the door behind me, I descended the wooden steps that led to the parking lot. Neither cars nor people revealed themselves, awarding me the eerie sensation of being the last human standing. Only the blue jays came to greet, gifting me miniature symphonies composed of their harmonious tweets.

I absorbed the serenity for a moment, appreciating the placidity Mother Nature so kindly offered, before carrying myself to my destination.

My journey consisted of me ambling along a narrow sidewalk, where the evidence of humanity snapped at my attention: vehicles racing along the cement, rumbling like beasts; packs of my peers, conversing with reddened noses and scarfs looping around their necks. Not a single "Hello" made it past my lips—a fact I didn't mind one bit.

Eventually, the finish line drew near in the distance, and I fished out my phone from my pocket to check the time.

7:37.

Looking good.

I sent my focus back to the endgame—a grand facility, its base mimicking the length of five football fields and the width of two. But rather than the generic body of a single structure, the shape aligned more with a cluster of buildings, as if the architect clung to an artistic vision. Narrow skywalks connected the areas, their surfaces fixed with gaping windows on either side.

I ventured across the parking lot and towards the entrance, where double doors of glass and metal awaited to welcome me. A broad overhang held itself up above, adorning the letters **New Haven High School**.

As I drew closer, a girl who had been ahead held the door open for me.

"Th-Thank you," I uttered, awkward. My eyes couldn't even meet hers.

She simply smiled, then split off in a different direction once she had entered behind me.

I braced my thin heart, my feeble confidence that forced the lion to chuckle.

Then, before I knew it, I marched deeper into the jungle of wolf packs and misfits.

* * *

Silence, echoing across the classroom air, sonorous enough that our heartbeats drummed against our ears. Well, that and the rapid strikes of the chalk scratching against the blackboard.

Throughout the room, desks lay, arranged in neat order, each housing a student. Some napped. Some doodled. Few actually paid attention, myself included. I sat near the back corner, beside the line of windows that hoped to relieve my boredom through scenes of the ever-changing planet Earth.

Before long, the head of the class—a middle-aged white woman with silky, blonde hair and beryl-blue eyes—quit with the chalk movements, turning to face the class.

"Okay," she said, her voice light yet firm, "does anyone know how we would tackle this problem?"

I studied the equation on the board, unraveling the answer within seconds.

One girl raised her hand.

"Yes, Veronica?" the teacher asked.

"Sorry to ask, Ms. Diamond," the girl said, "but what variable are we solving for?"

The woman, Ms. Diamond, glanced over her work.

"Oops," she said. "My mistake."

With her chalk, she wrote $x =$ ___ towards the bottom of the board. Then, back to the girl: "You're solving for x."

"I see," the girl said. "Thank you." She proceeded to run her pencil against the pages of her notebook.

I just kept on staring at the clouds outside.

After lending us some time to think, Ms. Diamond asked, "Does anyone have an answer yet?"

Come on, people. Someone raise their hand.

"Anybody?" Ms. Diamond asked. "Veronica, do you almost have a solution?"

The girl shook her head.

"Sorry," she said. "I just don't understand how to get past this one part."

"It's okay. I'll admit, this is a difficult lesson." Ms. Diamond delivered her attention back to the entire class. "Does *anyone* have a guess? Don't be shy. It's okay to be wrong."

What she failed to realize: more than half the class had clocked into dream land.

Riiiiiiing!

An alarm, the school bell erupted through the room.

Ms. Diamond gave a soft sigh.

"All right," she announced over the rustling of shuffling backpacks, "your homework for tonight is to come up with a solution to this problem, so I hope you wrote it down."

To no one's surprise, barely any students gave any form of response.

I stood tall and began packing away my belongings.

As the students shuffled out the door one by one, Ms. Diamond returned to her desk in the corner of the room.

I dragged myself to the exit. But just before I could escape, my teacher called out to me.

"Jeremy," she said, "could I speak with you for a moment?"

I swiveled my body and took myself to her space. "Y-Yes?"

"I know it's time for lunch," Ms. Diamond said, "but there is something we need to talk about."

"It's okay," I assured. "I'm in no hurry."

"I need to know when you're going to finish your community service hours."

My stomach twisted into knots.

"C-Community service?"

"Yes. You're the only who hasn't done them yet."

"But aren't they not due till the end of the year?"

"That is true," Ms. Diamond said, "but you have to realize that forty hours isn't something you can just blow past. It takes time. Most kids start them at the beginning of the year and take a few months to actually get through the hours." She frowned. "It's February, Jeremy. School started in August, and you still haven't even started."

I lowered my head, my pupils quivering as my bile threatened to flood back up.

Gently, Ms. Diamond curled her fingers on my arm.

"Look," she whispered, "I know it's tough for you. Being anxious isn't fun, nor is it easy. But you can't just let it take over your life. Sooner or later, you're gonna have to fight back."

My teacher smiled.

"You're a smart boy, Jeremy, and you're one of my favorite students. That's why I don't want to have to hold you back just because you didn't do your part in helping this community. Do you understand?"

I gave a feeble nod.

"Yes, ma'am," I said. "I'm sorry."

"You don't need to be," Ms. Diamond insisted. "Like I said, you're an intelligent young man. If someone as hopeless as me could get through it, so can you. I believe in you."

Naturally, my lips curved into a small smile.

"Th-Thank you, Ms. Diamond," I said. "I appreciate it."

She gave my shoulder a pat then pulled her hand back.

"Don't mention it," she said with a charming grin. "Now get going, before they run out of food."

"Right."

I removed myself from the classroom and into the abandoned, locker-packed hallway, where the only noise came from the soles of my shoes tapping against the tiled flooring.

However, as I reached the cafeteria, the calmness withered away, the walls seemingly quivering with the boisterous chatter they faced. Elongated tables stretched across the spacious area, complete with benches that teenagers of various ages occupied. They laughed. They gossiped. They chowed down their slices of pizza and/or cheese zombies.

My gaze glued to the floor, I made my way to the back of the cafeteria, where the food was being sold. And after a rather awkward exchange with the lunch lady (as per usual), I brought my food to a surprisingly empty table, one which neighbored no specific clique.

My relief swirling to the heavens, I plopped down with ease onto a bench, ready to devour my meal—a salad.

I clapped my hands together and whispered, "Thanks for the food."

But just before I could satisfy the beast of my belly, the realization plummeted onto my head, cracking my skull wide open.

I . . . I forgot the fork . . .

Again.

I groaned, slamming my palm against my face.

I think I'm gonna have to eat with my hands again.

Suddenly, the plastic utensil popped up beside my salad.

"Huh?"

"Hi, Jeremy," a voice sang beside me.

I turned my head to find a trio of girls invading my space, one of them being the girl who had asked the question in class, Veronica.

She smiled sweetly. "Mind if we sit with you?"

"I-If you want to," I uttered, my cheeks blazing.

"Really? Thank you so much!"

Thus, the three of them took their spots at my table, Veronica next to me with the other two on the opposite side.

I merely stared at my salad as the three of them got cozy.

"You really saved our butts," Veronica said. "Every time we'd try to sit by ourselves, there'd always be a few guys who'd try to join us."

Of course. Classic horndogs.

"N-No problem," I said.

Veronica polished her grin.

With skin fair and a short, slender body, she appeared as the ideal high school girl (minus the super badonkadonks). Hair yellow like thunder glowed atop her head, its shape a basic ponytail. To further electrify, her eyes roared with the deep hue of blue purer than the finest of lightning bolts. Whenever she smiled, a silver retainer in her teeth would gleam, while tiny freckles peeked at the world from her cheeks.

Her outfit consisted of a violet hoodie with white drawstrings, blue jeans, and purple, low-top shoes.

"Th-Thank you for the fork," I managed to say.

"Oh, that wasn't me," Veronica said. She gestured to one of the girls across from us. "Amy, here, was the one who noticed."

The giver of the fork, Amy, smiled at me.

"I know what it feels like to be in that situation," she admitted.

"Th-Thank you, Amy," I said softly. "I appreciate it."

"Don't mention it."

Amy was a short, thin girl, much like Veronica, although her body had a more sand-like shading to it. The hue of her eyes matched that of her hair shaped like a bun—a delicate brown. Whenever she beamed, her pristine teeth would shine, letting the entire world be aware of her one-of-a-kind charisma. For an outfit, she wore a shirt striped blue and white, tight blue jeans, and white tennis shoes.

I stabbed my newfound utensil into the leaves. But before I could finally dig in, Veronica spoke.

"So, Jeremy," she said, "how come you were sitting by yourself?"

"I like being alone," I admitted. "It's easier that way."

"You're not wrong there, to some extent. But as they say, a meal is always tastier when you have it with other people!"

The other two nodded in agreement.

"E-Even so," I said, "I just prefer to not have to talk to anyone."

They gazed at me through pity-tinted lenses.

"But don't you ever feel lonely?" the girl beside Amy asked.

"No, not really. I'm just . . . here." I faked the content sprouting upon my expression. "Thank you for your concern, though, Jennifer. It means a lot."

The last of the trio, Jennifer, never stopped looking at me as someone who desperately needed a hug.

An average-looking teenage girl, she was (though not in a disrespectful way). Silky, hazel-colored hair plummeted down to her shoulders, complementing the fusion of jade and aqua swimming within her irises. To cover her svelte body— her white-as-a-swan skin—she wore a sweater striped black and green, jeans, and black, low-top shoes with white laces.

"Well," Veronica said, "if you ever wanna have your salad taste like heaven, you can always join us for lunch. We'd be glad to have you."

Both Amy and Jennifer donated their fruits of glee, genuine to the core.

"Th-Thank you," I said. "I'll be sure to keep your offer in mind."

With that, the trio began conversing amongst themselves, ready to devour their meals.

"Hey, Amy," Veronica said, "you saw that new *Song of the Fallen* movie, right?"

"Mm-hm!" Amy hummed. "It was phenomenal!"

Beyond that exchange, I tuned out the syllables, focusing only on me, myself, and I.

* * *

"Oh, no way," I whispered, my eyes scanning my computer screen.

I relaxed in my well-lit room, lying atop my bed, my back hugging the wall as I lay my laptop upon my lap. At my side, my window introduced me to the contrast—the sky of pure darkness, where only the clouds of midnight purple roamed like gentle giants.

I scrolled through the article before me.

"Danica Jenck, creator of web comic *Age of Valestone*, has decided to release the seventy-fourth issue early. This was due to the relentless messages she was receiving from fans insisting her to progress the story."

Hm. I guess if you just cry about it, you can make anything happen.

"I can't believe she caved in," I said. "I'll have to give it a read later."

Suddenly, my laptop began to ring like a cellphone, and from the corner of the screen, a notification surfaced.

Incoming call: Skygirl24.

In an instant, my heart warmed up, and I wasted no time clicking the *Accept* button.

Next thing I knew, the article on my screen had been overtaken by the image of a girl seated in front of a webcam.

Flawless,

in every way, shape, and form.

Around my age, she was, only her beauty rivaled the purest of gods. She had smooth, unmarred skin, white as a dove, fitting perfectly with her slim figure. A vivid, mystical blue glowed in her eyes, while her silky hair shaded like a raven fell gracefully to her waist. Her cheeks had a pinch of pink from the blush, and her crisp eyelashes whispered sweetness. She wore a set of retro-purple pajamas with dancing pandas printed from head to toe.

"This is on . . . I think," the girl said. "Er . . ."

"You look like you're having trouble," I chimed in.

A raised eyebrow, as the girl met my eyes.

"Jeremy!" she sang, squeezing my heartstrings. "Hello there!"

I waved. "Hey, Avella!"

"What's up?"

"Nothin' much. Just doing some research on my computer."

"Research?" Avella frowned. "Did I catch you at a bad time?"

"No, not at all," I assured her. "I say 'research' but, really, I was just reading some articles. Did you hear about the *Age of Valestone* update?"

"Update?"

"Yeah. I guess Danica had to release the next issue early because her fans wouldn't shut up about it."

Avella leaned in closer in the webcam, highlighting the detail in her skin.

"*Nani!?*" she exclaimed. "You're yankin' my chain! You gotta be."

"Too close," I said. "And no, ma'am. I just saw the news before you called. Apparently, they spammed the heck out of her."

Avella backed away to normal distance, and I could see her expression shift from shocked to suspicious.

"Heh~?" she asked. "Is that so?"

"Avella . . ." I said. "Don't tell me . . ."

"I didn't spam her!" Then, in a murmur: "I only asked once."

I chuckled. "You never were the patient type."

"Can you blame me? That comic is off the hook! Time just flies when I'm reading it!"

"I'll have to agree with you there. Whenever I pick it up, I just can't put it down."

"Right? It's like, uh, like soda—you know it's bad for you, but you just keep coming back for more!"

The two of us let loose our laughter.

After settling down, I asked, "So, how's Golden Gate?"

"Good," she told me. "Remember that drawing contest I told you about?"

"Yeah. How'd you do?"

Avella shot me a thumbs up. "First place!"

"Really? That's great, Avella! You've gotta show me the drawing that won it all!"

"But of course, my good sir."

Avella left the screen for a second, and when she returned, she set her art face down on her lap.

"Are you ready, Mr. Jeremy Mitchell?" she asked. "Is your mind prepared to be blown away by an image of such epic proportions?"

"You tell me."

"Well, all right. Get ready to order a new pair of glasses, 'cause you asked for it."

She held up her art, revealing a painting of a red rose attached to a blue stem. Everything, from the boldness of the curves to the intricate shading, convinced me that this piece had been crafted by hands that rivaled Da Vinci's.

"Wow," I uttered as I studied the drawing. "That looks amazing, Avella. It looks so . . . life-like."

"Thank you, thank you," Avella said, acting as if this were her award speech. "I do try."

She quickly broke out into a soft giggle, and I did the same.

Avella then set the painting aside.

"So," she said, "how's New Haven? Still the same as I left it?"

"Just about," I answered. "Oh, I did forget the fork to my salad today, though."

Avella appeared . . . unimpressed. "Again?"

"Let's not judge here. It's a common mistake."

"Sure it is. Like how I forget a spoon when I'm eating soup. Totally normal."

"I feel like you're mocking me."

"What gave me away?"

I chuckled once more.

"So," Avella said, "did you end up eating with your hands again?"

"Not exactly," I answered. "These girls I know decided to sit next to me today, and one of them saved my bacon."

"Is that right? Did you talk to them?"

"Avella, we've known each other for ten years. I think we can both agree that I'm not, exactly, the biggest talker around."

My best friend sighed as she gave me a small smile. "Jeremy Mitchell, are you ever going to attempt to make any friends in high school?"

"Doubt it. Besides, I have you."

"Yeah, but I'm about two-point-seven-thousand miles away from you."

"Still, just being able to talk to you like this from time to time is fine with me." Upon my lake of emotions, the waves of joy rippled pleasantly. "You're the only one that really knows me."

"But, Jeremy"—Avella's demeanor sank with gravity—"what'll you do once I'm gone?"

I refused to let go of those beautiful waves.

"Well," I said, "I take it that the only way I'm gonna lose you is if you die. And while I will get lonely not having you around, I'll be okay, because I'll keep reminding myself that someday, I'll come back to you. I'll find you in the place after this one."

Avella, too, had her own waves, evident by her cheeks becoming as red as strawberries.

"Oh, Jeremy," she sang. "You're making me want to come back to New Haven right this second!"

"I'll always be here, waiting."

My best friend beamed. "Once again proving why you're the bestest friend I've ever had!"

"Why, thank you, my kind lady."

For a little while, the two of us ventured into that special place, where the rabbits roamed and the petals never ceased to sway, where the sun always welcomed us, inviting us to bask and behold.

The space where our sorrows knelt before our joined hands.

"Well," Avella said after some time, "it's getting late, so I better get going. Got a test tomorrow and I needs to study till the sun returns!"

"I respect that," I said. "I think. It was fun talking with you, Avella."

"You, too, Jeremy!" She sent me a wave. "I'll see you again tomorrow, okay? Goodnight!"

I matched her gesture. "Goodnight, Avella."

Her character soon snapped away from my computer screen, delivering me back to the Danica Jenck article.

I just kept staring at my laptop, wondering if there really was a name for this coziness I felt in my chest.

It Begins . . .

It'd be two, right?
Or maybe three?
But if I carry that over . . .
Within the library, I sat, pencil in one hand, calculator in the other. Before me, lying atop the table of wood, my math homework smirked, overjoyed at my apparently low IQ.

I rocked back and forth in my chair, contemplating and contemplating, my eyelids sore.

Five . . . Five . . .
By now, just the thought of digits rattled my brain.

At least I could drown in the calmness of the atmosphere—soundless, save the murmurs of the other students.

I brought my head down to the table, shutting my eyes.

Tired.

The lunchroom boomed with adolescent conversation— teens laughing, grinning, scarfing down their overpriced meals. The silent soldiers held no room to fight, the tables packed from one end to the other.

Amidst the youthful banter, the entrance to the school swung open, and in waltzed a pair of distinguished individuals.

The first: a light-skinned man, his stature bold and altitudinous. Defined muscles all around, invigorating his air of intimidation. A blue like sapphire thrived in his irises, while his hair, sinking down to his neck, consisted of a wavy feel, dark like a vulture's wings. The same shade, the stubble on the lower half of his face was crisp, refined. His outfit appeared professional, yet casual, with the only outstanding aspect being the cloth that concealed the entirety of his right arm.

The other: a being that had been born from the soul of science fiction. A meager robot, their body enjoyed the casing of pure bronze and silver, dense enough that bullets would never hope to mark a dent. Their head took on the shape of a rectangular prism placed on its side, the squares facing the front and back. On the face, a camera-lens-like spectacle zoomed, a solid orange dot resting dead center. Metallic spheres connected the being's joints, swiveling with each of their movements.

The duo approached the front counter, the metal man's feet clanking quietly with each step taken.

When they reached, the middle-aged woman on the opposite side handed them a wary look.

"May I help you?" she asked.

The kempt man cleared his throat.

"Ah, yes," he answered. "I am here with the SPU—the Suicide Prevention Unit."

The woman raised her eyebrows. "Suicide Prevention Unit? What in Sam Hill are you talking about?"

"You must not have been informed. Your school scheduled for us to have a talk with the kids about the dangers of suicide and self-harm."

"Hold on." The employee turned to her coworkers, unconvinced. "Hey, Janice!"

A faint voice spiraled from deeper in the office. "Yeah?"

"Could you come out here for a second? I gotta ask you something."

"Sure thing!"

A moment later and another woman past her prime joined the scene, her reaction to the odd pair the same as the initial employee.

"What, um, what seems to be the problem?" the newcomer asked.

"They said they're from the SPU," the first woman explained. "Did you schedule for them to be here?"

"I did, but I, um, I wasn't expecting . . . *this*."

"Allow me to explain," the man offered. "We at the SPU try to reflect the message that image doesn't matter, that visual appearance does not define who you are as a person."

The women shot their eyes to the robot. "And him?"

"He is the representation of what the inner-human appears as when they have been neglected."

Still, the office ladies refused to board the train.

"Worry not," the man implored. "He is not a real robot; merely a man in a costume."

"Well, of course it's not real!" one of the women exclaimed. "What year you think this is? Three thousand?"

The man chuckled. "You're a funny one." He then swiveled his attention to the cafeteria. "I see the students are having lunch. Would it be all right if I spoke with them now?"

"I don't see why not," one of the employees said. "Seems like the perfect time. I'll send the check to your company's address."

"That would be greatly appreciated. Thank you." The man turned to march towards the young'uns. "Let us go, Dikadus."

"Sir," the robot answered, his vocal cords digitized.

As they watched the odd pair amble away, one of the women couldn't help but have this eerie sensation bubble within her stomach.

"I need to research who we schedule more carefully," she admitted.

"Mm-hm~," the other hummed.

The mysterious man and his fellow of metal delivered themselves to a narrow stage placed near the rows of tables—a circular platform of shaved cobblestone with a microphone planted towards the front.

It didn't take long for the curiosity to buzz like bumblebees.

"Who is that?"

"He looks sus."

"Is that a real robot?"

"Are you retarded?"

The man approached the mic stand.

I had never sighed so hard in my life (and I was black).

"I swear, we did not learn this," I argued, rubbing my eyes. "Ms. Diamond is trolling us. She has to be. Right?"

I rocked in my chair once more, my daydreams spreading their wings for flight.

I wonder what Avella's doing right now. Probably sketching something when she should be paying attention.

I imagined my best friend drawing happily in her sketchbook, right as the teacher would call on her to answer a question or read a passage. A snicker slipped out as I pictured her flustered face.

What the heck are you doing?

As my imagination built upon itself, reality yanked itself back to its space, its form a voice—a man's voice—projecting from the cafeteria.

"Hello there, children," he said. "How are you all today?"

Normally, I'd drown out the white noise, but seeing as how these math equations loved pimp-slapping me every which way, I decided to actually give a damn today and listen up.

The man scanned the sea of noiseless children.

"You all look like you're having a good time," he noted. "I take it, though, that you're a bit confused. Don't know who we are."

"You're tech support, aren't you?" one teenager taunted.

Laughter erupted all around the house.

Even the speaker joined in, albeit to a smaller degree.

"Tech support?" he repeated. "That's a good one. Unfortunately, though, we aren't such upbeat company. My friend and I are actually from the SPU—the Suicide Prevention Unit."

Rumbling from the teens once more, only this time, in gravitatious whispers.

Suicide Prevention Unit? They're gonna talk about that now? When everyone's eating?

Without realizing, my fingers curled up into fists.

Why even call in people to talk about this? It's not like it's gonna change the way anyone thinks. They've called in so many "inspirational" people this year, telling us how they reached the peak of their life. Don't get me wrong, that's great to hear, but it's not like I'm suddenly gonna change my entire outlook on life just like that.

The voices edged to the tip of the abyss, never breaking free but getting beyond close.

At the end of the day, I'll always believe I'd be better off six feet under.

The crowd settled down.

"I suppose we should just get this started," the man said. "No use in beating around the bush, not with a topic such as this. My first question: You all know what suicide is, yes?"

Answer: an awkward hush.

"All right . . ." the man bounced back. "Well, in case you didn't know, suicide is the act of taking your own life. Now, who in their right mind would ever want to kill themself? Life is so great!

"The answer to that, ladies and gentlemen, lies in that very claim—'life is so great.' Because for some, life isn't so great. For some, their eyesight lives only in black and gray, the colors of the world drained away. They have forgotten what happiness even means. But fear not, because such a feeling can be recovered!"

The speaker pointed to a girl. "You there. Did I mention that your outfit is spectacular today?"

The teen blushed, smiling shyly. "Thank you."

"See that?" the man asked the crowd. "All it took were a few kind words and that girl's day has been made. And that's what we need in this world: kindness. Kindness in how we speak to people, kindness in how we treat them. Not just to our friends, not just to our families, but to every person we come across. You may not know it, but a single 'Hello' can save a life. I promise you that. A simple 'Hello' can cure the soul."

He pointed to another student. "It could cure you!"

Another. "It could cure you!"

Then, to the whole: "In this fight against loneliness, we must stand together! In this fight against this colorless world, we must work together to bring the shades back! Otherwise, we're all doomed."

He spread his arms. "So, to that girl holding her books close to her chest, tell her she looks lovely today! To that boy sitting alone, join him, assuring him that he, too, can matter, that everyone on this planet may matter, so long as their heart beats with good will!"

Like firecrackers popping off, cheers and applause exploded across the cafeteria, with some students wearing moist cheeks from their dribbling tears.

The man continued.

"Let's say we practice this kindness!" he suggested. "Believe it or not, I actually know of someone from this school. A boy. I've known him for quite some time, and I can tell that he is in pain. He is the quiet type, but his expression tells a hundred— no, a thousand words! He is distressed. He is alone. But let's go forth and remind him that he may fight the good fight along with the rest of us! How does that sound?"

More cheering, urging the very ground to tremble.

The man grinned. "That's the response I like to hear. So, without further ado, can we have Jeremy Mitchell come to the stage?"

Frozen, as if I bore rigor mortis, as if my limbs had forgotten the very concept of motion.

Did he just say . . . my name?

Slowly, I sent my gaze to the library entrance.

"Jeremy Mitchell?" the speaker called out. "Where are you? Come on, don't be shy."

My lungs suffocated beneath my shallow breaths.

Why would he call me? Just who the hell is this guy?

"We know you're here today. Don't make us hunt you down."

My fingers quivered. My saliva flooded my gums. No room to just . . . to just breathe.

I went to collect myself, shutting out all the background noise.

I can either do two things: show myself or stay in here. If I stay in here, chances are, they're just gonna come get me. If I go out . . . If I go out . . .

Just the idea of having all those stares latch to my skin had my stomach gurgling.

I think I'm screwed either way.

In the end, I decided to face the music, because if I was gonna have all the attention shoved down my throat, I'd rather not have the tag "Coward" hovering above me as it happened.

Even as my muscles screamed for me to stay the hell down, I lifted myself to my feet, bringing myself from the land of books to the spacious balcony that overlooked the cafeteria.

I studied the area, my focus locking to the stage, where an odd duo presented themselves.

As our gazes met, the more human one burst with delight.

"There he is!" he cheered.

Like wolves catching their prey's scent, my peers hooked their concentration onto my person.

My heart sank.

"So nice of you to, um, join us," the man said. "I don't wanna sound pushy, but do you think you could come down here? It'd make things easier."

"You have the wrong person." It took everything just to shove those letters out.

"But when I called for Jeremy, you came out. Can't quite say that's coincidental, can we?"

"No, I am Jeremy Mitchell," I explained. "Just not the one you're describing. I'm not sad or alone or anything like that. I'm as happy as can be."

"Really?" the man wondered. "You don't look too happy to me."

Because you just became a pain in my ass.

"It's okay to be honest," the speaker said. "No one's gonna judge. I think it'd be better if you just came down here, don't you think?"

"I don't think so," I answered. "I'm Jeremy Mitchell, and I'm satisfied with my life. But I'll let you figure that one out."

I readied myself to return to my homework.

"*Hey!*"

A hasty shift in nature, the man's tender visage eaten alive by sternness.

He glared at me.

"Get your ass down here," he hissed.

A loud quietude followed, more volume than any conversation could hold a candle to.

I just held more tightly onto the guardrail, listening to my gut instinct to stay the hell away from that human being.

"So," he growled, "I take it you're not gonna come down?"

Hell no.

The mysterious man smirked. "Fine. Have it your way. Dikadus, bring him to me."

"Sir." At once, pressurized flames spurt from the metal man's hands and feet, and the students gaped in awe as he took flight, setting himself down near me atop the balcony. A *klank!* chimed upon his landing.

The hairs of my body stuck up as I forced my feet back.

He just stared.

Ominous.

Intimidating.

But most of all, terrifying.

Before I could even think of bolting away, the robot stomped towards me, and when he reached, he snatched my collar, hoisting me into the air.

I wrapped my fingers around his arm, my teeth clenched as I struggled to free myself.

No luck.

With the strength of Twelve Labors, the man of metal hurled me over the railing, and my spine cracked in three different spots as I crashed into the table, splitting the steel in two. Pain gripped my innards, the intention to let go an absolute zero.

Shrieks of terror broke through as my peers dispersed, clearing the new battleground.

The man approached me and knelt down, his lips now twisted into a crooked shape.

"Well, now," he said, "you just had to make this difficult."

I shot him a shaky glare.

Another *klank!* as the robot planted himself back beside his master.

"We didn't have to go through all this," the man admitted. "You could've just been a good little boy."

"Hey!" someone shouted.

Our vision converged on the newcomer—the school security guard, his forehead ripe with sweat as he took aim with his pistol. "Freeze!"

The robot began to advance, but the leader of the attack halted his servant.

"This one's mine," he said. Then, to the keeper of the peace: "Do you really think your toy can harm me?"

"Don't tempt me!" the guard warned. "I'll give you another reason to wear those bandages!"

The man just elevated his amusement. "Is that right? In that case, please, enlighten me. I beg you."

The security guard wasted no seconds, pulling the trigger.

Pop!

The handgun's barrel howled as the muzzle flashed white.

But as the bullet spiraled to the man's bandaged arm, it did nothing more, ricocheting off to tumble to the floor.

Not a single scratch.

"See?" the vicious terrorist said. "Before me, your weapon is beyond useless." Malevolence crept into his demeanor. "Allow me to show you . . . a *real* tool of destruction."

He trained his hand to the officer.

Foomp!

Quicker than a comet, a blast of energy exploded from the man's palm, and as it zoomed to the security guard, it ripped clean through his chest.

In a smooth motion, the innocent soul collapsed to the ground, his chest leaking crimson as the lights of his eyes withered away.

More cries of horror echoed like some sick symphony.

"Humans . . ." the mysterious man hissed. "So primitive. So naïve."

The cloth around his arm soon burned away, revealing an armored limb of black and blue metal.

"You're a thousand eons too young to be challenging me."

I gaped. "Who . . . Who are you?"

His answer: crookedness that would force even the Devil to reconsider his existence.

"Let's just say, I'm not from the SPU."

He knelt back down beside me.

"Now, if you could so kindly hand over the Gemini Fragment, I can make your death as painless as possible."

"The what?" I asked.

"You heard me. Give. Me. The. Fragment."

"I-I'm sorry. I-I don't know what you're talking about."

The monster sighed, pinching the ridge of his nose.

"Playing dumb, are we? All right. Have it your way, Mr. Mitchell. Dikadus, why don't you convince our friend here to tell the truth?"

"Yes, Master Veltrix."

My teeth chattered as the beast of metal stomped towards me, his footsteps resonating with my deepest, cruelest nightmares.

Once in my bubble, he grabbed me by the hoodie once again and flung me to the side, right into the school's trophy case. Glass shattered over my body as I dropped to the ground, gasping for air.

No time to rest.

Before I could even think, the robot was already before me once more. He coiled his cold fingers around my neck and slammed me against the busted container. He then slung his free knuckles right into my stomach, squishing my organs.

Saliva flew past my lips as an indescribable pain warped my innards.

"Ready to talk now?" the man asked from afar.

"I . . . I don't know what you want," I admitted. "I really don't."

Another sigh.

"It's a shame," he said. "Really, it is. I wanted to make your suffering quick, but it looks like I'll have to beat the answer out of you." Again with the nastiness of his nature. "Don't worry. Blood cleans well off Dikadus. You won't get him dirty."

A savage, the robot flung me across the cafeteria, towards the front desk.

"Nobody move," the man told the crowd. "Nobody blink. Nobody turn away. Just watch what happens when you don't do as you're told."

Fwoosh!

The man of metal jetted forward, his fist cocked back, his knuckles starving for my liquid scarlet.

I flinched. Braced myself.

This isn't looking good, Avella.

Klink!

The cry of metal clashing metal, of forces of equal might battling for the throne.

I peered ahead, and like a miracle dribbling off God's fingertips, protection barricaded my existence.

Its form: a trio of teenage girls.

One held a sharpened sword, which she thrust against the metal man's forearms, holding him back.

The next, an archer, letting loose a duo of arrows, one for each of the metal man's shoulder blades. He jerked from the impact.

The last, a vibrant blur of cherry as she dashed forward, bashing her foot into the robot's torso with the sweetest of roundhouse kicks.

My assailant soared back from the counter strike, grinding his body against the floor until he paused near his master.

The mastermind raised an eyebrow. "Oh, my. What do we have here?"

My protectors made a formation at my front, their battle stances firm, without gaps.

In a general sense, they could be ID'd as clones—fair, unblemished skin, healthy builds. But upon closer inspection, I could admire closely their vivid individuality.

At the center stood a beautiful girl who could convince me she originated from classic Japanese mythos. Hair, an alluring silver, stretching down to her shoulders, each strand the epitome of perfection. Her eyes captured the same shade as the blade of her broadsword—a rich cherry blossom, lively enough that one could go lost from a mere gaze. She dressed herself in a white nylon jacket with a pink outline, a skirt and thigh-high socks—both black—and onyx sheepskin boots.

Next, the girl on the left. A cool character, she made herself to be, her expression never straying from barren, as if emotions fled from her reality's paradigm. Straight, violet hair fell to the mid-section of her spine, matching well with the royal purple surrounding her pupils. The lower half of her outfit matched that of the girl of silver hair; however, the top half consisted of a white button-up shirt, short-sleeved, balanced by a tie hued like obsidian. In her hands glared an elegant bow, already reloaded.

Finally, the girl on the right—the one whose very spirit thundered through her body. Curly and tousled, her hair flaunted luscious thickness, covering most of her back as it rained downward to her waist. Even the curls she had for bangs boomed with volume. In each strand, a shade riper than any cherry, livelier than any cardinal, thrived; however, her eyes took greater care of such a shade, imploring every ruby gemstone in the galaxy to grow envious. She wore the outfit of a red nylon jacket with a black outline, and a bottom half which mimicked those of the sword and bow-and-arrow. Her fingers curled around a refined golden spear.

"I suggest you stay back," the girl of silver hair hissed. "Otherwise, we're gonna have problems."

"And who might you little girls be?" the mysterious man asked.

She of the cherry hair smirked. "We're the ones who are gonna kick your butt if you even think of touching him again."

"Affirmative," the archer confirmed. "This is not a battle you will win."

"Is that so?" He of the steel arm analyzed my protectors, soon coming across the sentiment of surprise. "Well, would you look at that? It would appear that Zekrians have blessed our presence."

The girl of silver hair tightened her stance, her caution solidifying.

"Guys," she said, "be ready for anything."

The other two complied, prepared to strike back in an instant.

Tension,

slithering between the opposing forces, imploring each side to march with that first step.

The metal man had already removed the arrows from his body, his own weapons begging to be unleashed.

"Master Veltrix," he said, "may I dispose of them now?"

"No," his master answered. "There is no need. As of now, our chance to steal this Fragment has gone away. But another will come. Rest assured. Besides, who would've thought that *three* Guardians would rise to the occasion."

The trio of girls never let their guard down.

"We will return when the opportunity presents itself," the man said. "By then, I will have enough to craft the Gemini Stone. And you can be certain that I will burn the Zekrian Empire to ashes. I will have the Sentinels licking my heels for mercy."

In his eyes burned a sickly passion, that of a being who hungered for nothing more than the despair of any and all.

The mysterious attacker turned his attention to me.

"Until we meet again, Mr. Mitchell," he said. "After all, you have something that I so desperately desire.

"Let us go, Dikadus."

"Sir."

The pair stuck close to one another, and with one final wicked visage, they faded from existence until not a single trace of their character remained.

Till the very end, my saviors didn't lower their weapons, and even when the threat had vanished completely, they didn't take the risk. It was only after the absolute certainty of safety had embraced them that the girls finally relaxed a little.

"Phew!" the cherry-haired girl expressed. "Now *that* was intense. I seriously thought we were gonna have to fight a robot. He looked like a straight-up psychopath."

The silver-haired girl simpered. "No kidding."

"This is no time to be joking around," the violet-haired girl noted.

"Faith is right. We need to get moving."

The trio had their weapons vanish from sight, digitized into the air.

The girl of silver hair then approached me, offering her hand.

"Come on," she told me. "We need to go."

"G-Go where?" I asked.

"No time to explain."

She grabbed my wrist and hoisted me to my feet, her strength bordering on superhuman.

"Ow," I groaned.

"Are you okay?" she asked. "Can you walk?"

"I-I think so."

She quickly passed me off to her of the cherry hair, who gladly held my hand like a head-over-heels girlfriend.

"Heyo!" she sang.

My cheeks heated up like tiny furnaces as the warmth of her palm blended with my own.

"Okay, let's get a move on."

The girl of cherry blossoms started her way towards the school entrance, and the other two followed suit, dragging me along.

They watched as the quartet withdrew from the scene, their jaws hung low as they refused to believe the events that had just unfolded before them.

Beyond the Boundaries
of Earth

I stumbled clumsily along the side of the road, struggling to keep up with the three girls. Luckily, she of the cherry hair glued her hand soundly to my own.

"H-Hey," I said. "Where, exactly, are we going?"

"No time for questions," the silver-haired girl replied. "Just keep moving, please."

"You're kidding me . . . You can't even tell me where we're going?"

The girl of the spear smiled my way.

"How 'bout I give you a hint?" she offered. "It's the place where you go to sleep."

Where I go to sleep . . . ?

Puzzle pieces, connecting, crafting the picture in all its clarity.

As if flames brushed against my face, my cheeks went red hot.

"We're going to my *house!?*" I cried.

"Bingo!" she praised. "I'm surprised you didn't notice, though. I mean, you go this way to get to school, don't you?"

I inspected our surroundings, the familiarity sinking in like a needle. The street signs. The stoplights. That rock I nearly tripped over. (This morning, actually.)

"Fair enough," I admitted. "But still! Why are we going to my house?"

"Just please, keep moving," the girl of silver hair insisted.

The cheeriest of rubies giggled softly.

"You're a curious one, aren't ya?" she asked.

You say curious; I say concerned.

In time, the four of us arrived at the parking lot of my apartment complex, right to where the steps leading up to my home began.

We stopped there.

"All right," the silver-haired girl said, "you guys go get the you-know-what. I'm gonna see if I can contact Sentinel Jax."

"Roger," the violet-haired girl acknowledged.

She commenced her ascension.

But as soon as her foot scraped the first step, I blurted out, "Now hold on a second!"

The archer paused her journey, and the three dug their attention into me.

"Just what is going on?" I demanded. "You can't just barge into my house like this!"

"We'll explain everything in a little bit," the silver-haired girl promised. "Just follow those two for now. Okay?"

"But—"

Cutting me off, the swordswoman stuck her fingers into her mouth and blew, firing off a whistle that could've most certainly pierced every planet in our solar system.

Once finished, she brought her stare to the skies, waiting.

"W-What are you looking for?" I asked.

My answer: a majestic creature gliding across the canvas of azure; an animal the color of a dove (aside from its aqua wings), the elegance of a blue jay, and the size of a vulture.

It lowered itself to our level, sinking its claws tenderly into the silver-haired girl's sleeve.

"Hi, Peeka," she said to the bird. "I have a message for you to deliver to Sentinel Jax." She brought her lips in close to the creature's ears and whispered, nodding her head with the end of each sentence.

Once finished, the girl leaned back.

"Did you get all that?" she asked.

Tweet! Tweet! the bird cried.

From out of nowhere, magenta sparks began snapping into existence from thin air, breaching the space beside us. And with each moment, the bits of electricity enlivened, widening and emboldening until, ultimately, fusing together to forge a mythical spectacle—a sight that took my comprehension and shredded it to microscopic bits.

A . . . A wormhole . . .

Like the ones you'd see in science-fiction films.

Its glow bounced off our skin, its roar low and humble as its center swirled with ripples.

The girls treated the phenomenon like business as usual, whereas my eyes bulged right out of my skull.

"Remember to bring us back the reply, okay?" the swordswoman reminded the bird.

Tweet!

The creature detached itself from the girl and soared right into the wormhole, no hesitation.

And once all of it, from beak to talon, had vanished, the wormhole followed suit, erasing itself to return the parking lot's boring state.

I backed away from the trio, alarmed.

"W-What the hell did you do to me?" I hissed. "Spike my food? Slip me some drugs? Because wormholes should not exist!"

"Is that what you call them?" the cherry-haired girl asked. "We just call 'em 'portals.'"

"Right . . . Portals . . ."

I have to be dreaming. I have to be.

"Now isn't the time for that!" the silver-haired girl exclaimed. "We can't just stand around here. Ruby and Faith, you go with Jeremy to get the thing. I'll stand guard."

"How do you know my name?" I asked.

The girl of strawberries mimicked a creepy expression. "Because we learned it when we planned to abduct you! Ooh~. Scary~."

She soon whimpered as the violet-haired girl bonked her on the noggin.

"Not helping," she said.

Without a second thought, the duo then continued their ascension to my front door.

"Just *wait!*" I cried. "Wait."

Again, the trio froze, their focus stitched onto my person.

"Look," I continued. "I-I don't know what's going on here, but I think you have the wrong person. I'm just a nobody. I'm not special. Listen, I appreciate you saving my life, but I'm not your guy. I'm sorry."

What came after: a thunderous silence.

Maybe I convinced them?

"You are far from correct," the violet-haired girl said. "After all, did the man from earlier not attack *you?* Did he not request for *you* in front of the entire student body?"

Each of her points felt like jabs rocking my ribcage.

I felt tiny.

"Y-Yeah . . ." I uttered.

"Look." The girl of cherry blossoms perched her hand on my shoulder. "You're the guy we want. No doubt about that. I know you're confused. I know you want answers. We will gladly give them when the time comes. But that psychopath with the robot could come back any minute and try to kill you again."

I swallowed the lump in my throat.

"Right now, I just want to get you to a safe place," she explained. "Somewhere where we can protect you better. So, please, trust us."

Her sincerity never wavered, her sense of mind never straying to a wobbly front. She carried with her this bubble of a caretaker, of someone I wouldn't mind cherishing my life, even though I had only just met her.

"All right," I said. "I trust you."

She smiled. "Thank you. I appreciate it. I really do."

"Eh-hm!" The cherry-haired girl cleared her throat. "Not that I like breaking up the wishy wash, but a killer robot is out there plotting to destroy us all. Can we get a move on?"

Serious faces, back on.

"So," I said, "what do you need me to do?"

"I need you to grab something for us," the silver-haired girl answered. "Nine years ago, you were given a gift from a man with white hair. Do you remember?"

How could I not? Even now, after all this time, the scene plays and replays in my head. I still remember his promise—to cure me of the monsters rattling where my happiness should bloom.

I was still waiting.

"Yeah," I told her. "I remember. But how do you know about that?"

"Like I said, I will give you your answers when the time comes. But for now, I need you to cooperate."

"Right. So, you just want me to bring this gift out?"

The girl of cherry blossoms nodded.

"Yes," she said. "Easy, right?"

I have trust issues when it comes to "easy" things. They said kindergarten was "easy," but I had never struggled so much in my life.

"I hope so," I muttered.

"Don't worry." She of silver hair gestured to the archer and spearwoman. "Faith and Ruby, here, will go with you to make sure nothing happens."

The girl of violet hair replied with nothing, whereas the cherry-haired girl shot me a thumbs-up.

"I got yo back!" she assured me.

Riiiiight . . .

"I'll stay here and keep guard," the silver-haired girl concluded.

"Got it."

With that, I made my way up the staircase, leading the archer and spearwoman to my humble abode. But as we reached the front door, a realization slapped me right across the face, bringing me to a daze of sheer stupidity.

I sighed.

"Shit."

"What is the problem?" the violet-haired girl asked.

"My key," I explained. "It was on my lanyard, but I think that robot guy broke it when he threw me."

"Not an issue."

The archer directed me to the side, then bashed her foot into my door, ripping it off the hinges as it swung open.

"Dude!" I cried. "What the hell! You can't just break my house! I have to pay for that!"

"We have more pressing matters at hand," she argued, her expression still blanker than a sheet of paper.

The cherry-haired girl waltzed right in, cheery as could be. "Excuse us."

I cringed at the damage.

Mr. Romero, I thought, *please don't busta my ass.*

"Ooh~," the cherry-haired girl sounded, snooping around my kitchen. "So, *this* is what a boy's house looks like."

Flustered once again.

"P-Please don't look around too much," I begged. "And sorry for the mess."

"Mess? What mess? Your place looks cleaner than mine!"

"Indeed," the violet-haired girl chimed in. "I was expecting you to have dirty magazines lying around."

Face, boiling.

"Well, I don't!" I promised.

The cherry-haired girl leaned in close and whispered, "That's what the internet is for, right?"

What is wrong with these people?

I rushed past them and to my bedroom.

Upon entry, the girl of strawberries whistled. "Not enough erotic material for my tastes."

Would you quit with the horny banter!?

I lowered myself near my bed, then shoved my hand deep into the underside. My fingers brushed against a mound of clothes, but after dismantling the mini mountain did my fingertips come across something cool and hard.

I fished out the item, exposing to me and the girls the gift I had received nine years ago: the triangular gem hued sapphire, housed in a glass case as tiny orbs rotated around it.

Even now, the shimmer snatched my breaths away, my awe inexplicable.

My company shared similar sentiments. (Well, one did; that archer, she did not want to let any emotions soak through.)

"Whoa," the cherry-haired girl marveled. "So, that's a Gemini Fragment. I've never seen one up close."

"Is this what that guy wanted?" I asked.

"Most certainly," the violet-haired girl confirmed. "Now, let us return to Luna before her mood sours."

Compliant, the three of us exited my room to leave my house. But right as we came to that crossroad between my living room and kitchen, the girl of cherry hair gaped at the former, her fascination dazzling like homemade stars.

"Holy crickets!" she exclaimed. "I didn't know you had a *GameMaster 6000*!"

Why would you?

"Y-Yeah," I said awkwardly.

The spearwoman quickly joined her hands and stared at me like a beggar. "You gotta let me play that!"

"R-Right now?"

"Mm-hm! I've been dying to try it out!"

Like a mother steering her child away from the candy aisle, the girl of violet hair pinched her partner's earlobe.

"Ow!" the cherry-haired girl hollered. "Ow! Ow! Ow!"

The archer sighed. "It is similar to raising a daughter."

"I was just kidding, Faith!" the girl of cherry hair insisted. "When we get back! When we get back!"

But the violet-haired girl refused to believe, and with her remorse lifeless, she dragged the spearwoman—the one who had literally roundhouse-kicked a robot—to the front door.

"C'mon, Faith!" the girl of cherry hair cried. "Let me go!"

"We cannot afford to waste time," the archer explained.

I watched the two withdraw from the scene, utterly speechless.

What am I getting myself into?

The archer reappeared at my porch.

By instinct, I flexed my ears.

"Are you coming?" she asked.

"Y-Yeah," I said. "On my way."

Thus, a cub leaving the den, I stepped away from my apartment for what I could only assume would be a long, long time.

The archer stuck with me as I shut the door. (Yeah, that thing did not look right.)

"My apologies," she offered. "I am unaware of the exact customs of this planet."

I'm pretty sure not kicking down doors is just common sense. Then again, I saw a bird fly through a portal, so maybe I'm the dumb one here.

"Don't worry about it," I told her. "Fingers crossed I don't get robbed."

The two of us joined the rest of the quartet downstairs, with the addition of a returnee—the wormhole bird.

The girl of cherry hair stroked its chin as the creature once again perched upon the silver-haired girl's arm.

"You get cuter by the day, Peeka!" she cheered.

Tweet!

Tweet!

"I'm glad there weren't any complications," the silver-haired girl said.

"I beg to differ." The girl of cherry hair rubbed her reddened earlobe. "Faith nearly ripped off part of my head. That's physical abuse, ya know!?"

Again, the archer offered no remorse. "You say physical abuse, I say necessary discipline."

The spearwoman sharpened her glare.

"Now isn't the time, guys," the girl of cherry blossoms noted.

Eventually, the girl of cherry hair softened her face.

"You're right, Luna," she said. "I'm sorry."

Aw, man, I thought. *Now I* really *have to let her play my game when we come back.*

"Any response from Sentinel Jax?" the violet-haired girl asked.

"Yeah." The girl of silver hair, with her free hand, held up an object the size and shape of a USB.

She pressed her thumb against the button up top, causing digitized sound waves to flow across the device's surface.

Shortly after and a voice poked into our bubble, one that lugged me right back to that fateful night.

I squeezed the cube in my hand.

It's him.

"Guardians," he said, *"this is Sentinel Jax. First off, I'd like to thank you for protecting Jeremy when you did. We had been suspecting suspicious activity for some time; however, we did not expect the threat level to escalate so abruptly. You have my thanks for your actions.*

"Thanks to your report, we have been able to paint a clearer picture of the situation. There is a man out there hunting the Gemini Fragments, and he intends to use all means to obtain them. This, of course, includes killing the Selectors and their Guardians. We cannot allow this man to succeed

under any circumstances. If he does, it will mean the end of all galaxies.

"Now, in regards to Jeremy: I understand and completely agree that Zekra is the safest place for him right now. However, this could very well be what this man, Veltrix, is expecting. A trip here could spell disaster, and that's the last thing we need. As much as I hate to admit it, as you three are now, you are not capable of facing Veltrix. That is the sad truth. Please understand.

"That being said, just because Jeremy can't come to Zekra doesn't mean I want him staying on Earth either. He has now been introduced to his life as a Selector, so I can't have him walking around in ignorance any longer. He needs to know how to defend himself, and to do that, he needs a weapon.

"That is why I am sending you an STS and asking that you escort him to Glaileid. There, you'll find Mr. Tovius Giles at Atlas Tools and Mechanics. *Once you meet him, ask for order Two-One-Five. He'll understand. Oh, and if he asks you which way the river flows, tell him, 'to where the heroes may defy it.'*

"Good luck and stay safe, Guardians. Take care of Jeremy and each other."

Once finished, the miniature device returned to its original state.

The girl of cherry hair crossed her arms.

"What does he mean we're not strong enough?" she huffed. "We nearly kicked his butt in that cafeteria."

"No, he's right," the silver-haired girl said. "Back then, I hate to admit it, but I was a little afraid. Not of him, per se; more of that robot. Everything about him just seemed so . . . off."

"Besides," the violet-haired girl chimed in, "we must think about this objectively. If this Veltrix truly means to collect the Fragments, then he must possess frightening strength to support his confidence."

A balloon popped, the confidence of the cherry-haired girl deflated.

"I guess you're right," she admitted. "By the way, what's he sending us?"

Right on cue, another wormhole— er, portal, blinked into existence before us, only this one had five times the intensity of the last. Bigger. Louder. As energetic as an electrified black hole.

And through it glided something that blew me away, not from awe or fascination but from sheer surprise.

A . . . A subway car. Or at least, part of one, like the ones you'd find zooming across the New York railways. A shiny silver body. Headlights. Grooves running along the sides, parallel to the thin red lines stretching from one end to the other.

However, some aspects did set this particular cart apart from Earth's: for one, the bottom had no wheels, with the vehicle opting to hover above the ground; for another, broad cylindrical cones jutted from the back, ready to boost this thing to the speed of light.

"The STS?" I asked.

"*Sentinel Transportation System,*" the violet-haired girl explained. "What the Sentinels use for means for travel. Such spacecraft are intended only for their use; we, however, are an exception."

"Not bad," the cherry-haired girl critiqued.

Well, when you compare it to the actual thing, this spaceship is actually pretty insane.

Despite the hesitation chaining my ankles together, I approached the pimped-out subway car, my protectors following close.

At our presence, the double doors slid open, and to these Sentinels' credit, the inside appeared as authentic as the outside. Two cushioned benches sat on either side, separated by a metal pole that extended to both the floor and the curved ceiling.

Towards the front sat a control panel packed with all sorts of complicated buttons and levers, the center decked out with a screen and holographic keyboard.

"Whoa," the cherry-haired girl said. "This place looks awesome."

"I agree," the silver-haired girl chimed in. "It looks so clean."

Now that, *you wouldn't find in New York.*

Tweet! Tweet! The bird sang.

"What was that?"

Tweet! Tweet!

"Oh, you're leaving, Peeka?"

Tweet!

The girl of silver hair stroked the bird's head.

"Okay," she said. "Thanks for all your help today. You did good!"

Tweet!

Blushing, the creature flapped its wings and soared out of the vehicle, leaving just the four of us to ride the ride.

The girl of cherry hair scoped around, confused.

"Wait a second," she said. "Where's the driver?"

"One is not required," the violet-haired girl explained. "This mechanism possesses autopilot. All one must do is enter the destination into the console."

Taking point, the silver-haired girl approached the front, and upon typing in the planet's name into the machine, the double doors snapped shut. Thick streaks of fire ejected wildly from the thrusters out back, urging us to take our seats as the shuttle launched itself right into the wormhole.

The whole experience was jarring to say the least. The walls warped like flesh with something squirming beneath. Every shade of violet and orange presented itself, even those I couldn't think imaginable. At some points, I figured the husky vines of electricity would tear our spaceship to pieces.

Luckily, though, that wasn't the case, and like a film reel clicking to the next scene, the view beyond the windows shifted from a giant's intestines to a canvas dotted with ecstatic glints and massive fluorescent globes.

The amazement washed over my vocabulary, shrinking me down to a single word: "Whoa."

"You get used to it."

I turned my attention to the girl of cherry blossoms who sat across from me.

She smiled. "After a while, the whole 'space' thing gets kinda monotonous."

"Trust me," I said, "I don't think *this* will get boring anytime soon."

I wish Avella could see it with me.

"Hey, Luna," the cherry-haired girl said, "how long till we get there?"

The swordswoman glanced at the console. "Uuuum. It says here . . . thirty-two minutes!"

The girl of cherry hair groaned. "Why is it so far away?"

That's far? *Where I'm from, it takes a while just to get to the moon.*

"Well, I think that's plenty of time." The trio looked to me. "Now you can tell me just what the heck is happening. One minute I'm doing my math homework in the library; the next, I'm getting my lights punched out by a robot! Just please explain to me what is happening."

Their answer: no answer.

One minute.

Nothing.

Two minutes.

Nothing.

Three minutes.

Nothing.

"Please," I begged.

"It's not that we don't want to tell you," the silver-haired girl said. "I just don't know where to start."

"Anywhere would be fine. I can follow along pretty well."

She chewed her bottom lip, pondering.

"In that case," she said, "I guess I'll start with the Sentinels."

"A good choice," the violet-haired girl commended, her nose buried in a novel of some sorts.

The girl of cherry blossoms leaned in close.

"Have you ever heard of the Sentinels of the Universe?" she asked.

"The who?" I asked back.

"Sentinels of the Universe."

"No. I'm sorry. It doesn't ring any bells."

"You don't have to be sorry. I wasn't expecting you to know. You *are* from Earth, after all."

"Yeah," the girl of cherry hair said, "you guys usually aren't in the loop."

Well, considering how we are, I don't blame you guys.

The girl of silver hair took a deep breath. "Okay. Allow me to give you a lesson."

I zoned in.

She began.

"Long ago, there once was a man named Zekrac. He was an extraordinary swordsman and sorcerer, his abilities second to none. Some even went as far to say he rivaled the gods.

"However, due to his capabilities, many villainous figures sought to persuade Zekrac into joining their ranks. They believed that with his power, they could take control of the universe for their own. They offered him many things: wealth, fame, glory.

"But Zekrac was of a pure soul and mind. He could see through their crooked ways and denied them at every opportunity. And seeing as he was a peaceful man, Zekrac never reaped lives. He only ever pushed the evil away.

"The villains, however, would not accept his unwillingness. They wanted his power beyond measure, and they were willing to do anything to seize it. Thus, on one sorrowful night, an assassin snuck into Zekrac's home and murdered his wife Juvilla. Zekrac had loved her more than anything, more so than his own flesh and blood. She was the one he could trust, the one who had more value than the universe itself.

"The villains believed that by killing Juvilla, Zekrac's heart would darken. He would see the nothingness that the galaxies provided and would abide to any advice given to him in how to heal.

"However, how Zekrac reacted surpassed the villains' expectations in every way. Rather than falling into despair, Zekrac had his vision emboldened, that of a peaceful reality. While mourning, he took that pain and forged a dream of a harmonious universe, one where no one would have to feel as he did.

"Thus, with his powers, Zekrac created the seven universal elements—aspects of the galaxies which he believed could maintain balance in order to keep the worlds from burning into chaos.

"For a long time, Zekrac wielded these elements himself, protecting them accordingly. But as you know, nothing lasts forever. As time progressed, he grew old, senile. He knew he couldn't defend the elements forever. So, before he passed, he assigned each element to an individual he could trust, someone he knew who was powerful but keen to justice and good will.

"Hence, the Sentinels of the Universe were born— seven courageous and distinguished individuals who each wielded an aspect of the universe, each responsible for protecting the worlds and their people. Generation after generation, the duty has been passed down, bringing us to today."

The silver-haired girl motioned her fingers to list off.

"First is the Sentinel of Reality: Athello. He is capable of restructuring the principles of the space we breathe in, transforming stars to planets and light to a phoenix.

"Next is the Sentinel of Wisdom: Gideon. He bears knowledge on all things that have existed, exist now, and will come to exist."

"Then there is the Sentinel of Destruction: Reaver. He is the harbinger of creation's antithesis, possessing power capable of erasing entire galaxies with a single wave of his fist.

"The fourth is the Sentinel of Time: Codex. The laws and fundamentals of time are under her control, and she adjusts them accordingly to bring forth balance. She is also the only one in possession of an Infinity Weapon.

"The fifth is the Sentinel of Space: Tetra. As the sister of Codex, she controls the structure of the universe, as well as dimensions that lie beyond our understanding.

"The sixth is the Sentinel of Affection: Persephone. She shows proficiency at sensing the inner-emotions of all creatures and the true desires that sleep within, healing their fractured hearts.

"The last is the Sentinel of Light: Jax. He is able to purify the darkness of an individual's heart and soul, elevating their morale alongside any others who stand beside him."

The silver-haired girl sank back in her seat, exhausted.

"That was a mouthful," she said.

She of the cherry hair fired off an applause. "Good job, Miss Luna! I am well informed!"

"You should have already been," the violet-haired girl noted, her sights never abandoning her read.

"And there you have it," the silver-haired girl told me. "The Sentinels of the Universe. They all reside within the Zekrian Empire, which is our home."

"Zekrian Empire?" I echoed. "How big is this empire?"

My teacher considered the question.

"What was that empire you guys had?" she asked. "Was it Rom?"

"Rome?" I guessed.

"Yeah, that's the one. Now, imagine Rome, but instead of stretching it across your planet, stretch it across a couple galaxies. And that's just the physical empire."

I gaped. "That's, uh, that's big."

"And still growing!" she said proudly.

"Well, that's good to know and all, but where do *I* fit in all this? Why am I so important?"

"Oh, shoot. I almost forgot that part."

My teacher went back into lecture mode.

"You see, even with his divine powers, Zekrac couldn't efficiently maintain control over the elements of the universe, but he knew that he would need complete dominance if he had any hope of protecting them effectively. Hence, in order to amplify his strength, he forged an artifact known as the Gemini Stone. With it, he was able to protect the universal elements to the best of his ability.

"However, only Zekrac was capable of harnessing the power of the Stone without inflicting self-harm. So, when the Sentinels received the artifact, they split it into three fragments—the Gemini Fragments—thus erasing any form of temptation to mimic Zekrac's greatness.

"It wasn't until eons later, when the prime Sentinels neared the end of their journeys, that the Fragments took on a greater role. To become the next Sentinel, you have to be born with outstanding affinity for a universal element. The Fragments helped with this, pointing toward those who could become worthy of being successors. The Sentinels would hand the Fragment over to their chosen pupil, and from there, the gem would act as a sort of generator, feeding its energy to the individual to prepare them for their role.

"These people became known as *Selectors*."

I just stared at my lap, my world spinning on its head faster than a hurricane. Sentinels? Protectors of the universe? Selectors? I was just the boy who did well in school, the boy who kept to himself as he waited to grow up so he could reunite with his best friend.

I had my plan mapped out, pixel to pixel. But now, that plan had been torn off the wall, replaced by a diagram too complex for human comprehension.

The girl of cherry blossoms lay her hand tenderly on my knee.

"Look," she said, "I know it's a lot to take in."

"No kidding."

"You should know, though, that you're not the only one going through this. There are two others just like you."

"And you know them too!" the cherry-haired girl blurted out.

The leader of the pack annoyed, the girl of silver hair glared at her companion, and realizing her error, the cherry-haired girl quickly went back to admiring out the window.

"What's she talking about?" I asked.

The silver-haired girl sighed.

"We know who the other two Selectors are," she said. "And you know them too. But we can't tell you who they are. It'd be breaking our oath."

"Your oath? What oath?"

"Oath as Guardians."

I had never heard a person be so proud.

I still had no clue.

"As what?"

"Guardians. Protectors of the Selector," she explained. "When a Selector is gifted their Fragment, they are assigned Guardians who watch over them, protecting them from major threats, like Veltrix. However, a Guardian must only reveal themselves in dire situations, which this one was!"

"Relax," I told her. "I'm not judging you."

She giggled to ease her nerves. "Sorry about that."

I glimpsed at the trio. "So, you three have been watching over me all this time?"

The girl of cherry blossoms gave an excited nod.

"Nine years and counting!" she said. She gestured to herself. "My name is Luna Tenshi. As I said, I'm from Zekra, making me a Zekrian. I look forward to working with you in the near future!"

She then pointed to the apparent bibliophile. "This is Faith Linex. She, too, is a Zekrian."

"Pleasure."

The archer didn't even look up.

Is it?

Lastly, the girl of strawberries.

"They call me Ruby Storm!" she boomed, blasting away a knucklehead grin. "I'm also a Zekrian, but with my humor, you'd think I was from a world of comics!"

Riiiight . . .

But that lack of enthusiasm soon crafted itself into amazement.

"You've been by my side all this time?" I asked.

"Every day," Luna added.

"Th-Thank you," I said. "I really do appreciate that."

My lecturer blushed.

"No problem," she said. "It's what we're here for."

"Yeah!" Ruby chimed in. "And to kick the booty out of anyone who even *tries* to touch you!"

I chuckled, as did they.

And during that exchange, I felt something, swelling in my chest—a vibe I only basked in when I spent time with Avella. It was warm, pleasant, reassuring.

It was comfort.

* * *

The rest of our trip proceeded with all of us doing our own thing: Luna and Ruby napped; Faith lived in her novel; and I just stared out into the decorated void, contemplating the hell out of my existence.

Before we knew it, the intercoms fixed into the corners rumbled with life.

"Attention! Attention! Now arriving in the vicinity of Planet Glaileid! ETA three minutes before landing!"

The sleeping beauties groggily awoke from their land of sweet dreams.

"Hm?" Ruby hummed. "What's happening?"

Faith shut her pages.

"We have arrived," she said.

Beyond the front window, a sphere double the size of Earth accosted us, its surface coated with the most surreal of blues.

"Is that the one?" I asked.

"That is the one," Faith confirmed. "That is Glaileid."

The Master Craftsman
of the Universe

We punctured through the planet's atmosphere, ushering the speakers to deliver a message once again.

"Now landing upon the surface of Glaileid! ETA: thirty seconds!"

I lay my sights out the window, finding scenery that made the planet's shell seem like a facade.

My expectations: oceans upon oceans, burrowing down to the lowest depths, housing an orchestra of civilizations.

My reality: the most deserty of desert biomes. Dried-out, compacted dirt, eating up every inch of the ground as far as the eyes could render. Rugged cracks thick and thin marred the surface, as if it'd been stomped upon by giants. And like remnants of a once luscious paradise, shriveled leaves and plants scattered themselves throughout.

I concluded that the blue we'd spotted came solely from the sky up above, where belly-sized clouds rolled through beside a dull sun.

The more I thought about stepping outside, the more my stomach rattled like a maraca, my bile threatening to shoot up and burn my throat and gums.

"Nervous?" Ruby asked me.

"You've been watching me for nine years," I said. "I think you've noticed by now how outside isn't, exactly, my favorite place."

Just imagine it: everyone watching your every single move, judging every microscopic imperfection. You notice how heavy you're breathing, how that one piece of skin on your forearm just won't stop twitching, and you just pray that the attention doesn't get worse. Every conversation is an uphill battle; every lull, a victory riddled with fractured bones.

Luna curled her fingers around my own, blending her warmth into my hand.

"We'll be right by your side," she told me. "You don't have to worry."

From me, one last deep breath, loosening my muscles.

"Right," I said. "I got this."

She smiled.

Meanwhile, the shuttle quit with its forward motion, opting instead to descend until, ultimately, the inside gave a delicate tremble.

"We have now arrived at Planet Glaileid!" the speakers announced.

"Looks like we're here," Luna said.

The four of us lifted ourselves from our benches, and although my legs felt just a little bit more firm than jelly, I dragged myself to the double doors of metal and glass. Like before, they slid apart at my arrival, and as if Mother Nature practiced her cooking, a pleasant, earthy scent found its way into my nostrils.

We stepped out of the STS, our soles digging into what felt like chalk.

I glanced around, confused.

"U-Um," I said, "are you sure this is the right place? There's no one here."

"Just about," Luna answered. "It's not exactly where we want to be, but it's the closest we can get by vehicle."

"Then where are we supposed to be?"

She pointed. "There."

My eyes followed where she gestured, stumbling upon a blurry dark mass hibernating in the distance.

"What is that?" I asked.

"Where we want to be," Luna answered. She then led the rest of us towards the spectacle, with the other two girls shedding not a hint of curiosity. Meanwhile, my confusion hung over my head like a busted halo.

But as we drew closer to the sight, such a halo was mended, for the features of our destination became more defined with each inch gained.

A dome; or rather, an incomplete dome, the upper portion sliced cleanly off, exposing what I could only perceive as a new-aged New York. Elegant skyscrapers stretched to kiss the clouds, the sun's rays bouncing smoothly off their tinted windows. Vehicles sleek in model raced around the outside of the structures, hovering along the glossy roadways looping around the walls. The dome itself donned a body of finely cut bricks, each one coated onyx as an obscure blue etched itself in between.

"T-That cannot be real," I uttered,

"But it is, my sweet Earthling," Ruby confirmed.

Luna brought her finger to her lips. "Shh! We're getting close."

Ruby zipped her voice, whereas I raised an eyebrow.

The four of us soon reached a broad section of the dome that had been shoved in, forming the indent of a giant square. In front, a pair of armored soldiers stationed themselves, their rifles as intimidating as the maroon visors in their helmets.

"Welcome to Celestipool," one of them said once we'd reached. "Business or casual?"

"Casual," Luna answered, polite. "Just wanted to do some sightseeing with my siblings here."

Siblings?

The guard looked over the rest of us, especially at me.

No offense, Luna, but I don't think—

"Understood," the soldier said. "You have two hours before you must clear the premises."

Heh!? Are you serious? You must be blind! You have to be!

The guard tapped his finger against the side of his helmet.

"Four coming in. Open the gates."

The ground around us soon shook as the indented square split apart into two equal pieces.

"Have a nice visit," the guard said.

"Thank you so much!" Luna replied, cheery.

As my Guardians and I proceeded into the city, I tried my hardest to hide the genuine shock written over my expression.

Yes, of course. It's so obvious that we're related. Can't you tell by our skin tones? Perfect match!

Once I knew we were far enough away, I asked, "Why did you tell them we were siblings?"

"It's easier if we say 'casual,'" Luna answered. "Go the business route and you have to show IDs and licenses. Not really the funnest process. With 'casual,' we just have a time limit, and seeing as all we're doing is getting you a weapon, we should be in and out in a flash."

"I think you dropped the ball on this one, Luna." Ruby grinned. "You should've said we were Jeremy's wives! Then, we would've gotten extra time, if ya know what I mean."

Redness swarmed both Luna's cheeks and my own.

"Let's just go to Mr. Giles," she said.

Ruby giggled. "You're cute when you're flustered, Luna."

You are one odd girl, I thought.

However, my embarrassment blinked away as quick as it came, my fascination overpowering as the City of Celestipool received us with open arms. A liveliness showered across the streets of asphalt, the residents beyond jovial. To my surprise, most resembled humans, the same way my Guardians did—vibrant hair and eyes, although the shades of skin did vary. On the other hand, some individuals fit into my description of "that of another world": antennas poking out of foreheads; horns protruding from temples; third eyes (not the mythical ones).

On either side of the street, glass entrances into stores and restaurants begged you to feed them your wallet, the buildings packed tight like stacked building blocks. On the opposite end of the scale, the actual street vendors literally shouted for your bucks, their carts of merchandise appealing from every angle imaginable.

"There are a lot of people here," I noted. Half of me wanted to keep being impressed, while the other half wanted to blow chunks into the nearest trash can.

"What else did you expect?" Ruby asked. "This *is* one of the wealthiest planets in the universe."

"Wealthy?" I studied every detail of the city, noticing how elite everything felt, as if everything from the ground up had been crafted carefully by hand. "I can see that."

"All right, guys," Luna said, bringing us back on track, "keep your eyes peeled. Remember, we're looking for *Atlas Tools and Mechanics*."

"Affirmative," Faith acknowledged.

"Wait," I said, "I have a question."

"Go for it," Luna offered.

"Why do we have to come for this specific guy for help? What makes him so special from every other person who makes weapons?"

"Because he is of his own breed," Faith answered. "Having your weapon crafted by Tovius Giles is a privilege that even the Sentinels of the Universe do not take lightly."

"Sounds pretty important."

"Undoubtedly. After all, Tovius Giles is the Master Craftsman of the Universe."

Master Craftsman of the Universe. The name alone carried more weight than a bevy of stars.

"He is recognized as the greatest inventor in the entire universe," Faith explained. "His weapons and tools hold with them a uniqueness that draws out the utmost capabilities of whoever utilizes them. He can turn a cub into a wolf, a peacemaker into a monster. It is believed that he even forges the bullets for Sentinel Codex's Infinity Weapon—the *Celestial*.

"That is why you should feel honored to have your weapon designed by him. Having an item created by Tovius Giles would be akin to being gifted by the gods."

"A weapon . . . from the gods . . ." I couldn't believe the syllables slipping past my lips, let alone what they represented.

Should something like that really be in my hands? Wouldn't I just botch it?

I pondered upon the notion as we searched for the shop, in-between snickering as Faith scolded Ruby to no end. Apparently, our cherry-haired hero just couldn't resist the mouth-watering temptations of the food carts, laying her hands on every single sample. This usually ended with our archer nearly ripping the starving girl's ear off. With vicious remarks, of course. (My personal favorite was "You have the attention span of a newborn goldfish.")

But with pain (for one of us) came reward, for after around half an hour, we found ourselves present before a . . . rather dull shop—a basic cube-shaped structure with plain walls and windows. The only real splash of color came from the sign fixed near the top: *Atlas Tools & Mechanics*, the "Atlas" part a bold red.

"*This* is the place?" I asked.

"Not as flashy as I thought it'd be," Ruby agreed. "I was expecting more of a *in your face* kind of thing."

"W-We shouldn't make assumptions," Luna said, her own shock carefully hidden. Or so she thought.

Faith remained unfazed.

I think.

She only has one expression, so it's kinda hard to tell.

"This is how he wanted it," she explained. "Since he is acclaimed throughout the galaxies, there are many who seek to use his hands for sinister reasons. He is attempting to not stand out as much as he can."

"Then why would he live in one of the wealthiest cities out here?" Ruby asked.

. . .

. . .

. . .

"Personal preference," Faith answered.

Okay, now you're just bullsh*tting.

"Whatever the case may be," Luna said, "we need to get Jeremy his weapon, so come on."

She took the first step, pulling open the door of iron and glass. On cue, a soft *ding!* caressed the air.

We entered the shop.

Instantly, the vibes around us twisted to a more placid feel. The chitchat of the public that strangled us perished, conquered by a soothing silence that held our hands. The blazing rays of the sun, gone, dimness clutching the atoms from wall to wall. As for the floor, our soles no longer tasted the grainy asphalt, our footsteps now genial against the polished wooden floorboards.

Another atmosphere shift stemmed from the de-evolution of the era. The hints of the technological feats—the hovering cars, the holographic guides—all gone. Now, the sense of an Earth-like hardware store hammered us. Neck-high shelves arranged themselves in neat rows, packed with items familiar and not, from mere bullets to grenades layered four times over. On the walls hung various weapons like swords and tools like shields.

The one that hooked me, however, was the birdhouse.

Yes.

A birdhouse.

Like the one your grandmother would have in her garden.

I see the Master Craftsman of the Universe is all about creativity.

The four of us approached the glass counter occupying the front.

Behind that, curtains concealing a narrow opening swayed.

"Hello?" Luna asked. "Mr. Giles, are you here?"

The response: a gravelly voice spiraling from behind the curtains.

"Are you here for a pickup?" he asked.

"No."

"Then I'm afraid I cannot help you. My queue is full for the next few months, so you'll have to wait till then."

"I'm sorry," Luna said, "but this is important. Can you come out here, please?"

"I'm afraid I am quite busy at the moment," the man called back. "Whatever you are looking for, I cannot provide."

Luna balled up her fist, frustrated.

"I'm here for Order Two-One-Five," she said.

Next came nothing.

Part of me was expecting Mr. Giles to rush out and choke-slam one of us for still being here.

But instead, we just had the curtains to the backroom part, and through them ambled a man seemingly as old as Lady Time herself. Tall, slim, with white skin and wrinkles defined yet still aesthetically pleasing. Shortened hair that spiked up covered the top of his head, shaded like the puffs of a cloud, the same as his well-kept goatee. A serene fusion of blue and silver danced in his eyes, amplifying his collected yet intimidating demeanor. His style of clothing consisted of neatly ironed pants, a light undershirt with a button-up vest, and glossy business shoes. A magnifying glass shielded his right eye, which could've easily been mistaken for a monocle.

"I'm sorry," he said, "I didn't quite catch that."

He leaned on the front counter, his stare piercing right through us.

"Say that again."

I swallowed the lump in my throat.

Luna, on the other hand, kept her face solid.

"Order Two-One-Five," she said. "I'm here to order it."

Mr. Giles considered the request, his inhale more gravitatious than a dragon's.

"In that case, little miss," he said, "I ask you: Which way does the river flow?"

Our leader didn't even flinch.

"Where the heroes may defy it," she said.

A pause.

A moment that offered nothing but the anxiety that sh*t was about to get real.

But again, my expectations crumbled, for Mr. Giles merely smiled, pleased with the answer.

"You must be the ones Jax told me about," he said. "I've been waiting for you."

He straightened his stance,

whereas my lunch quit insisting on spraying over the weaponry.

"The name is Tovius Giles," he said. "Owner of this here shop, as well as the Master Craftsman of the Universe; although, who's paying attention nowadays?"

He studied us.

"Which one of you lucky souls is the Selector?" he asked.

I stepped forward.

"M-Me."

I refused to meet his eyes, as if my limbs would break off from all the quivering.

But Mr. Giles didn't seem to mind, offering me his aged hand.

I managed to match his gesture, the coolness of his fingertips breaching my palm.

"Nice to meet you, Mr. Selector," he said.

"I-It's Jeremy," I told him. "Jeremy Mitchell."

"In that case, it's a pleasure, Mr. Mitchell."

The urge climbed over my fears, sinking its claws into my iota of confidence, and I lifted my chin, meeting the gaze of a man whose intimidation had been snapped away.

Now, it was just a kind old man.

"L-Likewise," I said.

After he released my hand, Mr. Giles spoke to all of us.

"So," he said, "I take it you all know why you're here?"

"Yes," Luna answered. "We need to get Jeremy a weapon, and Sentinel Jax said you're the man to go to."

"A wise choice, considering how paramount Order Two-One-Five is."

"It's important?" Ruby asked.

"Oh, yes," Mr. Giles said. "After all, the last time that order was requested was during the Phantom War."

Instantly, the tension in the room thickened, my Guardians donning the faces they had when they faced Veltrix.

"Armageddon," Luna whispered.

"The very one," Mr. Giles said.

"W-Why's everyone so serious?" I wondered.

"Because it was a serious event," Mr. Giles answered. "The Phantom War was the bloodiest conflict this universe had ever witnessed. Death and despair littered the corners of every planet, of every galaxy. The very paradigm of existence was at stake.

"Order Two-One-Five was created by the Sentinels of that time to aid the then Selectors, who played a major role in the war. With it, the Selectors would be given strength that placed them on the same level as the Sentinels, the same level as Armageddon. This strength took the form of my greatest creation."

"The Gemini Tools," Faith whispered.

Mr. Giles appeared impressed. "I see we have a knowledgeable bunch."

He continued.

"Yes, the Gemini Tools—devastating weapons that hold the capability of erasing entire nations in a single sweep."

Sweat dribbled down my forehead, my fingers clenched with overwhelming anxiety.

I'm *supposed to have something like that. You're kidding me.*

"The universe must be facing serious trouble for Jax to call this order," Mr. Giles said. "In any case, I need *you*, Mr. Mitchell, to pick out a weapon of your choice. That way, I have a frame to work from."

"A weapon?" I echoed.

"Anything that fits you." He gestured towards his stocked shelves. "Have a look around. My inventory is endless. After all, an inventor needs his toys."

Suddenly, I felt Ruby tug at me sleeve.

"Hehe. C'mon, Jeremy," she said, her knucklehead smile loud. "I already know the perfect weapon for ya!"

"You do?"

Because right now, the only thing I can think of is a fork.

My Guardian of strawberries escorted me to a section of the wall where swords of all shapes and sizes glinted.

"Ta-da!" she sang. "You can get yaself a sword! That way, you'll look like the hero straight from the comics! Plus"—she gestured towards the Guardian of cherry blossoms—"Luna, here, can teach you all the tips and tricks!"

Luna raised her hands, smiling shyly.

"I've been studying techniques for eight years," she said. "I don't think Jeremy can learn all that with the time he has."

"Th-That's okay," I told her and Ruby. "I don't think a sword would really work with me. I'm sorry."

I could already envision it: me, facing the final boss, our clash ready to explode into anime-level proportions! But oof! I can't even lift my weapon 'cause it'd be too heavy.

Not the best way to go out.

Ruby didn't back down.

"Okay, okay," she said. "No sword, and that's all right." She gestured towards our archer. "How 'bout a bow and some arrows? Faith can snipe at things from light years away! I'm sure she can show you the ropes!"

"A moot suggestion," Faith said. "My training with my craft is similar to Luna and her blade. Hence, I cannot imbue into him the skills necessary within our strict time frame."

Judging by the lack of cursive in her message, I didn't think I wanted Faith to teach me, anyways. Nothing personal, but I had the feeling her "Good job"s wouldn't be all that inspiring.

"Th-That's okay," I said. "I don't think a bow would work for me, anyway."

Ruby frowned. "Now I feel like you're just shooting me down."

"N-No, really," I tried to justify. "I just don't think those weapons would suit me."

But Ruby's disappointment settled like stones sunk to the ocean floor.

"Ladies," Mr. Giles called out, "you have to let the boy choose for himself. Part of the Gemini Tool's efficiency lies in its master's fondness of the weapon. If he receives something he doesn't like, it'll just be that much more difficult for him to familiarize himself."

"He's right," Luna said warmly to Ruby. "We should let Jeremy find his own weapon."

My cherry-haired Guardian sighed.

"I was no help at all . . ." she groaned.

"There, there." A motherly touch, Luna stroked the top of her comrade's head. "It's okay. You tried your best."

Despite the guilt beating alongside my heart, I stuck with Mr. Giles's suggestion and browsed the shop on my own. I examined every nook and cranny of every shelf, every display case. I came across them all: rifles with a quartet of barrels;

halberds coated with poison; the birdhouse (which I had actually considered).

But in the end, I just couldn't find anything that suited the boy known as Jeremy Mitchell. Honestly, I just couldn't picture myself in the hero guise, my weapon held up valiantly as I conquered the battlefield.

My hope dwindled like stars blacking out.

But then I glanced towards Mr. Giles, who had been spectating me this entire time, anticipating my grand choice. At first, I did so out of nervousness for his level of patience; however, my attention quickly hooked itself onto the display case he had pinned to the wall, next to the drapes.

Nothing fancy; just a glass box.

In it, a simple rusted wrench lent its "Hello."

"What's in there?" I asked, pointing towards the item.

Mr. Giles turned his head. "Oh, *that?* Just a gift I received when I first opened the shop. I used to use it a lot, but as you can see, it has fallen to the tests of time."

"W-Would you be able to fix it a little?" I wondered.

The Master Craftsman grinned. "Curious, are we?"

I smiled shyly.

Jubilant, Mr. Giles retrieved the tool from its resting place and offered it to me.

"Give it a hold," he said.

So, I did.

A bit on the airy side, as if a single gust could snap it in two. Just a little longer than my forearm. A ruggedness swallowed the texture, the breaks from rust to worn-out metal clear as day.

In a fight against any actual weapon, this thing would crumble to dust beyond the first hit.

Yet, in this shop of daggers sharper than claws, of guns more dynamic than my entire planet, this wrench spoke to me. It was the odd one out; the underdog that still believed it could be fixed.

I liked that.

My lips curved. "I think I'll take this one." My sense of utter awkwardness kicked me briskly in the gut. "U-Unless, you know, it's not for sale. I-It was a gift, after all."

Mr. Giles chuckled.

"I think it'd be better in your hands than mine," he said. "With me, it hasn't seen any action. Perhaps you can give it the adventure it deserves."

Upon my pond of emotions, the ripples of bliss blinked from edge to edge.

My Guardians joined us at the front.

"Heh~," Ruby purred. "That's your weapon? Not too shabby, J-Meister!"

J-Meister?

"Will it be okay?" Luna wondered. "It looks a little beat up."

"Fear not, my dear," Mr. Giles said. "With my fine tuning, I can make this a Gemini Tool that lasts a thousand lifetimes."

I gaped.

That's a lot of lifetimes.

Mr. Giles offered his hand. "Now, if you would so kindly hand me the Gemini Fragment, we can begin the process."

I reached for my pocket, but Luna stopped me.

"What do you need the Fragment for?" she asked, nearly a growl.

"Don't worry," Mr. Giles said. "I was expecting this kind of reaction from the Guardians. I mean, your sole duty is to protect the Fragment and the Selector with your lives. I could understand why you'd have trust issues. Please, allow me to explain.

"There's a reason why only I am capable of crafting these Gemini Tools, aside from the fact that I created them. The birth of these weapons of mass destruction requires a very meticulous step: to insert the Fragment into the weapon of choice."

"Insert it?" Luna asked.

"Indeed. With the insertion, the Selector gains two advantages: one—the Fragment amplifies the weapon's power to heights unthinkable to even the gods; and two—the Fragment becomes considerably more difficult to steal."

"Because who in their right mind would challenge a person with such a weapon?" Faith concluded.

Mr. Giles grinned. "Precisely."

He offered his hand for the second time. "However, I cannot craft your Tool if you don't hand me the Fragment. I can assure you, as a man who can craft any gadget possible, using the Gemini Fragment for my own personal gain is very low on my list."

A valid argument, much so that Luna caved.

"Give him the Fragment," she told me.

"You sure?" Ruby asked.

"Yeah. Besides, Sentinel Jax trusts him, so we can too."

Thus, I fished out the glass cube from my pocket and plopped it onto Mr. Giles's palm.

"Magnificent," he whispered, cherishing the marvelous gem. "It's just as beautiful as the first time I came across it."

With his other hand, he lifted the wrench.

"I'll get started right away," he said.

"How long will it take?" Luna asked.

"Well, this is the creation of a kingly weapon," the craftsman said. "Twenty minutes?"

I'd love to see what he can do in an hour.

"In that case, I'm gonna go for a walk," I said.

I started my way towards the exit only to be stopped by Luna's grip on my wrist.

"I'll come with you," she said.

"N-No, thank you."

Her fingers tightened. "Wasn't a suggestion."

Based on her expression, the word "No" had no place in her vocab.

"R-Right," I said. "Let's go, then."

My Guardian nodded, letting go of my arm.

The two of us then vacated the shop.

"Have fun, you two!" Ruby said to the pair on their way out.

"This is not a trip for sightseeing," Faith reminded, her nose already in her book.

The cherry sighed. "Unfortunately."

Back to the Eden of technology, the sun's warmth hugging us like an old relative.

"So," Luna said, "where do you wanna go?"

"I was just planning on walking around," I told her. "Trying to get my mind right. You can follow me, but I'm probably not going to be saying much."

"That's fine. I'm your Guardian, so I'm going to protect you."

I blushed. "Th-Thank you. I appreciate that."

Hence, Luna and I waltzed across the streets of Celestipool, the magnificence of the city only evolving with every corner turned. Yet, my awe didn't live up to par, the cubs of my mind suffering against the hunter known as "Reality."

In time, we found ourselves at a spot sparse of citizens, where a guardrail offered an overlook to a manmade body of clear water. It looked like intricate crystals danced across the surface.

I rested my arms on the railing, peering out into that field of tranquil ripples.

Luna came up to my side.

"What are you thinking about?" she asked.

"How life can just change on the flip of a dime," I said. "I mean, last night, I was laughing in a video chat with my best friend. We didn't talk for super long, but that was easily the funnest part of my day. Now, I'm a couple galaxies away getting a weapon that could wipe my country off the map."

"I'm sorry. I know this is all sudden."

"'Sudden' would be an understatement."

Luna perched her hand on my shoulder.

"Just know that you're not alone," she said. "You have the Sentinels and us with you. You can count on us."

A genuineness blanketed her message, the words smooth like silk. Sadly, though, her kindness could do nothing for the manacles looped around my ankles, tugging me further and further down this abyss where not a single iota of my screams could be heard.

I gave a small smile. "Thanks."

Luna matched my expression.

"I'm sure Avella would be very proud," she said.

I furrowed my brow.

"How do you know Avella?" I wondered.

My Guardian put on a face as if she'd been caught in an affair.

"B-Because we've been watching you for so long," she said. "Of course, we'd know who you were friends with."

I shrugged, accepting the answer.

"Makes sense."

Luna sighed in relief. (And while I did notice, I just did not have the mental energy to care.)

Just then, she brought her finger up to her ear.

"What?" she asked.

A pause.

"Oh, it's finished? Okay, we'll head back now."

Then, to me: "That was Ruby. You, sir, are now the proud owner of a Gemini Tool."

My stomach gurgled.

"That was a fast twenty minutes," I noted.

"Time does fly when you're chatting it up," she said.

We started our trip back.

"By the way," I said, "if you have those earpieces, why did you use that bird back on Earth?"

"Signal doesn't go that far," Luna answered. "Only a few light years."

That . . . actually makes sense.

Retracing our steps, my Guardian and I returned to Mr. Giles's shop, the *ding!* greeting us as we opened the door.

Faith leaned against the wall, reading, while Ruby admired a spear of scarlet that hung near the front. Upon our entry, though, she turned her head to us.

"Welcome back!" she said.

Mr. Giles, who had been reading his own text, shut the covers upon our arrival.

"There he is," he said.

He then shuffled to his back room behind the curtains.

Meanwhile, my Guardians and I gathered around the front counter.

"He finished it?" Luna asked.

"Yes, ma'am," Ruby said. "Looked pretty proud. Couldn't see the Tool, though."

Just then, the Master Craftsman returned, a large piece of cloth covering his hands at his front.

He set the concealed item on the counter, eliciting a soft *thnk!*.

"I have your Gemini Tool ready to go, Mr. Mitchell," Mr. Giles said. "However, something peculiar did occur during the process."

Luna raised an eyebrow. "Peculiar?"

"See for yourself."

Mr. Giles unwrapped the Tool, revealing an object that robbed me of my breaths. My wrench, yet not my wrench. The rust that marred the metal had been destroyed, with the tool now wearing a body of shiny silver. Towards the head, the piece used to adjust the jaw had been torn out, replaced by that glorious sapphire gem. And acting as the epicenter, it sent glowing, pulsating, vein-like lines surging throughout most of the upper portion.

I only had one thing to say: "Whoa."

"Are you sure that's the same wrench?" Ruby asked.

"It was rather odd," Mr. Giles said. "I had never seen anything like it. The moment I embedded the Fragment into the tool, the entire composition of the gadget was altered. What was once simple iron is now pure zikranium."

Ruby and Luna practically creamed their skirts.

"Zikranium?" Ruby asked. "Are you serious?"

"U-Um," I said, "what's zikranium?"

Luna kept her gaze steady. "The hardest metal in the universe. Think of your diamonds, then multiply that by a billion."

Now I creamed my shorts.

"Even the *Celestial* would have trouble piercing it," Faith noted.

"Well, Mr. Mitchell," Mr. Giles said, "it would appear that you got the cream of the crop."

A lot of cream going around.

He offered me the wrench.

"Your very own Gemini Tool."

I clutched the cool metal between my fingers, the tension within me building as the Fragment called to me.

Erase entire nations in a single sweep.

Uncertainty coiled around my neck like a snake.

I turned to Luna. "M-Maybe you should hold it. You're more of the fighter."

To that, Mr. Giles chuckled.

"You're just like Jax was when he received his Tool," he pointed out. "You're nervous, Mr. Mitchell. You're unsure if you're worthy of such power. Just remember that you are a Selector—a future leader of all the galaxies. This is destiny calling, and destiny has grand plans for you."

He tapped me on the shoulder.

"Just believe in yourself as the universe believes in you."

I considered his wisdom, and although the doubt still clung to my feet, the chains it brandished loosened a little.

"Right," I said, smiling.

Mr. Giles did the same.

Luna bowed. "Thank you for your time, Mr. Giles. We apologize for dropping in so abruptly."

"No worries," the Master Craftsman said. "I blame neither you nor the Sentinels; I blame the bastards who would try to disrupt our peace."

"Agreed," Faith concurred.

"Well, then, Mr. Giles," Luna said, "we'll be taking our leave now."

Thus, my Guardians and I turned to head for the exit.

"Good luck on your journey, children," Mr. Giles said. "May your victory prove to be actualized."

"You know it!" Ruby cheered. "We're gonna rock this popsicle stand!"

Luna giggled.

We departed from *Atlas Tools & Mechanics*, the adventure, continued.

Where Hope Goes to Die

We marched along the arid desert, the City of Celestipool bidding us farewell in all her glory. My wrench tapped playfully against my thigh as it hung from the loop of my shorts.

Before long, the STS budded into view, prompting that sinking feeling in my gut to act up. The journey had only begun, yet I already wanted nothing more than to game out in my living room.

We held our place towards the front of the shuttle.

"All right," Luna said. "I'm gonna go let Sentinel Jax know we have Jeremy's weapon. You guys chill around here for a sec."

The girl of cherry blossoms brought herself to the back of the shuttle, leaving me with two very, *very* beautiful females. Needless to say, my hormones bonked me on the noggin, my self-consciousness rising to levels beyond imagination.

"I wonder where we're going next," Ruby thought aloud. She rubbed her stomach. "Hopefully somewhere with some delicious treats, 'cause I am *starving!*"

Hnnng! my stomach whined, right to the beat.

Thank you, Life. You never let me down.

Of course, my embarrassment pooled in my hot cheeks.

Ruby smiled. "I see I'm not the only one. Hehe! Say, Jeremy, what kinda food are ya into? What right now is making ya scream, 'I gotta eat that'?"

I thought for a second.

"I-I wouldn't mind some spaghetti," I said.

"Spaghetti, huh? Not bad, not bad. For me, I'd *kill* for some rice and curry! But guess what?"

"What?"

A feline ecstatic, the girl of cherries lunged onto me, wrapping her arms loosely around my neck.

"Spaghetti is my second favorite food!" she bellowed. "Just further proving that we're destined to be the best of friends! Hehe!"

Too close.

Too close.

Too close.

Too close!

Everything, from her candied shampoo to her feminine scent, washed over me, striking my heart with too many beats to be considered healthy.

Luckily, I had a distraction in the form of Faith, who just stared into the distance, her lips locked.

A lone figure.

"W-What about you, Faith?" I asked. "What's your favorite food?"

Ruby quit rubbing her cheek against my own, also curious of her friend's answer.

"My favorite food?" Faith poked her chin with her thumb, the circuits of her mind surging with activity. And once her computations ended, she spoke back to me. "Hamburgers . . . I suppose."

"Hamburgers?" I asked.

She nodded.

I twisted my face in true awkward fashion. "C-Cool."

Meanwhile, Ruby cast a face as though she'd just cracked a mystery.

"Now it makes sense!" she said.

"What does?" Faith asked.

"Well, I've been wondering why you've been putting on weight." Ruby pointed at her waist. "Right around here."

I.

Was.

Flabbergasted.

See? This is why I don't talk to people. Because I know I would be dumb enough to let something like that slip.

The rebuttal?

From the archer, a reaction that diverted from the usual (which I probably should've expected). Rather than glaring with in-your-face fury, Faith just nodded.

"I see," she said calmly. "Well, while hamburgers do grant immoderate weight gain, curry has been proven to be the ideal meal for excessively idiotic individuals such as yourself. I can understand why you would select it as your favorite."

D-Damn.

That hurt my *feelings.*

Ruby shook her fist, her teeth clenched like a wolf's snarl.

"What was that!?" she growled.

"I can assure you that I did not stutter," Faith said.

The tension between the two only intensified, squishing me to the point where my actual body could suffer damage.

By the grace of the gods, though, the girl of cherry blossoms returned to the scene, reviving my hope of a bloodless bloodbath.

Or maybe not,

for her expression—grave, sunk—suggested that she'd just stormed the shores of Normandy.

"Luna?" I asked.

The other two quit with their bickering right away, noticing, too, their leader's distress.

"What's up, Luna?" Ruby asked. "Did you find out where we're going next?"

The silver-haired nodded weakly.

She then clenched her fists, her bones quivering.

"Why do we have to go there?" she muttered. "Of all the damn places."

Ruby stepped to her leader to offer comfort.

"Luna, relax," she said. "Where are we going?"

The girl of cherry blossoms took a deep breath.

"Sentinel Jax," she said, "wants us to go to Xerges."

As if bullets ripped through their skin, my other Guardians threw away any jovialness they held dear. Even Faith, whose lips kept level, had discomfort creeping through.

"You're lying . . ." Ruby whispered.

"I wish I was," Luna said.

The odd one out, my confusion flashed at every angle like a beam spiraling from a lighthouse.

"What's wrong?" I wondered.

"Just get in the shuttle," Luna told me. "I'll explain on the way."

With no other option, I obeyed and shuffled into the STS, my Guardians joining me against their will. And as the double doors slid shut, Luna typed the destination into the front console, her fingers stiff and sluggish from letter to letter on the keyboard.

Once finished, she took a seat on a bench like the rest of us.

In one continuous string, the STS engaged in flight— thrusters spitting streaks of flames, followed by the clean propulsion off the desert floor.

Like the switching of wallpaper, the scene outside the window melted from an alluring blue to an empty void where no man would dare to tread.

A loud silence stuffed the innards of the shuttle, my Guardians prepping for the fight of their lives.

"Xerges, huh?" Ruby said softly. "Not ideal."

"Sentinel Jax wants us to head there to help Jeremy," Luna explained. "He wants Jeremy to learn how to fight with his Tool, and he knows someone from Xerges who can train Jeremy."

"Sh-Should I be worried that you guys look like hell?" I asked.

"No," my cherry blossom Guardian assured. "We *will* protect you, whatever it takes. But where we're going now is *very* different from where we just left."

"Even that is an understatement," Ruby groaned.

I yanked the cat out of the bag.

"What's so bad about this place?" I asked.

"Imagine the most heartless place you can think of," Luna told me. "Now multiply that cruelty ten times over and you have the bare minimum of what goes down in Xerges."

My arms stiffened.

"Xerges is the trash can of the cosmos," she continued. "It's where the scum goes to congregate. The bandits. The bounty hunters. The assassins. Anything vile that you can do to another person, someone on that planet has accomplished."

"It is where hope goes to die," Faith said. "Why Sentinel Jax knows an individual from Xerges is beyond my comprehension."

Luna shrugged.

"For us, though, it's even worse," she said. "A good portion of Xerges's residents were once Zekrians, banished because of their crimes against our kind. Because of this, Xergesians hate Zekrians from the pits of their souls. There's a good chance that if our identities are found out, we could get rushed and killed on the spot."

My toes just wouldn't stop twitching, my lungs still as my breaths barely made it past my lips.

We're not going to a planet, I thought.

We're going to Hell.

Faith noticed my withering composure.

"Selector," she said, "make sure to keep your Tool out of sight. We must divert as much attention away from us as we can."

"Right." I grabbed my wrench from my shorts and tucked it beneath the underside of my hoodie.

The rest of the trip couldn't have gone any slower, as if Miss Time herself did not want us to endure this suffering. Everyone was on edge; even Ruby, who at this point rivaled Faith for best deletion of glee.

But Lady Fate didn't care for our needs, and before I could finish my umpteenth prayer, the speakers of the shuttle vibrated to life.

"Attention! Attention! Now arriving in the vicinity of Planet Xerges! ETA: Three minutes!"

"Game time," Ruby whispered.

I peered out the front window to see where we were headed: a menacing globe darker than a crow's eyeball, with only certain sections highlighted by glows of orange. The remains of ships orbited the sphere like deceased insects, their sizes and decay varying. The bowtie—a thin layer of smog encapsulating the planet, as if to attempt to hide the cruelty that cracked its knuckles.

A little further in and we glided through the atmosphere, coming upon another Celestipool, only not nearly as technological or animated. Wherever I looked, murky, rundown skyscrapers stood, their sides riddled with holes and grazes. Pipes ran along most of the alleyways—the perfect place to hide a body.

The STS carried us to a shipyard, landing in an open section. Immediately, eyes wandered to our shuttle, which had a cleaner body than most of the spaceships around.

"We have now arrived at Planet Xerges!" the speakers announced.

"Remember, everyone," Luna warned, "don't make any eye contact. If we mind our business, they'll mind theirs. And if anyone asks, we're from Glaileid. Understood?"

We nodded, not a single one of us willing to abandon the shuttle.

But the journey called for this event, and we had to face the music with chins held high. Otherwise, we were gonna be eaten alive.

Thus, as Luna rose to her feet, we backed her up, and like doe stepping into the wolves' den, we left the sanctity of the STS.

Instantly, stenches worse than cigarette smoke assaulted my senses, nearly forcing me to stifle my coughs.

Overhead, a lifeless plain of gloom stared back; an eternal night that was anything but serene.

"Okay, guys," Luna said in a low voice, "we're looking for *Rikaden Bar & Meals*. Glance around, but don't make it too obvious. Last thing we need is for someone to ask if we need help."

"Because that usually adds up to us getting robbed," Ruby concluded.

Hence, as we searched for this building, we strained the hell out of our nonchalant skills. My rule consisted of scoping around for a few seconds, then look back down. Scope around for a few seconds, then look back down.

Unlike Glaileid, the pathways here lent a feeling of claustrophobia—cluttered and narrow, much so that not all of four of us could even walk in a straight line.

At least the Xergesians didn't study us as much as they could've, because judging by their characters, any one of them could've had me whiting out from sheer terror. Burly, monstrous figures adorned with weaponized prosthetics, torn eyepatches, and horns that could puncture right through my intestines. In essence, any one of them could've grabbed me and snapped me in half, just like that.

Thankfully, my person remained intact, and my anxiety could finally tidy up as our goal came into view.

A basic structure shaped like a cube, the walls tasting of wood as the multiple doors shown consisted of glass, each leading into a different store.

Above one of the doors, a neon sign glowed: *Rikaden Bar & Meals.*

"Thank the Sentinels," Ruby said as we approached. "I was ready to whip out my spear so quick."

"It's not over yet," Luna said. "Let's just hope Mr. Rikaden isn't like the other people living here."

She pulled open the door, and together, we helped ourselves inside.

He eyed them from behind a wall, a shadowy figure dressed in a cloak.

And as he watched the children enter the restaurant, he brought his crimson-skinned finger to his face.

"Scar," he said, his voice croaky, "I have him."

6

Selector-in-Training

Bar talk, popping around us like a stream of beer bubbles. Everywhere I looked, a violet lighting engulfed the space, from the leather booths to the left to the long wooden counter to the right. The population of outside had been translated into the bar, with nearly every seat housing a mean-mugging thug.

At least they didn't have their weapons?

(Thank God for common courtesy.)

"I don't like how packed it is in here," Ruby whispered. "If things go south, we're gonna be in for a rough time."

"Then let's hope it doesn't get rough," Luna said. She scanned the crowds. "Where is he . . . ?"

Her eyes stopped.

"Gotcha."

She led us to the wooden counter, near the far end, away from the potential murderers.

"Where is he?" Ruby asked.

Luna nodded her head towards a man stationed behind the counter. Middle-aged. Muscular build, outlined by his tight white tee. On the opposite side, bagginess thrived in his camouflaged pants, right down to the combat boots. His skin's shade copied my own, tasting that delicate coffee brown. Unlike me, though, the only hair he had grew around his lips— a scruffy beard. As for his head top, the sheen of the lights bounced off the perfect sphere with ease. A pair of dog tags hung around his neck by way of silver chain.

He busied himself with wiping a glass cup.

Must be the bartender, I thought.

In time, the man noticed us, much like most of the patrons, and keeping his glass with him, he ambled over our way.

"Sorry, kids," he said, "this is no place for you guys." Deep tone.

"We know," Luna acknowledged. "But we're looking for a man named Timothy Rikaden. You wouldn't happen to be him, would you?"

The bartender lifted an eyebrow.

"Depends on who's asking," he said.

Luna leaned in close. "Nano sent us."

At first, the man coughed up confusion.

"What?" he asked.

"Nano," Luna said.

Upon the repeat, the bartender examined our faces, and finding no bullsh*t, he gave us an answer.

"Stick around till I close up," he ordered.

"Understood," Luna said. "We'll be right here."

So, taking our seats on the swivel chairs before the counter, we waited.

And waited.

And waited.

You know that feeling when you're there but not really? Like, you're present physically, but up there in the head, you're blowing dandelions into the wind.

That was me, except instead of dandelions, I blew pissed off hornets. And as they rushed back at me, I bobbed and weaved, threading the needle from their stingers. An infinitude of thoughts jounced around up there, frying my brain to the point that the matter physically boiled.

Well, at least that killed time,

because once I'd zoned back in, the boisterous bar quieted, the booths emptied out along with the swivel chairs.

I even got to watch the final patron make his exit.

"Later, Rike!" the alien called out. "Same time next week?"

"Hell yeah, brotha!" the bartender hollered.

The creature handed us one last curious glance as he vacated through the front door.

The bartender stepped over to the exit to hang up a *CLOSED* sign, then shut the curtains.

He then regrouped with the four of us.

"Okay," he said, "let me ask again: What did you say?"

"Nano sent us," Luna repeated.

"Nano as in . . . ?"

"As in Sentinel Jax."

To this, the bartender groaned.

"He can't even write me a letter," he whined, "yet that jackass had the audacity to send four children. Ain't that a little backwards?"

"I-I don't think you're supposed to send children at all," I noted.

The man chuckled. "Fair enough."

"Sooo," Luna said, "are you Mr. Rikaden?"

"I am he," he answered. "And judging by Nano's decision to send you out here to Xerges, I'm guessing he needs something?"

"Something very important." The girl of cherry blossoms directed the focus to me. "We need you to train this boy."

"H-Hello," I uttered, eyes to the floor.

Mr. Rikaden folded his arms. "And who might this be?"

"This is Jeremy Mitchell," Luna said. "He's Sentinel Jax's Selector."

"A Selector?" Mr. Rikaden repeated. "You want me to train a Selector?"

"Yes. Sentinel Jax thought that given your background in war, you'd be a good fit as Jeremy's teacher."

"But isn't this boy *Nano's* Selector? Why do I have to train him?"

None of us could give an answer.

Mr. Rikaden raised a hand.

"Never mind," he said. "Again, since Nano put you through the trouble of coming here, it must be important that I do it. Plus, I do kinda owe him at the moment, so this should be a good way to clean the plate a little."

To me: "Tell me, boy, where are you with fighting?"

"U-Um . . ." I started. "I-I've never really done it."

"Well, judging by the fact that you're not even looking at me, you must be some kind of pussy."

I tensed up.

Ruby narrowed her eyes.

"That wasn't very nice," she hissed.

"Neither is being in a fight," Mr. Rikaden challenged. "You can't go into this with only half a heart. Every punch has to have weight. If not, you lose before the battle even starts. You can't win by being a pussy. I can guarantee you that."

I slouched, my confidence shattered.

"But"—Mr. Rikaden grinned—"it's okay to start as a pussy."

Taken aback, I finally lifted my gaze to meet his.

"There's no shame in being small," he said. "It's only when you *stay* small that you lose respect. Tell me, boy: you wanna stay small?"

I clenched my fists.

"N-No," I said. "I-I want to grow."

"Now *that's* what I like to hear."

Mr. Rikaden stepped towards his shelves of colored bottles.

"Come with me," he said.

And we did, joining him at a steel panel he had hidden behind the counter.

"Let's go somewhere a little more appropriate," Mr. Rikaden said.

He lifted the panel, which turned out to be a hatch, revealing a narrow staircase that descended.

"Hoo-ooh~," Ruby sang, excited. "Just like the movies."

Mr. Rikaden went down first, and single file, we tailed him.

After passing the bottom step, we arrived at a dojo-like room, spacious enough to host a party. Tan mats covered the entirety of the floor, while one wall had been decorated with a row of body windows. At certain sections sat exercise equipment, from those machines where you could bend your knee backwards to a punching bag that looked mean enough to clap back.

"Welcome to my training hall," Mr. Rikaden said. "Usually I come down here when I need to cool my head, but starting today, Mr. Selector, this is where you're gonna get stronger."

Our veneration stirred across our faces.

"And I thought the stuff at the Academy was insane," Luna said.

"Indeed," Faith added. "The equipment here is incredibly superb."

"Well, when you're a veteran for the biggest empire in the universe," Mr. Rikaden explained, "you tend to get some perks."

Please don't put me on the machines.
Please don't put me on the machines.
Please don't make me run.
Please don't make me run.

I recalled all my time in gym class, my stamina and strength more mediocre than mediocre. The Pacer—crushed me. The Mile—murdered me. Don't even get me started on the suicides.

Mr. Rikaden turned to me. "All right, Mr. Selector, let's get this started."

A-Already?

"The first thing we need to do is establish your baseline," he said. "Figure out from where can we start building you up."

Mr. Rikaden clapped his hand, causing square sections of the ceiling to slide open, and like angels descending, sleek androids plummeted through the openings, their silver bodies crystal-clean as they did their superhero landings. The menacing auras in their magenta eyes strangled any confidence that I had hoped to bring to life.

"What are those?" Ruby asked.

"Sparring bots I made," Mr. Rikaden explained. "Don't think for a second that I'd be practicing my moves with some air."

Cautious, I fished out my wrench from my hoodie, holding it before me like a sword.

"Nice weapon," Mr. Rikaden complimented. "Little unusual, but I think it fits you perfectly."

Glad I wasn't the only one that thought so.

My Guardians watched from the side, along with our host.

"Okay, Jeremy," he said, "I'm gonna send the bots at ya. All I want you to do is try to beat them. Don't worry about destroying them. They're as solid as rocks!"

Believe me, the last thing I'm worried about is beating them too bad.

"You ready?"

Nope.

"Y-Yeah."

"Okay. Level three! Let's go!"

Like starving wolves, four of the robots arose to charge towards me, their knuckles hungry for my bones.

Oh boy . . .

The moment the first bot reached, I blindly swung my wrench, bashing through nothing but the open air.

In retaliation, the robot smashed its fist right into my chest, shooting aches through my torso as I collapsed to one knee.

And seizing the opportunity, a second bot curled its fingers around my hood to hurl me across the room, breaking my spine as I crashed into the wall.

"Ow . . ." I groaned as I lay face-down on the mats.

Ruby cringed. "Ooh~. That looked like it hurt."

"That's 'cause it did."

No time to relax, for the gang of metal men had already begun jogging towards me.

I scrambled to my feet.

"Take your time!" Luna shouted from the sidelines. "Find the openings!"

Once in vicinity, I swiped my wrench once more, again connecting with nothing but air.

If these robots could laugh, they would.

Wham! a robot's fist cracked as it sank into my gut.

Saliva burst from my mouth as I gasped for air.

The PTSD rushed into me like a drug—the ruined cafeteria; the psychotic man of metal, beating me to a pulp; the crookedness of Veltrix's grin.

My instincts snapping open, I smashed my wrench against my assailant's chin, forcing his body to jerk back from the impact.

"He got one!" Ruby cheered.

"Can't relax just yet," Mr. Rikaden said.

Wham!

A solid hit, right at my spine, firing an electric shock across my entire body.

Like before, I stumbled to my knee, and like before, the robots wasted no time flinging me against the wall by the hoodie.

By now, my body screamed to just stay down.

That's a . . . That's a good move. I can see why they'd do it again.

"Hey," Luna whispered to Mr. Rikaden, "isn't this a bit much? I mean, he's never been in a fight before. Not as himself, anyway."

"What do you mean, 'not as himself'?" Mr. Rikaden asked.

The girl of cherry blossoms considered her next sentence.

"Never mind," she said. "The point is, this boy has no combat experience, yet you're essentially just ganging up on him."

"That's the point," Mr. Rikaden said. "Look at him. He's not confident one bit. That's why he's just swinging that thing around aimlessly. He doesn't think he can land a shot, so he's hoping luck will help him out."

"But he just landed a hit," Luna noted.

"Because something triggered in him for a second. I saw it in his eyes. Whatever had punched him in the stomach left an impression."

The cherry blossom knew just what that "whatever" was, and she couldn't blame Jeremy for not forgetting.

"We need to keep him in this high-stress situation," Mr. Rikaden said. "That way, he can get pissed off; he can get frustrated. If we can get his emotions to fuel his movements, he'll get stronger, because at this moment, he doesn't have a purpose to fight."

But as the hours passed, the situation did not improve. The metal men did not let their ruthlessness die down, their thirst for the human boy's blood. They thrashed. They beat.

They tore him to shreds, at one point even jabbing their feet into his limbs as he just lay motionless on the floor.

"Enough!" Luna bellowed. "Kill the bots!"

Despite his reluctance, Mr. Rikaden shrugged and announced to his training hall, "End combat!"

Their fangs satisfied, the metal men backed off the Selector, returning to their original positions in the corners of the room.

Luna rushed to Jeremy, kneeling before him.

"Jeremy, are you okay?" she asked, worried.

He simply groaned, sitting himself up. Blood leaked from his lips as bluish bruises marred his face.

"This is too much," Luna said. "We need to take it slower."

"No, we don't," Mr. Rikaden said. "The situation's dire, right? If that's the case, we don't have much time. It'd be easier if he had even an iota fighting experience, but since he doesn't, we need to push him past his limits. Otherwise, he's not gonna stand a chance against whatever's threatening you all."

I clenched my teeth, defeated.

"I'm . . . I'm sorry, everyone," I whispered. "I'm sorry for being weak."

Exasperation erupted from the bartender, and his handle rough, he grabbed me by the collar and yanked me towards him, bringing my face mere inches from his own.

"You're a future Sentinel of the Universe!" he growled. "A future protector of all of us! So, would it kill you to just man up!? Stop being such a coward!"

My Guardians already had their weapons trained on Mr. Rikaden's neck.

"Let him go," Luna growled. "*Now.*"

Mr. Rikaden sucked his teeth, then shoved me away.

"Maybe Nano was wrong to send you here," he said. "No point in a lost cause."

"Or maybe Sentinel Jax should pick better friends," Ruby hinted.

The tension skyrocketed, a clash nearing the cliff to drop off.

I could barely stand. My face, my legs, my fingers, all of them were numb to the core. But my heart, that kept its integrity, and I could finally feel something beneath the base begin to sway—something hot, fiery.

"M-Mr. Rikaden," I said.

"What?" he hissed. "Gonna ask me not to give up on you? A little too late for that."

"No. Nothing like that."

The bells lined themselves before my understanding; I just needed to figure out how to ring them.

"You have war experience, right?" I asked. "You were a soldier?"

"That's right. I fought for Zekra for many years. Went through things that make me afraid to close my eyes." He folded his arms. "And I'm just a normal man. *You* . . . You have all this potential, all this power, yet you choose to be weak."

Luna narrowed her eyes.

"I *am* weak," I admitted. "I've never done anything like this before, and I'm terrified. Of course, I don't want to get hurt, but more than anything, I don't want to show my shortcomings. Because when you lose, it's because of your inadequacies. It's because you failed to meet the standard."

Those hands of the abyss stretched out to my toes, their bony ends brushing against my uncertainty.

The voices murmured.

Those damn voices.

I just don't want to keep proving that I am *a waste of space.*

"What's wrong with being scared?" Mr. Rikaden asked, genuinely confused.

First bell, rung.

"You'd have to be pretty damn stupid to not be afraid," he said. "But what brings out greatness is overcoming that fear. What turns you into someone worth respecting is when you can charge headfirst, confident that you'll be on top."

I lowered my head.

"I just . . . don't know how to be confident," I whispered.

Mr. Rikaden offered a simple answer.

"Have purpose."

Second bell, rung.

"Know why you do the things you do. Believe in the things that will help push you through. I fought in wars not to be the better warrior but to protect my home and my loved ones. That's what kept me going."

"Same with us," Luna added. "When we saved you at school, Jeremy, we were petrified. But we wanted to protect you. That's why we moved forward."

"Fighting to protect . . . ?"

I pondered upon the notion, the foreignness of it all.

"I've never fought to protect anything before," I said. "Everything I've had has either been given or taken."

Sorrow unfolded between Luna and Ruby, their memory etched into their wall of mistakes for eons to come.

"So, you have nothing now?" Mr. Rikaden asked.

"Not quite." I thought of that grand girl, that human being who always held me close, keeping me safe from the relentless loneliness. "I have someone worth protecting, and I can't let anything happen to her, no matter what."

Mr. Rikaden approached me, cautioning my Guardians; however, rather than bullying me, he tapped his fist against my chest.

"Then you keep that feeling," he told me. "You keep it tight, and you let it ride with your movements. You let it fuel your passion. If you do that, your fear will become nothing more than a side thought. If you do that, you will be untouchable. I promise you."

The harmony blended together, those bells performing a perfect symphony, remedying the certainty that could never find its luster.

I bowed my head, my resolve pieced together.

"Please, Mr. Rikaden," I said, "don't give up on me. Teach me how to be a real Selector."

The bartender was taken aback at first but soon found his smirk peeking through.

"That's the kind of face I was waiting to see."

Tinkering, his hands gloved, his tools wrestling inside the robot's spine. Wires of all lengths, all shades, protruded through. Yet, the man of metal never pushed his motions, his body as lifeless as a statue as he lay on the operating table. All around, glass cabinets packed with vials and jars watched with curiosity, their surfaces decorated with glimmers from the hexagonal lights fixed to the ceiling.

"Just a few more adjustments," Veltrix said, playing with the circuitry. "Shouldn't be too long."

He stood beside the downed servant, his nose crammed into the innards as he let not a single detail pass him by.

"My apologies, Master Veltrix," Dikadus said. "I have failed to accomplish your first task."

"This defeat was no fault of your own," the master said. "Although they appear human, and although they were just little girls, those Zekrians are not to be underestimated. Add the fact that they were trained Guardians and even I would consider calling them monsters. I mean, just one kick and your entire inner workings were misshapen."

"My apologies for being weak," the metal man offered.

Veltrix set aside one tool, laying it on the copper tray beside him, in favor of another.

"Again, no fault of your own, Dikadus," he said. "I am your creator, so it is only right that I take responsibility for where your capabilities lie. Had I taken extra steps in reinforcing your body, in giving you more superior weaponry, well, we may have been able to take Mr. Mitchell's Fragment then and there. But the past is the past, and any shortcomings that dictated such events fall upon me, not you."

Another tool swap.

"That isn't to say that you are without perfections. I like to think that within that head of yours, I instilled the very essences of my character—the aspects that I take great pride in, that have allowed me to be where I am today: my intelligence; my ingenuity; my ruthlessness. Simply put, Dikadus, you are the me that I can keep building and building upon. You may become the perfect Veltrix."

The metal man proposed no insight, no retort, his apparent destiny no harder to swallow than a microscopic pill.

Eventually, Veltrix set all his tools aside, finishing his work by shutting the robot's torso.

"Have a move around," he suggested, pulling off his gloves.

So, Dikadus did, sitting himself up to perch upon the table. His gaze stuck to his fist as he clenched and re-clenched.

"Feeling well?" Veltrix asked.

"Yes," Dikadus answered. "Thank you, Master Veltrix."

The master smiled. "It is no problem of mine, Dikadus. I am happy to fix my boy."

The robot planted himself on the ground, his stance tall.

"Now," he said, "we may challenge those Guardians once again."

"Slow yourself, Dikadus," Veltrix urged. "You've only been repaired, not upgraded. Besides, I've already hired some helping hands to seize Mr. Mitchell, so we should be seeing him very shortly."

"What of the other Selectors?"

The master grinned. "Worry not, my boy."

He aimed his palm to the space before him, summoning a considerable holographic model of Planet Earth. At one section, a tiny red dot blinked, decorated with the string of text, "Golden Gate, New York."

"I already know where the other one is."

Change of Course

Several days later . . .

Everything. Just. Hurt.

And even that claim would be me underselling. My veins burned. My bones creaked. Every time I coughed, a metallic taste splashed across my tongue; half the time, I figured a piece of my lung had come up.

But I stayed on my feet.

Even with a blurred vision, even with Death himself scraping his scythe against my back, I kept my stance firm, my chin held high.

Before me, the girl of cherry blossoms positioned herself, her fists raised, her gaze acuate. Sweat dribbled down her forehead, soaking into her clothes as her body suffered through the same wear and tear as my own.

"Ready?" she asked me.

I steadied my wrench,

then nodded.

A beast set loose, Luna rushed towards me, her speed impeccable. And as she tore through my personal space, she launched her fists into a furious combo.

Wham!

Wham!

Wham!

I briskly shot up my arms in defense, absorbing the strikes. But against those punches—those hardened jabs more impactful than a crashing comet—my limbs crumbled against the strain.

Even so, I never let my focus splinter, observing each move as carefully as I could.

"Don't forget to breathe," Luna told me.

Inhale.

Exhale.

Left hook.

Right jab.

Inhale.

Exhale.

Solid connection.

Knuckle graze.

Inhale.

Exhale.

The opening.

Seizing the window, I knocked away Luna's knuckles with my wrench, throwing her off balance.

"Not bad," she praised.

Not finished.

Look for the opening, I remembered.

I freed up one of my hands, then hurled it towards her cheek.

Thnk!

Before my fist could land, Luna swung her foot, blocking my attack with her own.

Our power ground against one another.

"You're doing well, Jeremy," she praised. "But . . ."

Luna cranked up her dial, blasting me with a spike in strength that shoved me back, forcing me to waver. Before I could recover, she went for another kick, smashing her sole into my chest.

I spit up a gasp as I collapsed to the floor, and at this point, my exhaustion surpassed the point of understanding; unless it was for the universe's mightiest massage, I was not getting back up.

"I lost . . ." I choked.

My silver-haired Guardian approached me, offering her hand.

"You lost the battle," she said, "but with your progress, you'll win the war."

I gave a small smile. "That's good to hear."

I accepted her help, having her hoist me to my feet, followed by me leaning on her for support.

Mr. Rikaden settled near the sidewall, one eyebrow raised.

"This don't make a whole lotta sense," he said. "You asked me to train you, yet I just sat here each day."

"Because he needs to learn the fundamentals," Luna noted. "You were trying to have him run six light years before he learned how to walk."

The bartender shrugged. "Worked with me."

My Guardian merely rolled her eyes.

"In any case," she said, "I think you're really getting the hang of this, Jeremy. You're not just swinging your Tool randomly anymore."

"There's a purpose to your movements," Mr. Rikaden added. "Very nice growth, considering it's only been a few days."

"What can I say?" I asked. "It's the Selector in me."

The barkeep chuckled.

"Well," Luna said, "I say we call it for today. We actually have to leave for a bit to get some more supplies. Running low on food."

"I have stuff you can eat," Mr. Rikaden said.

"If you think I'm trying any of that, you've lost your mind," Ruby remarked. She lay on the floor nearby, just now waking up from her nap. "I've seen the sludge you serve up there."

"It's not . . ." From the bartender, a second thought. "Yeah, it's pretty bad. How was I supposed to know these bandits would gobble anything up?"

"You are what you eat," Faith noticed, seated against the wall with her novel in her hand. "And they happen to eat scum."

"You really know what to say when you wanna talk."

The five of us grouped up in the center of the room.

"So?" Mr. Rikaden asked. "What are your plans?"

"We're gonna stop by Voladea for a bit," Luna answered. "Stock up on supplies."

"And chow down on some fine dining!" Ruby cheered. "I hear the food there makes you keep coming back for more!"

"I needn't remind you that this is not a vacation," Faith said.

Luna's cheeks reddened.

"I wouldn't mind some restaurant-quality food," she admitted shyly.

"I-I just want something," I chimed in, adjusting myself to stand on my own.

Mr. Rikaden chuckled.

"You four really do make a solid group," he noticed. "You click like Nano and I did back in the day. Man, I remember this one time I threw him into a . . ."

His remembrance trailed off, possibly because we were handing the most judgy of looks.

"Just know that I think you're gonna do fine," he said. "You'll have each other's backs." The barkeep focused on me. "And you'll each be able to stand on your own."

My pride coated my skin like a tattoo, one that I'd be glad to show every day.

"You're welcome to come back here to train," Mr. Rikaden said. "Just relax when you use this room."

He gestured to a fractured mirror on one of the walls.

"Repair's aren't free."

"I-In my defense," I began, "I didn't think the wrench's handle would get so slick."

"Backwards thinking," Faith pointed out. "You were drenched with sweat. The outcome was highly predictable."

"Th-Thanks, Faith. You know just how to make me feel better."

"It is no problem."

Mr. Rikaden just laughed as he made his way to the staircase.

"I'm gonna go make sure I'm ready to open tomorrow," he said. "You kids stay safe, and just know that you're always welcome here."

Before he commenced his climb, he turned his head to me.

"And Mr. Selector . . ." He grinned. "Let me just say that you are no lost cause. Not by a long shot."

On the outside, I offered a hint of delight, but inside, the fireworks lit off in all directions, banging and popping with ecstasy.

His message complete, Mr. Rikaden vanished from the dojo to tend to his shop.

"Well," Luna said, "why don't you and I get cleaned up, Jeremy? Then, we can head out."

"Sounds good to me."

She handed me my original outfit—the red hoodie, tan cargo shorts—so that I could swap out this muscle shirt and these basketball shorts. (I guess the STS was faster than I originally assumed, because Ruby and Faith brought me this workout outfit in record time.)

I was also handed a towel to dry myself off from all this Jeremy juice.

Ooh, I didn't like the way I said that.

I brought myself over to a corner to change but quickly stopped as I noticed the girls' gazes stuck to me like honey bee stingers.

"U-Um," I said, embarrassed. "C-Could you look away, please?"

They kindly listened, although Ruby giggled.

"You are just the most adorable boy," she joked.

Once we had finished our cleanup (difficulty insane thanks to my screaming aches), we commenced our own exit, gifting Mr. Rikaden a farewell and thanking him for his hospitality as we made ourselves scarce from the bar and headed back to the shuttle.

From there on, it was just smooth sailing, the tension of the bandits evaporating as the STS glided away from the hellhole and into the endless void of space.

I melted onto my bench, my eyelids just begging to be shut.

"Phew," Ruby sounded, "I am so glad we're leaving that place."

"Agreed," Faith said. "Even if it is merely temporary."

"Hey, Jeremy?" Luna asked me.

"Yeah?" I asked back, my eyes shut, my head tilted back.

"When we were fighting all those times, you never swung your wrench at our faces. Why was that?"

"Because you're girls, and I was assuming you all wanted to keep your faces pretty."

So smooth.

So lady-killer like.

So not me.

What the hell did I just say?

Panicked, I glanced around the shuttle, spotting two of the trio splash upon the pond of embarrassment. (You could guess which one didn't.)

I sighed.

I'm sorry, Avella. Please forgive me. I promise, I'm not a smooth criminal.

"Speakin' of what we wanna keep," Ruby said, her cheeriness returning, "I'd love to see you keep going up, Jeremy! You being a Selector is no joke. You caught on really fast."

"Mm-hm!" Luna agreed. "Of course, we're not finished with the fundamentals just yet, but you're learning really well.

If anything, just remember the things I tried to hammer into you."

"Breathe," I recalled. "Always be aware. Believe in yourself."

That last one might take a while.

The girl of cherry blossom basked in her thrill.

"You're gonna be surpassing us in no time," she said.

"I don't know about that one." I gazed at my bruised hand. "But I like where I'm going."

Maybe,

just maybe,

the path to my ideal starts here.

Maybe this Jax guy wasn't lying about curing me.

I glanced back up, and it was then that I caught wind of a shooting star, dazzling as it came towards us.

"Hey, Luna." I pointed towards the spectacle. "Do you always see stuff like that?"

Luna peered out the window, and spotting the glimmer zooming towards their shuttle, panic oozed from her veins.

"That's pretty co—"

"Get down!"

Suddenly, my Guardian grabbed me and hurled me to the ground with her, just as the star rammed into our shuttle, exploding into a cloud of monstrous flames.

The STS trembled from the impact.

Kaboom!

Ruby and Faith jumped to their feet.

"What's going on!?" the Rose exclaimed.

"It would appear we are under attack!" the archer deduced.

Kaboom!

Another hit, this time on the opposite side of the shuttle, rocking the inside.

The girls and I slid all over the floor.

Not too long after did a red light begin to flash from wall to wall.

Luna scrambled to the front console.

"This is not good!" she bellowed. "We need to get these defenses up!"

"There aren't any," Faith said.

Despair caved into the cherry blossom's petals.

"What . . . ?" she asked.

"The Sentinels didn't believe that they required weapons for this spacecraft, so they didn't bother installing any."

"You've gotta be fu—"

Kaboom!

Another deep impact, the starving flames grazing across the windows.

"Left engine has been disengaged!" the speakers announced. "Now to switching to manual support."

From the console, a steering wheel popped out, daring a soul to take command.

A task for the leader.

Luna jerked the wheel, her movements stiffened by the mechanism's stubbornness.

"We have to land this thing!" she bellowed.

"But where!?" Ruby cried, clinging to a pole for dear life.

"Anywhere!"

Kaboom!

"Right engine disengaged!" the speakers announced. "Critical damage has been sustained! Repeat: Critical damage has been sustained!"

"I can see that!" Luna cranked the wheel to the side. "Crap! This isn't where I wanna go!"

Despite the unwillingness of my limbs to squirm, I grit my teeth and lifted myself up, just in time for the shuttle to nosedive towards a globe, flames eating away at the metallic shell.

Faster.

Faster.

Faster.

Our speed boosted to a million miles per second, mimicking well the racing of my own heart.

"Get ready!" Ruby cried.

I braced myself.

"Jeremy!" Luna's voice echoed as everything faded to black.

8

Insanity Has a Voice

Blurred words, scurrying into my ears, carving themselves into my brain's curvatures.

Their messages, decrypted.

Their familiarity, absolute, despite the debris tumbling off the details.

I know them. I know this.

It was like a droplet hanging off the tip of my tongue, but no matter which way I tilted my head, I just couldn't coat my entire mouth. I couldn't dive into the full taste.

Blurred words, poking at the itch in my head.

Then, a hush,

as if all melody knelt before Lady Silence, as if the concept of sound had been wiped away with a single sweep.

There was nothing.

Then, there was everything.

Suddenly, the shades of my vision returned to me, transporting me to the origin of all forms of chaos. Sirens blasting in the distance. A vehicle flipped on its hood sprawled, vast flames and voluptuous smoke savoring the air from the underside. In every inch, the elements roared with definition, as if the whole had decided that it could never be drawn from hand. Everything else, however—the street, the sidewalk, the sun—took on a fuzzy outline, like a camera that couldn't focus on it all.

"S-S-S-S . . ." whispered the wreckage; or more specifically, murmured the corpses buried beneath—a man and a woman. Their flesh had been charred, disfiguring most of their traits, morphing them into creatures that even Satan would have to turn away. Melted eyes. Burnt hair. Revealed bone, solid white as their blood had boiled to nothingness.

The woman forced her hand towards me, her one good eye glistering with agony.

I hurled my hand back to her, only to realize that my fingertips wouldn't scrape against hers. No matter how much I pushed, no matter how much effort I bled, the result remained the same.

Come on! I begged. *Please! Let me save her! I can save her!*

The flames grew richer, overpowering the smoke, shaking the heated metal of the vehicle.

Let me reach! I can reach!

Soon enough, the pair became engulfed in the hill of red and orange, turning their frames into mere silhouettes.

Don't take them from me!

I had everything.

Then, I had nothing.

Boom! the wreckage howled, erupting into a sierra of fire and automobile fragments.

A damaged door flew towards me, ready to smash against my torso.

But, just before my sternum could break apart, a miracle descended upon me:

I opened my eyes.

I awoke to find myself lying on the ground, my head throbbing every which way. I shut my eyes tight, then reopened them, easing the pain a bit as well as refreshing my fuzzy vision.

Thus, the pair of sheepskin boots resting before me could be seen as clear as day, along with the warm, sock-covered legs acting as my pillow.

Where am I? I wondered.

My answer: the gentle, rhythmic humming of a female, just a foot or so away from my ear. As a bonus, a hand ran lovingly along the top of my head, the fingers poking through every curl of my hair.

Curious, I turned my head, spotting the captivating face of my cherry-haired Guardian. Her lips curved sweetly as she set her sights forward.

"Ruby?" I asked softly.

The girl of strawberries sharply quit her humming, her smile widening even more as she noticed me.

"Jeremy!" she cheered. "You're finally awake! Hehe!"

As if they kissed stovetops, my cheeks burned up at the intimacy of the distance, and I hastily loaded my stare back to her boots.

"W-What are you doing?" I asked.

"What do you mean?" she rolled back.

"I mean . . . Why am I lying here?"

"Well, I couldn't just let you sleep on the ground, dummy. That could really mess up your neck, and we can't have the next Sentinel of Light take over with a bad posture now, can we?"

"Oh . . . Makes sense . . ."

"Right? So, I just did what any reasonable person would do, which is give you the most super-ultra-mega lap pillow in existence!"

Reasonable, huh?

"By the way," Ruby said, "I've been told that my legs are as soft as clouds." She leaned her face in. "What's your opinion on this?"

Well, she wasn't wrong.

I'm sure you've heard of Einstein's claim: "Put your hand on a hot stove for a minute, and it seems like an hour. Sit with a pretty girl for an hour, and it seems like a minute."

Boy, do I wish I could get that minute, because I don't think my hormones can take much more of this!

Anxiety, please, behave yourself!

"I . . . I agree," I admitted. "They're pretty soft."

"Right?" I had never heard a prouder person. "I knew you'd feel that way."

A piece of rock tumbled before my Guardian's soles.

"Hey, Ruby?" I said.

"What's up?" she asked playfully.

"Can . . . Can I get up now?"

"That's up to you. Just know that if you leave now, you're always welcome back at Ruby Storm's lap pillow service, free of charge!"

"I'll keep that in mind."

I wasted no time getting out of there, soothing my squirming nerves.

Glancing around, I could tell that we were in a cave of some kind, the walls jagged as rocks and boulders jutted out like a sort of collage. No illumination to speak of, save some brilliance luminescing towards the front.

"Where are we?" I asked.

"Not where we want to be."

Up ahead, Luna and Faith huddled around a globe-shaped hologram.

The girl of cherry blossoms smiled my way.

"Glad to see you're okay," she said.

I lifted myself up, my heels digging into the compacted dirt graced with shriveled leaves and puny twigs.

I then approached the duo, the radiance of the hologram gradually seeping into my hoodie.

I knelt down beside Luna to study the globe.

"Is this where we're at?" I asked.

"Looks like it," she answered. "Gridlock: a tertiary planet deemed unfit for complex organisms to live on. For the small fry, though, it's Heaven."

"No Voladea, then, huh?"

"It would appear not," Faith noted. "We had been shot down, and this planet was our only option."

"Either that or float through space for all eternity," Luna added.

"Who shot us down?" I asked.

"We're not entirely sure, but if we had to guess, we'd say mercenaries."

My fear coiled around my throat.

"Mercenaries?" I asked. "But why?"

"Because Veltrix is a smart man," Luna answered. "Rather than going for the Fragments one by one, he's going for the quick game. Hired arms equals more helping hands, and I'm sure he has the bucks to pay for them."

Unease dug its claws deep into the chest of my peace of mind.

"Have you tried contacting that empire of yours?" I asked.

"We did," Luna said, "but we can't reach Peeka. Whoever's behind this put down jammers, blocking us out from everyone else. It's just us here."

I swallowed the lump in my throat.

"The best we can do now is wait and think," Ruby said, lifting herself from her comfortable spot on the ground. "I'm sure we all still need to recover from the whole crash-landing dilemma."

"You seem rather nonchalant given the circumstances we're in," Faith pointed out.

The cherry-haired girl stretched. "If we're not in tip-top shape, we're gonna lose. It's that simple."

The archer's eyes soon gleamed with annoyance.

"That attitude of yours," she said, "I wouldn't expect any less."

Ruby narrowed her eyes. "What's that supposed to mean?"

"I'm simply implying that your way of thinking is rather . . . *ignorant*."

Enmity shaded the Rose's petals, and she stomped towards the group.

"Define 'ignorant'," she requested coldly.

Faith stood tall herself.

"You guys . . ." Luna said. "Now isn't, exactly, the best time to be arguing."

"No offense, Luna," Ruby said, "but would you mind shutting up for a few seconds."

The girl of silver hair widened her eyes with shock.

"I know you're our leader and all," Ruby continued, "but sometimes, you have to let the team settle things for themselves. Besides"—she pointed at Faith—"I'm getting sick of Miss No Emotion over here treating me like a child."

"I'm merely highlighting the obvious," Faith hissed. "As far as I can tell, you possess the mental capacity of a disabled chimp. Up to this point, only Luna and I have been utilizing our thinking power, whereas you're just here to be here. You make no contributions to the team, nor do you want to."

"Faith!" Luna exclaimed. "You know that's not true."

"Yeah!" Ruby said. "I think the team effort should be split into equal shares."

"Your words differ profusely from your actions and choices," Faith argued. "You make no effort to contemplate on the possible outcomes; instead, you simply take action in the moment, giving absolutely zero consideration to the aftermath."

The girl of strawberries quivered as she clenched her fists. "You know what, Faith . . ."

Luna hoisted me to my feet and escorted me to a safer distance away from the two.

"You're gonna wanna back up for this," she suggested.

I held my breath.

"Nobody's perfect!" Ruby cried. "At least I'm trying!"

"You call that trying?" Faith mocked. "If that is your limit for effort, then I am utterly embarrassed to claim you as a comrade."

"Well, at least I know how to crack a smile! Would it kill you to show some emotions once in a while?"

"While it is true that I do not show any signs of emotions, I cannot visualize how that and my intelligence hold any sort of correlation. As expected, your incomprehensible brain functionality would jump to a meaningless conclusion."

A tear rolled down Ruby's cheek as her glare became bolder and bolder with hatred.

"Faith . . ." she whispered.

On the other hand, Faith merely viewed her comrade with genuine boredom.

This is only gonna get worse, I thought. *I have to do something.*

"Hey, guys," I said, "y-you don't have to fight."

"Stay out of this, Jeremy," Ruby hissed.

"But friends shouldn't—"

"I said stay out of this!" A howl that froze my character. "This is none of your business! Besides, how would you know how to deal with us? You're just a damn loser!"

That one bullet, shredding through my chest, then circling back to tear away again and again. The specks I had witnessed here and there, promising in their guidance, erased in one clean sweep.

That hope that died before it could even leave the womb.

"*Ruby!*" Luna roared, furious.

Even Ruby had realized her error, her remorse supplied as soon as her venom was spat.

The boy stared aimlessly at the ground, his eyes watery.

"Y-You're right . . ." he choked. "W-What am I thinking? I'm sorry."

Ruby pushed her hand towards him. "Jeremy . . . I . . ."

"As expected," Faith said, "your ignorance has led to the devastation of another's emotional state."

Swift as the wind, Ruby's viciousness returned, her glare right back on the archer.

"Oh, shut up, Faith!" she growled intensely. "You always say things at the worst possible time!"

"I'm merely stating what needs to be said."

"Yeah, well, maybe you should stop doing that and just read the freakin' mood!"

Who am I kidding? She's right.
I am a loser.
All I'll ever be is a loser.
This world has so many great people, so many characters that just fit. They have the charisma. They have the charm. They have it all that makes you truly believe that they deserve to be here.

Then, there's me. I can barely look people in the eyes when I talk to them. I push away the ones that are nice to me, because I know that I can never live up to their expectations. I only have one friend, for crying out loud! And I'm sure that even she is tired of me. They all are.

All I ever do is make mistakes.
All I ever do is bring people down.
I really don't belong in this universe, nor do I think I ever will.

I should've just stayed in that car . . .

An agreement, spawning from the demons thriving in my abyss, snarling from those hands that swayed from the shadows, their hunger endless for my being.

The beats of my heart quickened, the vibrations pounding in my eardrums.

Thump!
Thump!
Thump!

All at once, the heat of my body dissipated, as if ice clung to every centimeter of my veins.

My limbs quivered.

My sweat ripened.

I started panting like mad.

Breathe, I told myself. *Please, just breathe.*

No dice, my lungs shriveling from the impact.

Then, they scurried through—the voices, like spiders burrowing into my flesh.

"*Useless . . .*" they whispered. "*You're so very useless . . .*"

"No . . ." I choked softly. "Please . . ."

"*Worthless . . . So very worthless . . .*"

"Don't do this to me . . ."

"*End it all . . .*"

I cupped my hands around my ears.

"Please . . . Leave me alone . . ."

Ruby and Faith barked and barked, stirring the solutions washing through Luna's mind.

I need to break them up, she decided.

However, her resolve soon collected itself elsewhere—towards the teenage boy who trembled as he wept.

"Jeremy . . . ?" she uttered. "Jeremy!" She scrambled to his side, perching her hand on his shoulder. "Jeremy, what's wrong?"

The boy said nothing.

Desperate for help, Luna looked to her comrades.

"Guys!" she cried.

But it was pointless, the archer and spearwoman battling it out, their words their weapons.

"Damn it." Back to the jumble of broken pieces. "It's gonna be okay, Jeremy. Just stay with me, okay?"

"Worthless . . . You are so worthless . . ."

My sanity neared that breaking point, filling my head with itches that I just couldn't scratch. Just scratch the itch! JUST GET THE FUCK OUT OF MY HEAD!

"Alone . . . You are so alone . . ."

Something latched onto my shoulder—a short figure with long, black hair, the facial features scribbled out. Through its front rushed incomprehensible garble, like an orchestra where all the notes had been disfigured.

I shut my eyes as tight as I could.

"Please . . . Just stop . . ."

The boy dropped to his knees, bringing Luna down with him as she hugged him close, stroking his hair.

"It's okay," she whispered. "It's okay."

But his pieces refused to be collected.

As Ruby continued with her growls, Faith glanced around to please her interest, and it was only then that she finally caught wind of the withering boy and girl desperate to save him.

"Hey!" Ruby hissed. "The least you can do is listen to what I have to say!"

But her malice, too, faded as the real plight unfolded before her.

"Jeremy!" she cried, rushing to him along with Faith.

"Finally, you two noticed," Luna groaned.

"What's wrong with him?"

"It's his psychosis."

"But it has never been this severe," Faith noted.

"Something must've really set it off," Luna explained.

A lover, guilt nuzzled Ruby's neck.

More of the figures, surrounding me on either side. Like the first, their faces had scribbly lines running across them, their words nothing more than a mishmash of blur.

But the one of clarity did soon present itself; first with the arm of pale skin, phasing through the wall as its bloodied claws planted themselves on the rocks. Then came the head, features nonexistent save the grin it gleamed through its blood-soaked fangs. Scarlet droplets splashed onto the dirt, dirtying the shriveled leaves.

The boy hastily broke free from Luna's hold, hurling himself back to the furthest wall possible.

"Get away from me!" he screamed. "Stay the hell away from me!"

They sent their stares to where he lashed, finding only a barren wall.

"Jeremy," Luna said to the boy, her tone hushed, "there's nothing there. Calm down."

Inevitable, the creature warped through the rocks completely, landing creepily before me as flakes of dried blood fell from its limbs.

"*Waste of space . . . Such a waste of space . . .*"

It took a step forward.

I . . . I couldn't move, the claws of the abyss looping around my ankles like manacles, the shadows pinning themselves to my shoulders, locking me down.

"Please . . ." I begged.

"*Alone . . .*"

"Don't do this to me . . ."

"*Worthless . . .*"

"Spare me . . ."

A beastly roar, the creature lunged forward, its jaw unhinged to latch evenly across my skull.

I had nothing.
I still had nothing.

Evening.

The sun barely kissed the horizon, the soft orange radiating off the skyscrapers' stacks of windows. Down below, the home commute boomed, car horns snaking through the air as traffic cluttered up.

They relaxed atop a rooftop, basking in the scenery.

"So, this is Golden Gate," Veltrix said. "Although the humans are rather inferior, I must admit that this city is nothing short of astounding. I'd even size it up with somewhere like Altharia."

He angled his attention to a particular framework of steel and concrete.

"I'm certain that she's in there, my boy. So, if you may."

"Sir." The man of metal trained his hand on the area, and like a metamorphosis, the hand morphed into a hefty cannon, the inside etched with lines of circuitry.

He charged his weapon, collecting energy.

Then, he let go, firing the mass of burning atoms towards the windows.

9

A Guardian in Distress

Again with the awakening, the sparks of my mind popping as my engine heated up. One by one, the senses revived themselves, clicking and clicking until my consciousness blended back to the baseline reality.

I lay on my back; only this time, the makeshift pillow of clouds didn't cushion my neck. Instead, I had the coolness of the dirt to embrace. A terrible haze clouded my thoughts, like ink diluting a glass of water. Nothing really hurt; everything just felt . . . off, or rather, foreign. My eyelids kept demanding to shut on me, and the fatigue of my limbs bubbled from the deepest core to the outermost surface.

My sights roved across my surroundings.

Still in the cave, the walls of rocks enclosing like sides of a tomb.

Towards the far end, the archer relaxed, whisking herself away to the pages of her novel.

Across from her, she of the cherry blossoms crouched, examining the globe-like hologram.

No one else.

Where's the other one?

Using the wall for support, I lifted myself up, then sauntered over to Luna.

Her attention spun to me as she heard my footsteps.

"Glad to see you feeling better," she said heartily.

"Thanks," I replied, my awkwardness flickering. "S-Sorry you had to see that. Truth be told, it hasn't been that bad in a long time."

"It's okay. This is a new part of your life, and I think calling it stressful would be an understatement."

No kidding.

"Part of me was expecting something like that to happen," Luna continued. "I just wish our situation for when it occurred was more manageable."

"Sorry."

She smiled. "Not your fault."

I glanced around a second time.

"By the way," I said, "where's Ruby?"

Piece by piece, the cherry blossom's petals withered.

"She's, um, she's gone," Luna said softly.

"Gone? She left?"

"Yeah. After you fainted, she and Faith went at it again. At some point, Ruby just had enough, so she stormed out. I tried to stop her, but . . ."

Shame mutilated the rest of Luna's message.

I rubbed her shoulder.

"I-It's all right," I told her. "At least you tried to get her to stay. That shows that you actually care, and that's what really matters."

The girl of silver hair simpered.

"I'm the leader," she said. "I'm supposed to be the glue that holds everyone together, you know? But it just feels like I could be doing more."

"You can't please everyone."

Not even yourself, I've learned.

"Do you know where she went?" I asked.

"No idea," Luna said. "She didn't say anything, and I've been trying to see if I could find her on this map, but I've had no luck."

She rubbed her eyes, highlighting the bruises etched into her knuckles.

"What happened there?"

"Oh, this?" She caressed the injuries. "Let's just say, I got kinda frustrated. May have punched the wall a couple times."

"And she did not hold back," Faith commented.

Nearby, a portion of the wall had been caved in, cracks breaking through in every direction.

Remind me not to make her mad.

The guilt, however, soon splattered across my painting of indifference, disfiguring the image.

"Sorry," I said. "You guys are all clearly struggling, yet here I am passing out. I'm pretty lame."

"You're not lame, Jeremy," Luna told me. "You're you. Nobody's perfect; we all have our kinks, our shortcomings. In the grand scheme of things, we're in this together."

The seriousness returned.

"I just hope we can find Ruby before it's too late."

"Too late? What do you mean?"

"Like I said, everyone has their kinks. Ruby may show herself as this cheery, fearless girl, but deep down, she has her own issues. I think this new direction in our lives has taken its toll on her, which is good in a way. She can finally let it all out. But she shouldn't be alone when she loses it. We need to give her that support system."

Unexpected to my past's notes, my confidence switched gears from the usual nosedive.

"We'll find her," I said.

Luna's morale rose up to my own.

"I know we will."

Just then, rustling toppled from the opening to the cave, where the darkness invited us.

And more brisk than an officer's draw, my Guardians spawned their weapons, their stances ready for battle.

"Who's out there?" Luna hissed. "Ruby, is that you?"

The answer: a tiny black object rolling in like a dead cockroach. Upon closer inspection, I found its construction similar to that USB device Luna had used at my apartment.

"Jeremy, stay back," she ordered.

I retreated to the farthest corner.

Our leader then tiptoed towards the device, fully expecting it to transform into a killer android or another of the like. However, the item did no such thing, even as she poked at it with her blade.

She investigated the dusk for another round, and only after finding no characters did she settle on grasping the gadget, laying it in her palm.

Right on time, the object's surface lit up with blue luminance.

"Hello? Is this thing on?"

The speaker: a voice furthest from our favorite Rose, heavy and grim.

"Looks like it. Hello there, kiddos. First of all, I have to give you props on staying in there for so long. I figured you midgets would come scrambling out for food or water by now. You must be stacked up.

"Then again, maybe not, since we found one of your little chicks fleeing the coop."

My stomach gurgled as Ruby's weakened groans came through.

"Shh, shh," the voice said. *"Relax. Don't make me rip up that pretty face of yours. Now then, I know you're in there, and you have what I want. I think we can make an arrangement. You give me Jeremy Mitchell, and I'll make sure that your friend here doesn't end up with more red than she already has. Tell you what: I'll even give you an hour to decide! Aren't I just generous, boys?"*

In the background erupted manly cheering.

"You'll know where to find us. Don't be stupid."

The device shut down, supplying the cave with a boisterous silence.

Luna looked back at us, dread dulling her cherry blossom irises.

For my part, I vomited into the corner.

Saving the Rose
of Joy

Thirty minutes passed, and none of us could say a goddamn word. Thus far, the chapters of our story had flowed seamlessly, the bumps so short that even the blind couldn't decipher them. But this . . . This predicament didn't just warp the timeline; it mutilated the path, tearing those next pages into jumbles of messy scraps.

And the worst part:

my story was only gonna get worse from here.

That epilogue reared its head, polite like a maid, wondering if I was ready to follow her lead.

"I'll go," I said.

A concerned mother, Luna gazed at me.

"What?" she asked.

"I said I'll go. Clearly, they're only after me. Whoever was talking didn't mention the Gemini Tool, so I'll hand it off to you, then you can give me to them. This way, Ruby gets to come home."

"Have you lost your mind? If we give you up, they're gonna take you to Veltrix, and what do you think he'll do once he finds out you don't have the Fragment?"

"Kill me."

I didn't even flinch.

Luna's lips quivered. "How can you say that so easily?"

"Because it doesn't matter if I die! Look, I'm a Selector or whatever you call it, right? You find people like me in the universe, right? I'm easily replaceable. But the Fragment, that's what important. That's what we can't give up. So, you're gonna hand me to those creeps, then you're gonna take that wrench back to your empire and find a new Selector. Ruby stays alive and the universe is safe. It's a win-win."

"It's not a win-win if you die! You must be protected—"

"Your job is to protect the Fragment! Keep that safe and everyone gets to live on. If I die, nothing changes."

"Is that how Avella would feel?"

I narrowed my eyes. "Don't you dare bring her into this. She would do a whole lot better without some insecure idiot who can't even look people in the eyes!"

"I don't think you get it, Jeremy." Passion blew across the cherry blossom, lending her petals a beautiful tint. "You're precious, you idiot, and I want to protect you not as your Guardian but as your friend." She clenched her fists. "I'm not letting you go."

My position stayed as firm as the manacles strangling my self-opinion.

"I'm not gonna let anyone die," I said. "Not for me."

The alpine impasse, its zephyr of tension fluttering all around us.

"No one has to die," the archer assured.

Luna and I turned our eyes.

"Faith," our leader said, "do you have a plan?"

"More or less. We're certain that there's no way to spy on us here, correct?"

"Should be the case. They only know that we're in here, and you and I scoped out the place after we got the message."

"Then this should work," Faith muttered to herself. Then, to us: "Hear me out."

* * *

Nature's waste crunched beneath the weight of their footsteps, their heels digging into the moistened soil littered with dead vines. All around them, tropical trees grand like giants cast shadows, their leaves thick enough they had to be shoved aside just to pass through. Up above, a blanket of pure gray played spectator.

"Are we almost there?" Jeremy asked.

Luna flipped her hand over, projecting a small-scale hologram of the planet onto her palm. To one section, a bevy of still red dots stood their ground.

"Yeah," she answered. "I'm still trying to figure out if their signatures were always on the map."

"Most definitely not," Jeremy concluded. "They must've hid their signatures until we received that message."

"They're smart; I'll give 'em that."

"They *are* hired guns."

"Fair enough."

Eventually, the duo stumbled upon a change in scenery: the head of a massive spaceship, poking through the tree line, somehow emboldening the army of dull clouds.

"We're right here," Luna said.

The two rushed through the rest of the tree maze, breaking through the edge to plant themselves upon a voluminous, grassy plain.

"It's about damn time."

Up ahead, an elevated ridge showed, and residing upon it, a grim character twisted his grin. A humanoid wolf, his frame gracile yet fortress-like. His outer fur smirked dark gray while the inner portion resembled a stained moon. The obsidian of his scleras contrasted prominently with the crimson of his slit pupils, the same hue as the scar shredding diagonally along his right eye. A vest of armor covered his torso, its surface adorned with clips and magazines, while a plasma rifle readied itself behind his back.

The wolf examined his dirtied claws.

"I didn't think you were going to show," he said. "Sure took your sweet-ass time getting here." He grinned, his fangs yellowed. "Guess I was wrong."

Luna glared with cold eyes.

"We don't leave our own," she hissed.

"Oh? But isn't that what you're about to do right now?"

"Jeremy isn't Zekrian; he's just a human." She gnawed off a piece of bottom lip. "Easily replaceable."

"Fair enough," the villain agreed. "Humans are just a dime a dozen. Hell, if this wasn't a request, I'd blow his head off just for the fun of it."

The boy couldn't have been less fazed.

"By the way," the wolf said, "wasn't there another one of you? Where's the one who had the book?"

"We didn't bring her along," Luna explained. "Can't be sure that you'll keep your word."

From the wolf, a wider smirk.

"Judging from your tone," he said, "I take it you know who I am."

"I do. You're Scar, the most infamous mercenary there is. You use women as tools and will defile anyone standing in your way. "

"You're not as dumb as you look. Anything for a paycheck. I have pussies to mangle!" He gestured to his armed comrades stationed at his sides. "Ain't that right, boys?"

Their excited cheers shook sickeningly in Luna's gut.

"Can we just get this over with?" she growled. "No point in the delay."

"Whoa, whoa, take it easy," Scar said. "Relax. It's not like either of us have anywhere else to be, right? Why don't we take our time and get to know each other? Don't you wanna know how I snatched your friend to begin with?"

The cherry blossom grimaced.

Please don't sneeze.
Please don't sneeze.
Please don't sneeze.

I made my steps featherweight, praying that not a single atom of attention would be drawn to me. Trees in every direction, hopeful that my senses would be jarred. But I came out on top, scurrying through the maze until reaching near the backside of the colossal spaceship. The entrance had been flipped open, a threatening alien stationed on either side, armed with energy weapons.

Hidden behind a bush, I punched through my train of thoughts, busting each window until the one discolored shard of glass spilled onto my toes.

I grabbed a rock nearby.

Here's hoping those games weren't BS.

I flung the pebble into the forest behind me, banging it against the bark of a tree.

Dink!

As planned, the guards swiveled their heads, their firearms ready.

"Not it," one of them said.

The other shook his head, muttering as he approached my position. "Pussy."

I crouched low, my forehead drenched with sweat as the alien marched past me. Then, once he had gone far enough in, I tiptoed to his back and swung my wrench.

Wham!

Like beating a loaf of ham. A meaty thud popped as the guard dropped to the dirt.

"Cutter?" the remaining guard called out.

He, too, came close, and once in range, I bashed his skull as well, wiping his lights.

I eyed the downed men.

Yay!

Maintaining my stealth, I ventured over to the ship's entrance, hiding behind a wall to peer inside.

No guards in sight.

Nice.

I journeyed deeper in, creeping through the steel hallways, the natural light fading as the lit panels fixed into the ceiling became more prominent.

A handful of forks in the road, and on the latest one, my hands were tied, footsteps rising steadily from one of the choices.

Distressed, I rushed down the desolate path, snaking into a doorframe and hiding behind it.

I waited.

Please don't come here.

Please don't come here.

Please don't come here.

The shuffling steps grew louder and louder, but thankfully, they became softer once again, the Doppler Effect soothing my confidence.

Oh, thank God.

"Where the hell did I put it?"

I froze, the syllables behind me calm as night.

In slow motion, I turned my head, discovering that I had ended up in some locker room. At one of the iron cabinets, a merc dug through the contents. Luckily, he faced the other way, but I knew it wouldn't be like that for long.

Gotta think.

Gotta think.

Another discolored shard, directing me to jam myself into a corner of the room. The lockers had enough bulk that they could easily hide me.

So, I followed through, my muscles clenched as I squirmed into position, crouching down.

He searched and searched and searched.

"I could've sworn I put it in here," the alien said.

Look, man, if you've been at it for a while, chances are, whatever the hell you're looking for isn't in there!

. . . As you can see, I can't always be patient.

At long last, the merc just gave up, shutting his locker with annoyance.

"Forget it," he cried. "I'm sure it'll come up." As he walked out the room: "I'll just ask Zikey for his girly mag."

Really? All that effort for some porn? Now that's *dedication.*

Once in the clear, I let loose a hefty breath, my anxiety level just a little below crippling. But I had to keep pushing, whatever it took.

Ergo, I carried myself back into the hallways, and before long, my destination rolled to my reality; its form, an armed merc guarding a complex door.

That's gotta be it, right? I figured. *Question is, how am I gonna get him away?*

The third shard, "epiphany" written along the front.

I'm a madman for this one.

Hidden behind a wall, wrench in my hands, I tapped the edge against the steel.

Thnk!

Thnk!

"Hm?" the guard hummed, followed by his advancement to my position.

I prepped for the beatdown.

Not yet.

Close.

Not yet.

Closer.

Not yet.

Nose poking into frame.

Go time!

I bashed ruthlessly the underside of the merc's chin, knocking him out cold in an instant.

I am scarily good at this.

No time to waste, I hurried to the abandoned door, only to find out that it was locked, a card reader glued to the left side.

Why make things easy, right?

Prediction. I traveled back to the downed guard, and after frisking his body did I locate a credit card lookalike buried in his pocket.

Thanks, brotha.

I went back to the locked door, slipping the card into the slot.

Beep! the machine sounded, the mechanisms of the door clicking and thumping not too long after. Next thing I knew, the barrier of metal slid upward, revealing a room no larger than a walk-in closet. No guards to fear; only a feminine figure plopped down in the back corner. Her strawberry hair appeared messy, her left arm battered and bruised with internal damage. White bands of cloth bedizened her body, from the one shielding her eyes to the ones wrapped around her wrists and ankles.

"W-Who's there?" she asked weakly, terrified.

I drew closer to crouch down beside her, then removed her blindfold, letting her vibrant cherry irises be admired once again.

"Jeremy?" she asked. "Is that . . . Is that really you?"

"I'm gonna get you out of here," I promised. "Just gimme a second."

Stashing my wrench in the loop of my shorts, I undid my Guardian's restraints, then tenderly helped her to her feet.

"You okay?" I asked. "Can you walk?"

"Y-Yeah." She gazed at me, her disbelief limitless. "You came . . ."

I grabbed her hand. "Come on. You can stare at me all you want once we get out of here."

I dragged her out of her cage, and right as my foot passed the doorframe,

Beep!

Eh-ooh!
Eh-ooh!

Eh-ooh!

Piercing, a thunderous alarm erupted from within the ship.

Scar lifted his brow.

"Well, well," he said. "Looks like our little pig is trying to make a run for it." To his comrades: "Why don't you go check on her? Make sure she's okay." An underlying viciousness took root in his words.

The mercs nodded, with several fleeing the scene. Still enough around to trouble Luna and Jeremy, though.

"Is it bad timing?" Scar asked the cherry blossom. "A coincidence? Or did you just try to screw me out of a paycheck?"

Luna's caution pulsed like a shockwave.

"I don't know what you're talking about," she said.

"I think you do. I think you were trying to fuck me. And the only ones who get to fuck good ol' Scar are his many wives! Boys, time to be mean!"

At once, the mercs trained their rifles on the duo.

Luna held her arm to her side, and like a familiar, her pink blade digitized into reality, the hilt glad to be in her grasp.

"Faith," she said to Jeremy, "I think it's time to drop the act."

"Agreed," the boy said.

Except, as specks of blue light encased his being, swirling around him like a tornado, as his person became concealed completely, the identity bloomed with mystery. But once the spectacle had been cleared, it was not Jeremy but Faith who now faced the pack, her bow loaded and ready to headhunt.

"Impressive," Scar commended. "It almost makes me want to kill you with mercy. But there's no mercy here; only the savages and the slaves, and we're all savages around here! Ain't that right, fellas!?"

The bandits hurrahed, their wild sides breaching through like new personalities.

Scar grinned. "Let's start this party."

The hunters complied, and their hesitation zero, they pulled their triggers, sending wave after wave of projectiles zooming towards the Zekrians.

Her teeth clenched, Luna swiped her sword with fury, slicing apart the bullets that zipped her way.

Meanwhile, Faith sped to cover, then cleanly drew back her arrow, picking off targets.

"Not ideal," I groaned, the alarm pounding into my eardrums. Uneasiness surged through my nerves, breaking down my blessed gift of complex thought.

"Jeremy," Ruby said, "which way did you come from?"

"That is a very good question," I told her, flustered.

"Hey!" From down the hall, a pair of mercs emerged, their weapons trained on us. "Don't move a muscle!"

Pretty sure that's the way, too.

"Come on, Jeremy!" Ruby jerked me the opposite way, guiding me.

Pew! Pew! Pew!

Opened fire, the energy rifles bellowing as their bullets rushed past Ruby and me.

Not good. Not good. Not good. Not good.

We sprinted through the seemingly endless spaceship, outrunning the bandits but having no idea where we could meet daylight.

"R-Rub—"

I stopped myself.

Ruby just got kidnapped. I can't rely on her right now; at least, not for everything. Come on, Jeremy, you're badass when it comes to school. Use that big brain!

I swiped my hands at the notions, the poor ones phasing through my hands like phantoms, until one of tangibility soared into my grasp.

It's a gamble, but it's better than running this marathon.

"Ruby," I said.

"Yeah?"

"You're strong, right?"

"Super strong!"

"Think you can punch a hole through the wall?"

We halted, and Ruby raised an eyebrow at me.

"Say what?"

"Punch a hole through the wall," I repeated. "Right now, we're running around like blind mice. It's a gamble, but if we're near the edge right now, it's our ticket out of here."

In the distance, the growls of stomping boots threatened us.

"Better than nothing," Ruby admitted.

She ushered me back then cocked back her fist, focused on the sheet of metal.

She thrust.

A cannonball busting a sea vessel.

Poong! the wall cried as it ruptured against the impact, forging a hole wider than a window.

And by the grace of God, the other side smiled at us with a scenery of greenery.

"Jackpot!" Ruby cheered.

"They're over here!" a merc hollered from down the hall.

"Time to split."

Killing my reluctance, I grabbed Ruby's hand and leapt out the ship, making a mad dash for the great beyond.

Fwoosh! Fwoosh!

Her precision, deadly.

Her mercy, boundless.

One by one, Faith picked off the mercenaries, her arrows drilling into their skulls, blanking out the whites of their eyes.

For her part, Luna unfolded her wrath, driving her blade cleanly through her foes' chests. With each kill, she shook the scarlet off her weapon.

At one point, a bandit crept up behind the cherry blossom, knocking her down before unloading his magazine. But just before he could complete the villain act, an arrow spiraled into his neck, stripping his life.

The Guardians nodded to one another.

"Come on!" Scar bellowed. "They're just some little girls! Let's end this already so we can get paid!"

However, his patience had been tested, for like frantic doe, his prey fled from the battlefield, bolting back into the luscious jungle.

"After them!" the big bad wolf hollered. "I wanna see their heads at my toes!"

Like a swarm of yellow jackets, the mercenaries still standing poured themselves into the sea of wood.

Scar began to do the same, just as a peculiar sight caught his eye: the ticket to his fantasies and his prisoner, scrambling into the far distance.

His face twisted with curiosity.

"I like what I'm seeing," he said.

He changed directions.

My Guardian and I darted through the jungle, trampling over the roots embedded in the ground. My lungs held up their white flag; same with my legs. Under any other circumstance, I would've dropped like a log. But my mind snatched the reins this time around, fueling my body with the hunger to keep pushing forward.

Before long, we found ourselves in an open plain of grass, the sides composed of leaning trees and aged shrubs.

After escorting Ruby to the center, I finally let go of her hand. I then slouched over and waited.

I know I say this a lot, but I'm gonna throw up.

If I saw a chunk of pink spill with my bile, I really wouldn't be surprised.

I glanced around.

"Which way was it again?" I wondered, breaths still running short. "That way?"

"Why . . . ?" I heard Ruby whisper.

"What?"

"Why would you save me?" Her anguish hugged lovingly the whole of her sleeve.

The answer was simple.

"'Cause you're my friend."

Beating down my expectations, Ruby scrunched her face and sobbed.

"I'm sorry, Jeremy," she said softly. "I'm so sorry, for everything up until now. I'm sorry for being an idiot. I'm sorry for causing you trouble. I'm sorry for being no help whatsoever. *I'm* the one that almost made you lose your mind. *I'm* the one who hurt you the most, even though I'm supposed to protect you."

"Ruby," I said, "I don't think now is the best time—"

"No!" the Rose whined. "I have to let it out. If I don't . . . If I don't . . . I'm just going to break."

Those beautiful petals shoved the focus away from themselves, pointing it, instead, to the whole, where the lilies and lilacs sagged like limp corpses. Her confusion showered all throughout, spilling from her clouds of hopelessness.

"I'm sorry, Jeremy," she whispered. "I just feel so weak. I feel like I have a million thoughts all the time, and I don't know what to do with them. I don't know what to think or how to think it.

"I make one mistake and just let it eat away at me. I'm trying really hard to be this happy girl, but my failures just keep haunting me, again and again and again and again. It's a cycle, and I just can't seem to find the end."

Then came her defeat.

"Maybe I really am just a screw up," she said. "All I can ever do is let people down. But it's hard because I don't know whether or not what I'm doing is actually right. I don't know . . ." Ruby angrily rubbed her hair. "I just don't know . . ."

This . . . This is strange.

Wasn't I the only one who had to peer into the abyss? Wasn't I the only one who had to wear those chains of solitude, forced to listen to the critiques of my darker half? Yet, as I hear you out, as I see the pain eating away at you, I can't help but spot my own reflection. I can't help but want to pick up your scattered pieces and stick them back together, to give you a hug and tell you it's gonna be okay.

I can't help but be the light you oh so deserve.

"And at the end of every day, I—"

"—wonder how you were able to make it through okay?" I guessed. "I know. I feel the same way."

From master to apprentice, I stroked the top of my Guardian's hair.

Her drizzle of confusion reshaped into curiosity.

"You wake up every morning wondering whether or not it's going to be a good day," I continued. "And when you think it *is* gonna be all right, you second-guess yourself. Sometimes, you even deny it. That way, you won't jinx it.

"When you make a mistake, you immediately blame yourself, and if you even *think* of pointing the finger at someone else, you beat yourself up. How can it be their fault? You're the one who's a loser, not them.

"But deep down, you wonder why no one ever taught you what to do—how to act.

"For you, making mistakes isn't doing the wrong thing; it's trying to figure out how to do the right thing."

I smiled.

"I know how you feel," I said, "because it's what I go through every single day. So, please, don't blame yourself, because ninety-nine percent of the time, it's not your fault. Like I said, no one ever taught you how to truly live, and that's okay. No one taught me either. We're all still learning.

"You just have to understand that life is always around the corner, ready to beat us down and make us submit. But you can't lose, Ruby! You're strong! I know you are. That's why, when life pushes you down, you can't just sit back up; you have to *stand* back up. Shine like the gem you were meant to be."

Ruby merely stared, as if the entirety of the universe gleamed before her very eyes.

"I . . . I don't know to say," she uttered.

"If it makes you feel any better," I said, "you were right: I am a loser. I'm the epitome of social awkwardness. I always feel like throwing up when I think about meeting people. I've been alive for sixteen years, yet I only ever spoke to one person. Everyone has their home; I'm just too afraid to build mine."

". . . That's not true," Ruby whispered.

Time for my own confusion as the Rose grinned.

"You have built your home," she said. "You have Luna, Faith, and me right here beside ya! You're kind. You're generous. You're forgiving. Even after the horrible thing I said to you, you still risked your life to save me. You're my knight in shining armor. That's why . . . I'll stay being your friend, no matter what! Even when you've grown up and become the next Sentinel of Light, I'll still be your friend! Even when I die and go to Heaven, I'll still be your friend! It doesn't matter when or where! In this universe or in the next, I'll always be right by your side!"

Ruby grabbed my hand from her head, embracing my fingers with her warmth.

"I'm sure Luna and Faith feel the same way," she said. "You may have been a loser before, but you're anything but that now!"

The valley of dusk had haunted me since the day I could dream, and for so long, I believed from the bottom of my heart that no amount of brilliance would sweep. Yet, here was this single speck, microscopic but as powerful as a sun.

Perhaps . . . Perhaps the light could thrive where reality refused to define.

"Thank you, Ruby," I said softly. "Thank you so much."

My Guardian giggled. "Don't ya mention it!"

"My, my, what do we have here?"

A carnivore in the midst.

As if an eraser swiped over our mouths, the jovialness of mine and my Guardian vanished. And as we turned our heads, we found a humanoid wolf leaning casually against a tree, baring his salivated fangs.

"That was pretty touching," he commended. "Almost brought a tear to my eye."

He sauntered towards us, his malice emanating like a rotten stench.

My joints locked up, my instinct to get away flatlining.

Ruby stepped to my front, protecting me with her arm.

"Stay back, Jeremy," she said. "I'll keep you safe."

"Hmm~?" the wolf hummed. "Trying to play the hero? You didn't look so confident when we snatched you up."

Ruby's glare only intensified.

A vicious liger, she darted towards her foe. However, her might could only bring her so far, for once in range, the menace killed her assault, bashing her cheek in with his paw.

My Guardian collapsed to her knees, and before she could recover, the wolf struck again, drilling the nail into the coffin.

The girl of cherry hair fell face-first onto the grass.

"Ruby!" I cried.

No response.

"Sorry, girly," the wolf snarled, "but this convo is for the dick swingers only."

He advanced towards me, casting his massive shadow over my modest frame as I equipped my Tool.

"So, human," he said, his eyes cold, "you got any motivational words for me? I've been feeling pretty down myself."

My vocal cords had been shredded to pieces.

What do I do? What can *I do? He's a freakin' monster. I have to try something . . .*

Desperate, I swung my wrench towards his skull. But to no surprise, he shut me down, snatching my wrist.

He chuckled.

"That was pretty dumb," he said. "If you're gonna hit, you gotta do it right."

Wham!

A solid connection, his fist sinking ruthlessly into my gut, into that spot that collided with my PTSD. Spittle fumbled out my mouth as I gasped for air and dropped to my knees.

The wolf gladly stripped the Tool from my clutches.

"You won't be needing this," he said, tossing it aside.

Then,

Wham!

Another meaty blow, this time to my temple, spiking my head with pain worse than a cluster of headaches.

I collapsed onto my back, and no matter how hard I begged for it, my movements just wouldn't translate from my brain to the rest of me.

Euphoric, the wolf stepped over me, then crouched atop my chest. And as his gaze pierced through me, his sadism surpassed the very rules of our actuality.

He extended his arm out, brandishing his acuate claws. Then, his mercy empty, he slammed down his paw, sinking the points into my stomach. Like knives, they felt like, poking at my intestines, slathering pain that made me scream like mad.

As the wolf pulled back out his natural weapons, the viscous liquid dribbled down, splashing onto the blades of grass.

My fingers quivering, I caressed my new wound, feeling a warm, thick substance stick to my palms.

"Stings, doesn't it?" the wolf asked. "Well, that's how much of a PAIN IN THE ASS YOU'VE BEEN!"

A burning rage lined his fur, and he delivered another beating to my head.

Wham!

In a snap, my vision blurred, the lens of my glasses suffering against the thin cracks that erupted.

"This was supposed to be an easy job!" the wolf whined. "Bring him the human and get paid! It was that simple, and yet, I have a field filled with my dead men! Do you know how much that's going to cost me? Do you!?"

My lips stayed locked, my only response to quiver.

"You made me look like a fool. You made Scar, descendant of the almighty Talis, look like a chump." The slits of his eyes darkened. "So, now, I'm gonna beat the holy hell out of you."

And he delivered on that promise, pounding every inch of my body with his hefty blows. My ribs shattered. My sternum wept. Fragments of my skull scraped against my brain, tampering with the memories I had stored there for sixteen years.

Avella . . . I thought, the pain worse than death itself. *Th-This isn't looking good.*

The strawberry, ripened once again, Ruby's consciousness returning as her senses struggled to electrify themselves.

The situation wasted no time dawning on her, however: her favorite human being beaten senselessly nearby.

"Jeremy . . ." she whispered weakly.

She went to rise to her feet, only to again stumble down.

I have to save him, she thought. *I have to be his Guardian.*

A cardinal, her hope began to soar away to a place unknown.

I will save him.

Lady Fate applauded the Rose's tenacity, and as a reward, she presented the girl with the wrench that lay just a little ways from her face.

The cardinal returned, its wings now enflamed like a phoenix's.

The wolf waved his paws, flinging off the carmine.

"Damn," he said. "My hands are killing me now."

I couldn't do anything even if I wanted to. At this point, the only path I hungered for was the way of the noose; that way, I could be relieved of this terrible, indescribable, excruciating pain.

When will it end?

A familiar inquiry.

"I think I got enough for one more," the wolf said. "Don't worry, though; it won't kill ya. After all, you're my ticket to a fine-ass paycheck."

He cocked back his fist.

I admired the golden gates of beyond.

"Time to hit the lights."

"Back the hell up!"

Wham!

The brutality of a rhino, my Guardian slugged my assailant in the torso, my wrench shimmering in her grasp.

The wolf was shot across the plain, rolling limply across the ground before coming to a stop.

Ruby's wrath blazed at the downed menace, but once she was certain he was down for the count, her expression softened.

She lowered herself to me, setting aside the Tool to hold me in her arms.

"Jeremy," she said, "are you okay? Can you hear me?"

"B-Barely," I answered. "E-Everything really hurts."

Shame flourished throughout the Rose's stem.

"I'm sorry, Jeremy. I'm supposed to be your Guardian. I'm supposed to protect you."

I just pet her on the head.

"You apologize too much," I told her. "That's my thing."

In turn, she handed me a feeble smile.

"Can you stand?" she asked.

"I-I think so."

She aided me to my feet, where the twinge of my stab wounds urged me to groan.

"Where does it hurt?" Ruby asked, worried.

"I'm fine," I said. "I just need to sleep for a while."

"With these wounds, if you sleep, you're not waking back up."

"I promise, I'm okay." I nodded towards the blood running down her forehead. "You should worry about yourself. You're hurt too, right?"

"This is nothing compared to what you got going on. Here, lemme have a look. I have to make sure you'll make it home."

"Really, you don't have to—"

"It'll only take a sec, I pinky promise."

The big, bad wolf, not ready to go down, to kiss his gravestone just yet.

I'll kill every last fuckin' one of them.

He began to hoist himself upward, his eyes brimming with nothing short of absolute savagery.

It came in an instance, this horror that beheaded my worst nightmares, that made the dusk beam as a suitable companion.

I watched as the big, bad wolf erected, his stance devolving from a poised human to an alpha beast. His brow furrowed as he bared his fangs, ready to pounce any second.

No time to warn.

No time to contemplate.

No time to even live.

Ruby's in front of me. If he comes here, he's gonna kill her.

I cringed at the mangled corpse of red, the still body that would forever gaze into my memories, asking and asking just why I couldn't step up to the challenge.

I'm afraid.

I'm very afraid.

One mistake here and I'm done for. We both are.

But I can't let it end like this. I can't let this bastard have his way, especially with what he's done to us. Most of all, I can't let him touch Ruby.

At long, long last, the next gear of "Jeremy Mitchell" jerked to life, the outline glowing as it delivered a new light into my perception. An arm, jabbing through the cocoon, hungering for the finished metamorphosis.

"I fought in wars not to be the better warrior but to protect my home and my loved ones."

"But we wanted to protect you. That's why we moved forward."

". . . what brings out greatness is overcoming that fear."

I get it now.

I finally understand.

When they told me why I should fight, I just nodded my head. On the surface, I had somewhat of an idea. I pictured Avella lying there, hurt beyond belief, all because I couldn't let my courage soar. I used that notion as thin fuel, mixing thoughts with my passion. I merely coasted by.

But this feeling right here, this craving that trumps anything my mind could argue, it's raw. No time to think. No time to consider.

I don't want my friend to suffer.

As she did so for me, I want to see her smile.

I want to protect her.

I need to protect her!

Everything shifted into slow motion, frame by frame, pixel by pixel.

Despite my injuries, despite my chances of surviving suffocating, I charged headfirst, confident that I could be on top.

The wolf lunged towards us, vicious.

I shoved Ruby to the side, and upon grabbing my wrench, I cocked the Tool back, clutching it as tight as I could.

You're not taking her from me!

Four inches.

Three inches.

Two inches.

One.

Before the beast could dine on our flesh, I swung my weapon, certain that not a single ounce of power was left behind.

Ping!

A shockwave.

Right as my Tool crashed into the wolf's jaw, a vehement flash of sapphire light erupted, blinding all who resided.

I heard the menace bellow in pain, and as the light dissipated, I watched his being fly back to where he once lay. His limbs now still, his eyes dulled, the left side of his face burnt off like rotten meat.

My limit shouted to me, informing that I had surpassed the boundary.

Still standing, I blacked out, coming back to only as my Guardian caught me.

"Jeremy?" she asked, astonished.

"I'm not letting anyone die," I whispered. "Not on my watch."

The girl of cherries smiled.

"Do you know the way?"

I nodded.

With Ruby holding me up by the shoulder, the two of escaped back into the jungle.

Luna stationed herself beside the spaceship's entrance, her uneasiness bubbling as her eyes bounced around the trees.

"Where are they?" she wondered. "They should be here by now."

Her prayers answered, the duo in question emerged, limping like war-torn soldiers.

At first, the cherry blossom breathed relief, but as their condition became apparent, her pupils quaked with horror.

She darted towards the couple, helping she of the cherry hair guide the beaten boy.

"What the hell happened?" Luna asked.

"We had some company on the way here," Ruby explained. "Things got ugly."

"I can see that." Luna studied the carmine dripping down Ruby's temple.

"I'm fine," the Rose said. "We need to take care of Jeremy ASAP. I doubt he's gonna last."

"Right."

The girls escorted their friend into the spaceship, laying him down on the steel flooring.

"Get us outta here, Faith," Luna instructed.

The archer, seated at the front, behind the wheel, lent her nod, and after tweaking a few levers, the ship's door shut, and the spacecraft boosted off the ground, zooming away from the atmosphere of this cruel, cruel planet.

"Where do we go now?" Luna asked. "Glaileid, maybe?"

"I say we go to Zekra," Ruby suggested. "Veltrix already showed his hand. He doesn't know yet that his hired help failed, so I doubt he's gonna try to shoot us down on the way."

"Please," Jeremy uttered, coughing blood. "P-Please, just take me home."

"We can't go back to Earth, Jeremy," Luna said. "That's why we—"

"*Please!*" He sobbed like a child. "Take me home. I just wanna go home."

Master of None

"Beautiful, isn't it?"

He rested upon a swiveling seat, a hexagonal table laid out before him. All around, charts and diagrams displayed themselves, a gargantuan map placed dead center.

Veltrix gazed in wonder, marveling at the scarlet triangular gem that shined between his thumb and forefinger.

"It took a long time to set this up," he said, "but the pieces are finally lining themselves together." His pride elevated to heights beyond the clouds. "Magnificent."

Dikadus stood by his side, listening patiently to his master's garble.

"I couldn't have done this without you, my boy," Veltrix said to his servant. "You should be very proud of what you've helped accomplished."

"Thank you, Master," the robot said. He then held out his hand. "May I?"

"But of course." Gladly, Veltrix laid the gemstone onto Dikadus's palm, and the robot turned away to admire it up close.

Veltrix rose from his seat.

"We are one step closer, Dikadus," he noted. "Pretty soon, we'll have the entire universe in our grasp. Even those blasted Sentinels will be begging for mercy."

Alluring, Dikadus found the gem, the scarlet gleam bouncing off his metallic front.

"Master," he said, "I don't believe that I ever asked, but why do you seek the Fragments? Why do you wish to possess the Gemini Stone?"

"Why?" Veltrix asked. "It's a simple answer, my boy: I want the power."

His visage softened. "My life has not been the easiest, Dikadus. The last several decades, I've only ever been kicked down, told to know my place. No one ever found the value in who I was, and it escalated to the point where even I was unsure of where I belonged."

Determination brewed within him like a cure.

"Now, I do know. I belong at the top. I belong where no one can compete, where my only judge will be myself. I will make those who belittled me pay with their skulls. Then, I will crush every single Sentinel for their idleness. They preach about bringing peace to all galaxies, but when it was my family starving, when it was my mother who was toyed with like a dog, no one came.

"When the dust has settled, no one will forget the name 'Veltrix.' When the last bullet has raced, the one planted upon the pile of corpses shall be me. I will become more feared than even that scourge Armageddon."

The man of metal merely kept his silence, his fixed facial features somehow reflecting contemplation.

"Master Veltrix," he said, "should I hold similar beliefs?"

Veltrix raised an eyebrow. "Where is this coming from?"

The man of metal faced his creator.

"You are my god," he stated. "You are the one who gifted me life. As such, I am curious if there is a certain way I should view this reality. Should I abhor it as you do? Or should I be grateful that there is a place for me to exist?"

Veltrix pondered upon his servant's reflection.

"I did not create you for any particular intention," he told his servant, "nor should I dictate how you view this universe. At the end of the day, you are you, Dikadus. You may be the culmination of my character; you may be a theoretical form of Veltrix that surpasses perfection; but at the end of the day, you are Dikadus—son of Veltrix, as well as his trusted partner. You are my greatest creation."

The message entwined with the electricity in the metal man's circuits.

"I see," he replied simply.

Veltrix swiveled around to face the grand map on the wall.

"We are far from finished," he said, "but I can taste our victory. It is inevitable, my boy. Together, we will—"

Kch!

It came in like a bullet, swift and precise, its purpose known from the moment it launched.

Veltrix gasped for air, pain stirring recklessly in his chest. And as he tilted his head down, he found a metal hand punctured through his torso, the fingers gripping his wire-packed heart.

He shook his focus to his creation, his pupils trembling with horror.

"Dik . . . adus?" the man called, blood pouring from his wound, dribbling down his chin.

"I am me," the robot said, "and because of such, my ideals do not align with yours, Master. I agree that the universe now, with its current paradigm, is flawed to a T. The way it is now, more lives like your own will suffer. However, the concept of a man in charge is ludicrous. The galaxies do not need a dictator drunk on his thirst for revenge; they need a rework, an implementation of how to act accordingly and justly. Only then will we be able to taste that peak of harmony, that ideal perfection that you had tried to forge within me."

Veltrix's vision blurred.

"I appreciate everything you have done for me, Master," Dikadus said. "You have given me the fortitude to stand on my own legs, the tenacity to believe with all my might that my vision aligns with the truest path. I am not a perfect version of Veltrix but a lifeform who can very well breach through the bounds of imagination. I can fix this universe."

A cloud of scarlet burst from the man's mouth.

"So," he choked, "this is where my dream ends?"

"No," the servant corrected. "This is where I carry on your dream, straightening the faults to elevate the perfection. This is where your dream fuels the passion for my own."

With each passing second, the man's consciousness flickered between this reality and the next.

"Promise me this," he uttered. "Promise me . . . that at the very least, you will make those Sentinels pay."

"*That* is a guarantee."

Kwsh!

His reluctance zero, the man of metal squeezed his fist, crushing his master's heart into a messy rag of meat.

The man known as Veltrix perished in an instant, dropping to the ground with a meaty thud.

The man of metal tossed away the proof of his kill, enclosing the Gemini Fragment tightly in his other hand.

"I will be the savior they need," he promised. "I will bring order. I will end suffering.

"The universe *will* learn."

Message from the Man of Metal

One week later . . .

Dimness swept through the area, the illumination stemming solely from the lamps hanging against the hazel brick walls. Tan tiles stretched across the floor, their obscure outlines prominent from end to end. The room itself mimicked the shape of an octagon, grand enough that many thrones would spit their envy. In one side gleamed a set of golden double doors, thicker than vault barriers, their surfaces engraved with exotic carvings. In front of the remaining walls, led in by a trio of staircase steps, lay chairs of solid gold, colossal enough to be fit for any king.

An occupant settled upon each seat, their features distinct and royal-like.

The first, a slender teenage girl, possibly sixteen years of age. Her height short, a delicate whiteness shaded her complexion, matching well with the aqua-blue of her eyes and adorable purple painted across her wavy, shoulder-length hair. For an outfit, she wore a sundress colored like doves, along with a bracelet of flower petals on both her wrists and ankles. The cherry on top, a crown of petals decorated the top of her head.

Next came another adolescent girl, stationed beside her of the many flowers. Her figure related to the other in every aspect, from skin complexion to slimness to stature. Only difference: her silky hair flowed down only to her nape, red like the bravest of cardinals with a tuft hanging on either side, held together by a black clip. Same with her eyes, a rich crimson that backed down to no force. She wore the clothing of an unzipped leather jacket, combat pants and boots, and fingerless gloves, all black like an icterid's wings. A sniper rifle leaned against the arm of her chair, its solemnity equal to that of her expression.

Beside her, a middle-aged man with rough white skin and dense muscular tone grimaced. Every detail of his being leaned towards the darker approach, from his unending irises to his short, spiky hair to the stubble spread across the lower half of his face. Even his clothing took the hint, his military jacket scowling as the sleeves rolled up to his elbows, as his jeans let barely any air through, as his military boots starved to stomp. The finishing touch, metallic braces looped around either of his wrists.

Across from him, another man pondered, and given his ancient aura, he seemed to grasp the entirety of wisdom to draw from. Features dug into his chalk-white skin gave a chiseled feel, like his pronounced facial lines and bulging six pack. A breathtaking silver engulfed his irises, while shortened hair shaded like a dandelion beautified his head. He wore nothing over his torso, covering himself only with baggy, black pants and roman sandals of the same hue. A red cloth clung to his waist, hanging down to his ankles.

Beside him relaxed a placid young woman, her prime at its pinnacle. Everything about her twirled around beauty, from her curvaceous, yet slim figure to her dainty, fair skin. Silky hair silver like steel dropped down to her spine's midpoint; as a disservice, however, her bangs concealed her right eye, letting only the left pocket of cherry-blossom pink be appreciated. Like the girl of many petals, this woman covered herself with a cloud-colored sundress, although she didn't own the accessories to enhance.

Then came the man who had roped Jeremy Mitchell into this battleground of the galaxies. Nothing of him had appeared aged, and he still wore the same outfit as when he first encountered the boy.

Lastly, amidst the center of the six individuals, a middle-aged man sat, one elbow pressed atop the arm of his chair. His complexion matched that of rich soil, offering little contrast to the shortened black hair atop his squared head and the neat goatee surrounding his lips. Even his irises followed the pack, dark like oil. His outfit consisted of a brown trench coat, the undershirt white, baggy pants, and average boots. At first glance, his muscular tone dipped to meager levels, but up close, it was apparent that he could take on a flurry of punches.

"I don't believe you quite understand the situation, Jax," growled the man of the metallic braces.

"Trust me, I do," Jeremy's gifter assured. "I just don't think we need to take such drastic measures."

"Drastic? There is a man out there hunting the Selectors. We must take precaution and begin training your boy."

"Listen to your words, Reaver: there is only *one* man we should be wary of. Surely he can be dealt with."

"That's what we predicted when Armageddon took action. Would you like to repeat history?"

The room clenched with gravity.

"We are still unaware of what this Veltrix is capable of," he of the grimace, Reaver, noted. "For all we know, he could be building an army this very moment. We must take precaution and prepare the Selectors for the worst-case scenario." To the entire room: "Who else agrees?"

The girl of the petals shot her hand into the air like a kindergartner.

"Ooh! Ooh!" she shouted. "I have an idea!"

"Silence, Tetra!" Reaver barked. "Your childish mindset will be of no use here."

Defeated, the flower girl lowered her hand.

The girl of the sniper glared coldly at Reaver.

"Watch your tone with my sister," she growled. "Otherwise, I'll rip your tongue out and smear the apology with your blood."

"Is that a threat?"

"It's a promise."

A hush.

"Now, now," he of the red cloth said, "let's settle down. Barking at one another will get us nowhere. Now, Tetra, I am certain that you have a grand suggestion, and I admire your bravery to bring forth your input. Well done."

The girl of the petals, Tetra, reignited her optimism, giggling softly.

"What about you, Gideon?" Jeremy's gifter, Jax, asked. "What's your stance?"

"My stance?" The chiseled man, Gideon, stroked his chin. "I concur with Reaver's belief, yet I oppose it. To concur would mean to overestimate, boosting our chance of success but straining our Selectors' limits in the process; however, if we underestimate, we could very well be piercing the coffin with the nails Veltrix longs for. I simply cannot decide."

"Overestimating guarantees our chances of survival," Reaver hammered in. "Have we not learned from the mistakes of our forefathers? I was there to live it."

"As was I," the young woman said. "I lived it more than you could ever imagine. That is why I am hesitant to instill that dread into my Selector. And while I do understand that no one is at the pinnacle of their strength, I believe in my girl. She can hold her own."

"That will be the cause of her demise, Persephone."

"Not if we can trust them."

"That's naive and you know it," the girl of the sniper argued. "Trust can only take you so far. Nothing beats evidence, and our history has shown that straying from Reaver's stance will cause our downfall."

"Excuse me if this seems rude, Codex," the young woman, Persephone, said, "but you merely know the history from which the pages cast definition. I breathed the Phantom War. I paid my price."

"As did I," Codex barked. "You think you were the only one affected? You may have been at the center, but you were merely the epicenter of the chaos trillions suffered through. I *refuse* to let this Veltrix become another core for our doom."

A standstill, either side refusing to budge even a centimeter.

"Do you truly believe Veltrix could be as fierce as Tarun?" Jax asked. "If so, then, my apologies, Codex, but you are a fool."

"Do not utter that name, Jax," the man in the trench coat growled. "He is undeserving of the respect."

"Sorry," Jax said. "Won't happen again, Athello."

The man of the trench coat, Athello, rubbed his eyes.

"I believe that either way, we will be facing conflict," he deduced. "Can we all agree on that?"

All around, concurrence formed.

It scurried in like an insect, this microscopic, eight-legged speck, mechanical by design. And once it brushed against the center of the room, it paused, its framework brightening in an azure glow.

"In that case," Athello continued, "we can also agree that—"

Veh-yoom!

A party crasher, a newcomer joined the table of the divine, his form that of a hologram, though his features stayed recognizable.

The man of metal.

In an instant, the seated ones snapped to the ceiling of their caution.

"Greetings," Dikadus said calmly, eyeing each individual. "I hope I'm not being a bother."

"How did you get in here?" Codex growled.

"More importantly," Reaver said, "who the hell are you?"

"I know exactly who that is," Jax informed. "He was with Veltrix when they attacked Jeremy."

Reaver raised an eyebrow. "Is that so?"

"I am he," the robot confirmed. "However, I must inform all of you that I am now at the head of the pack, for my master is now dead."

All around sprung stunned expressions.

"Veltrix is dead?" Gideon wondered aloud.

"How can we trust your word?" Athello asked the robot.

Dikadus darkened his stare.

"Because I'm the one who killed him."

The atmosphere went heavy.

"But worry not," the man of metal said, "for while my master may no longer be here physically, he has bestowed upon me his being and the spirit of his dream."

"And what would that dream be?" Codex asked.

Straight to the point. "To kill all of you."

Persephone skipped a breath.

"However," Dikadus added, "my motive does differ from my master's. Whereas he sought revenge, I view your deaths as a mere stepping stone to my grander vision."

"Your vision?" Gideon asked.

"Yes. You see, this universe is broken. The beings that occupy these galaxies can't help but act as savages, bringing only suffering to those like my master. Part of the blame lies in you Sentinels. Your positions are meant to bring harmony to the whole, yet I've seen nothing to signify unity. Chaos rampages through. Lives are extinguished, justly and not. This reality screams of imperfection, and I will not stand for it. Not any longer.

"I will fix this universe."

"Hoh~?" Reaver chimed, curious. "And do tell. What is your plan? Judging by your tone, I take it you have a proposal."

"It's simple," Dikadus said. "I will reset the universe."

Not even a flinch.

"Reset?" Jax asked.

The robot nodded. "We are past the point of on-site repair. No matter what anyone does, the universe as it is now will falter and crumble against the weight of its sins. I will be the savior that brings stability, and as my duty, I will obliterate all life that exists, saving the fate of those similar to my master."

Whereas most of the Sentinels donned grave expressions, Reaver couldn't help but chuckle.

"All life?" he repeated. "Every being in the entire universe? That is nothing more than a pipe dream."

"It's a simple calculus, Sentinel Reaver," Dikadus said, unfazed. "I can multiply at an exponential rate, wiping away entire galaxies in matters of time unfathomable. My vision is achievable, and I will proceed as planned."

"Even so," Athello interjected, "you are nothing more than a collection of scraps. Even with your grand numbers, you hold no chance of defeating us Sentinels."

"I beg to differ. After all"—he presented his scarlet gemstone—"I do have this."

The Sentinels sprung into high alert, save Persephone, who covered her mouth in horror.

"W-Where did you get that?" Jax choked.

"A little birdie dropped it for me," Dikadus answered. "Although, that birdie is no longer soaring."

From the young woman sprouted glistening tears.

"You're twisted," Codex growled.

"I prefer the term 'competent,'" the robot argued. "In any case, I recommend that you Sentinels simply stay where you are. There's no chance of your victory."

"We'll see about that, Dikadus," Jax hissed.

"'Dikadus' . . ." the man of metal pondered. "That is a name which belongs to one who knew not of his place, of his purpose. 'Dikadus' is no longer among us. From now on, you will now face the judgement of 'Dirodotus.'"

His message finished, the hologram blinked away, the man of metal off to his preparations.

The Sentinels merely sat in silence for a moment, digesting what had just unfolded.

"Do you see now?" Reaver finally asked. "Do you see why the Selectors must be prepared? This is power that now rivals even us Sentinels."

Persephone wept into her hands.

"I am with Reaver," Athello announced. "We must prepare the other two Selectors for this engagement."

"But, Athello," Jax said, "Jeremy isn't ready."

"Well, the universe is, Jax. We are dealing with a threat capable of obliterating us all. As much as it pains me to say, time is no longer a luxury we can afford."

Athello rose to his feet.

"This meeting is adjourned," he said. "Our very existence is at stake, so make all the preparations you can to ensure our survival."

The members of the divine dispersed, with Tetra ambling over to comfort the young, broken woman.

For his part, Jax merely stared before him with worrisome eyes.

It's Time

Oh my frick-frackin' goodness.

I never knew eating cereal could be so heavenly.

I relaxed in my kitchen, butt plopped down before my dining table. In my hand, a spoon, which I used to devour my *Fiber One*. Big bites, fast enough that at any given point, I had the cheeks of a chipmunk.

I missed you so much, Earth food.

Close to my breakfast, my math homework smirked, confident that its equations could bust a hole through my morning. Debatable. Or at least, I wished it were; life tested my patience, stringing together relentless pain in my ribs every time I gave even the slightest movements. The amount of breaks I had to take zoomed past what exponents could define.

Still, though, this cereal was definitely getting the short end of the stick.

I really should've let Ms. Diamond know I'd be gone, I thought, remembering the brutal lecture I'd been hammered with. Wolf bandits were no joke, but piss off an unmarried white woman and you will not hear the end of it. Now, I had a pile of worksheets thicker than my arm—all blank, all due by the end of next week.

Kill me.

Hoping to ease my mind, I twirled my focus around my consideration of what I would say to Avella. It had been a while since we last spoke to each other, and when I returned to my house, I hopped on my laptop to find out she had given me a ring. Only one missed call, but to us, a call that helped heal our fractured wings; at least, healed mine.

I wonder if she's mad. I hope she doesn't think I'm ignoring her. Sadly, I just can't say, "Hey, sorry I missed your call. I was busy fighting bandits on a jungle planet with a weapon I could use to wipe out the entire States."

But I can't act casually, either. I don't want her to think I'm too cool for her now. We do not need a precedent for shrinking our time spent together.

What if she hates me? What if she has a boyfriend now? I've been abandoned. Damn you, fate, for making me an important person! Damn you!

Thump!
Thump!
Thump!

A trio of knocks, stemming from my front door, hurling me out of my mushroom cloud of conclusions, right before Chaos Theory could start its engine.

"C-Coming!" I said.

I lifted myself up, groaning from the aches, then dragged myself to the entrance (which had thankfully been fixed). And after twisting the doorknob and pulling did I find my sights packed with the vibrant shades of my Guardians.

"Hi, Jeremy!" Luna sang, smiling.

"Yo-ho!" Ruby cheered, waving with her knucklehead grin.

"Hi," I replied. "What are you guys doing here?" My skin paled. "Please don't make me leave this planet."

The girl of cherry blossoms chuckled nervously.

"W-We're not going to a *bad* planet?" she tried.

My stomach squeezed itself.

"It is an emergency," she told me, some seriousness culminating in her aura. "Can we come in?"

"S-Sure." I stepped to the side, letting people of the female variety enter my home for the second time.

"Still as neat as when we first came here," Ruby remarked, glancing around. She then whispered to me, "You took my advice with the internet, huh?"

My cheeks blazed up, red as apples.

"I don't know how to respond to that," I admitted.

She giggled.

I was glad she did.

"Jeremy," Luna said, "do you have somewhere big we can go into?"

"His living room would be perfect!" Ruby assured.

The fact that you answered the question and not me is somewhat alarming.

"She's not wrong," I said.

Together, the four of us ambled over to where my game console lived, which Ruby quickly hooked her attraction to.

"Hey, Jeremy," she said, "you said you were gonna let me play next time we came over."

"I did?" I asked.

"Mm-hm!"

"But what about what Luna—"

"That can wait! Just let me get a couple games in and then—"

Swift as a hawk, her ear twisted as Faith pinched it with her fingers.

"I must say," the archer remarked, "you have the obedience of a child."

"Ow!" Ruby whined. "Ow! Ow! Ow! C'mon, Faith, you know I was joking! Lemme go!"

A tighter squeeze.

"Are you certain of that?"

"I am! Just lemme go! You're gonna rip it off!"

Choosing to believe, Faith released her partner's earlobe, allowing Ruby to massage her wound.

"That wasn't very nice," she groaned.

"Obedience is necessary," Faith argued.

I cracked a tiny smile.

Looks like not a lot's changed.

Luna placed herself at the center of the room, where she reached into her pocket to fish out an object shaped like a *Rubik's* cube, minus the color design; furthermore, the sides bore accessories—half-spheres of obscure glass that protruded outward.

"What is that?" I asked.

"A communicator," Luna answered.

"Communicator? Like a phone?"

She nodded. "There's someone who wants to speak with you face to face."

Oh, sh*t.

We're meeting even more *new people. Yay. Really, yay. It's okay, social anxiety; we'll pull through.*

Luna planted the device on the ground, and like lights warping through marbles, the half-spheres gleamed with a glow, accompanied by the sound of a mellow orchestra.

"It's ringing," Ruby said, animate.

Can't. I. Catch. A. Break? One week was not enough to heal from what I went through. I had to accept the fact that I own a weapon capable of erasing entire continents (which so happens to be right under bed); I got jumped by some robots; and I nearly got killed by some Halloween wannabe. To top it all off, I've had to meet a buttload of new people, like a trio of females *and someone who thrives off making WMDs. My nerves were not built for this. Right now, I just wanna eat and work on my homework. Give me a break. Please.*

The orchestra continued, lining well with the knots contorting in my gut.

You can do this, Jeremy.

Fists tense.

You can do this.

Flood of saliva.

You can do this.

Then, a hush, the orchestra blinking out of existence.

A smooth transition, a hologram emerged from the top of the cube, lengthening to the ceiling. And as my eyes stumbled upon the figure presented, a sense of silliness flicked me on the forehead. My muscles loosened, and my nervousness wriggled back into my pond of emotions.

You're not new, I concluded. *Not at all.*

He looked the exact same as the night we met, as if the passage of time wouldn't dare hold him down:

The man who gave me this life.

"Hello," he said, scanning the area. "Can you all hear me?"

There's no doubt.

"We hear you, Sentinel Jax," Luna said.

The man smiled. "Great! Good to see you looking well, Luna."

"Likewise."

Like a preschooler, Ruby shot her hand up.

"Ooh! ooh!" she called out. "Sentinel Jax, what's up!?"

"Ruby!" the man cheered. "Good to see you again! I see you're still gung ho."

An innocent child, the strawberry giggled.

Faith offered a slight bow.

"Good day, Sentinel Jax," she said politely.

"Hello, Faith," the visitor replied. "Have you finished that book I lent you?"

"Not yet. Although, my progress is coming along nicely."

"That's good to hear."

Finally, me.

"Jeremy . . ." the man whispered, as if he bore witness to a memory come alive.

"It's . . . you . . ." I uttered, just as speechless.

"It's been a while."

"Nine years."

Honestly, I didn't know what to feel. Should I have been happy that that scene from all those years ago would finally continue? Should I have been angry that he stirred the peace of my life? Or should I have been grateful that our promise may finally become more than mere syllables?

"How have you been?" the man asked.

"Not great," I answered, honest. "I had the crap beaten out of me every which way, and I have a pile of homework I have to get done by next week."

He chuckled. "My apologies for the former. I'll make it up to you."

I pointed to my new glasses. "You can start by paying me back for these."

"Did you notice those were new?" Ruby whispered to Luna.

She shrugged.

The man chuckled. "Will do." His visage straightened. "You have some questions for me, right?"

"Just a few," I said. "When we met that night, you kept me in the dark. But you're here now. So, I wanna know who you are, and I wanna know why you did this to me?"

"That is fair, and I truly am sorry for the agony you've been through." The man held his chin high. "My name is Jax, and as Luna and the others may have already told you, I am a Sentinel of the Universe—the Sentinel of Light. And I have chosen you, Jeremy Mitchell, to be my successor. You have incredible potential, and when the time comes, I would like you to become a protector of the galaxies.

"I understand that this explanation is more on the shallow side, but that's all I can offer you at the moment. Are you all right with that?"

"Yeah," I accepted. "I'm just glad I finally know your name."

The air between us softened.

"Okay," Jax said, his solemnity settling in, "time to get to business. Guardians, we have an emergency—a threat that jeopardizes all life in the universe."

All life?

I waited for the "I'm kidding."

It didn't come.

"Dikadus—or rather, Dirodotus—has begun executing his plan," Jax explained. "He wants to eradicate all life that exists in order to supply the galaxies with nothing but those of his kind."

The scope of the situation loomed over like a fortress.

"I didn't think Veltrix was that serious," Luna uttered.

"Veltrix is dead," Jax said.

From the throats present, gasps spurt.

"Dirodotus killed him," Jax expounded. "It's safe to say that he's a one-man show in this. But we can't take him lightly, not when he rivals the strength of us Sentinels."

"How do you know that?" Faith asked.

"Because he has a Gemini Fragment."

The news just kept getting worse and worse.

"Next, you're gonna tell me he shoots nukes for fun," I grumbled.

"We have no choice but to move forward," Jax said. "If we're not two steps ahead, we're done for." He then spoke to me specifically. "Jeremy, do you remember what I told you that night? What that Fragment could do for you?"

I nodded. "Get rid of the monsters."

"That time has come."

I tensed up.

"We can't delay it any further," my Sentinel admitted. "We need you to ascend now, Jeremy; otherwise, you won't stand a chance."

Face the monsters? Now? I know I've been waiting for this chance for nine years, but now that I have the option, I can't help but be scared out of my mind.

The voices, who tempted me into drilling a bullet through my brain.

The monsters, who proved that my nightmares bested Hell itself.

I have to defeat them? Can I defeat them?

"I know you're afraid, Jeremy," Jax said. "I know that this is sudden. But you can do this. You just became a full-fledged Selector, and already, you are fighting the good fight. It's been sixteen years, and still, you stand, denying those beasts of your mind. You're rising to the occasion. You're proving that you have what it takes to become what this universe needs. So, take this next step, Jeremy. Break out of that cocoon. For me. For your Guardians. For Avella."

Huh?

What is this . . . this feeling in my chest? What's my heart doing? It's burning, the same way it did right before I protected Ruby. There's this passion, this drive, this hunger. For sixteen years, I had been stagnant, barely marching along just so I could survive. But now, I want more. I don't want to crawl; I wanna walk; no, I wanna sprint. I wanna carry myself to the places that seemed so unreachable, the dreams that laughed in my face. I wanna gaze onward, my regret at my heels as I hold my chin high.

I wanna be someone my best friend can look at.

I wanna be more than what I am.

Resolve glistening in my gaze, I looked to Jax with impenetrable composure.

"Let's do it," I said.

My Sentinel appeared stunned at first, but in seconds, the visage of a proud father captured his expression.

He spoke softly.

"Looks like you're ready, after all."

Birth of a Savior

Zip! Z-Zip! ZipZip!

Sparks, dispersing like fireworks, adding a shade of warmth to the otherwise cool environment. Bionic limbs, zig-zagging over one another, their movements meticulous as they applied divine precision to their project.

Their craft? A still figure of metal lying atop the operating table, its aura menacing before it had even awoken. No more with the thin, scrawny limbs, feeble enough to be snapped; now, the body bore a more muscular, yet still sleek design, the defense of a fortress from its core to its shell. No more with the simple iron and copper; only the best of the best of the best for the apex predator—pure zikranium, shaded black like a crow's talons. All throughout, slits allowed the frame to breathe, and upon peeking inside, one could find a complex system of gears ready to rotate.

Zip! ZipZip! Z-Z-Zip!

Finishing touches.

The chest area split apart into two perfect squares, revealing a thinner layer of armor. And like the eye of a camera, that sheet of metal spiraled open, gifting full view of the intricate inner workings.

A messenger, an upright cylinder rose steadily through the torso, its top modified with a trio of triangular slots.

The heart—the scarlet gemstone which one of the bionic limbs carried over for dear life. Carefully, oh so carefully, it laid the jewel into one of the slots.

The little helpers then watched—watched as the torso closed itself, watched as the crimson surged through the innards, watched as their savior made his mark.

An orchestra, a soft *veeeem!* echoed from wall to wall, accompanied by the red glow glimpsing through the slits.

A moment later and the once blacked-out sockets on the head enlivened, giving birth to two scarlet dots.

A deep breath.

One, two.

One, two.

Adjusting to reality, the android arose, perching himself on the side of the table. He ran his fingers across his skull-shaped head, along the pseudo binoculars fixed to his forehead.

"Is this . . . me?" he wondered softly.

The simple machines quivered at his presence, as if a single gaze would rip them to pieces.

"I can feel it," he said, clenching his fingers. "This power. This control. This . . . purpose."

He lifted himself to his feet, his stomps issuing a hefty *klank!*. His equilibrium challenged him, but he won, no contest, feeling as himself in no time.

Soon enough, the man of metal marched towards the exit.

"Time to save the universe."

We All Have That "Other" Side

Ruby sighed.

"Oh. My. Goodness," she groaned. "Why do we always have to go to the faraway places?"

My Guardians and I rested within the STS, journeying through the void of space.

"Ruby," Luna said, "this place is the closest to Earth that we've had to go. We've only been in here for three minutes."

The strawberry sank into her bench.

"You say three minutes," she grumbled. "I say three *decades*."

The cherry blossom giggled.

"Where *are* we going, by the way?" I asked.

"Didn't we tell you?"

"No. When I came back from getting dressed, Jax was gone, and you guys shoved me through the front door." To Faith: "By the way, you owe my aunt and uncle two hundred bucks for that repair. They thought I threw a party or something."

The archer merely flipped the pages of her novel.

"I know not what you speak of," she said, uninterested. *That's not very nice.*

"Sorry about that," Luna offered. "I guess we were just in a hurry."

"That's fine," I told her. "We are on the precipice of total annihilation, after all."

"Well, if it makes you feel any better, we're going somewhere you should be familiar with."

It ain't Earth, so I already know I'm screwed. Then again, when isn't that the outcome?

"We're going to Saturn," Luna said.

"*The* Saturn?" I asked. "Like, the one I've heard of?"

"There's only one Saturn, dude."

"There are two Plutos, though!" Ruby chimed in.

"Say what?"

"Ignore her," Luna suggested. "It's an inside joke."

The spearwoman giggled, taking her gaze back to the window.

"But we're not going to Saturn specifically," Luna corrected. "We're going to one of its moons: Titan."

"What's on Titan?" I asked.

"The Temple of Arkon."

Whoever comes up with these pants-pooping names, well done.

"Th-That sounds like the arena of a final boss," I remarked, nervous.

"In your case, it kinda is. The Temple of Arkon was created by the prime Sentinels when the first generation of Selectors came through. It's a place designed to take Selectors to that next step, furthering their souls for the path of the Sentinel. Very few have seen what the temple actually looks like."

"I take it we're gonna be one of those few?" I asked.

My Guardian nodded.

I slouched over, struggling to level my breaths.

I talked a lot of game when I was with Jax, but truth be told, I am still afraid beyond belief. I don't know what to expect exactly, but I get the feeling that I'm gonna be hearing a lot of those whispers when push comes to shove.

I can do this, right?

"Hey."

A familial touch, as Luna rubbed my knee with her hand.

"Don't stress too much," she told me. "Don't overthink it. When you get in there, just be the best you can be. If you do, you'll win."

A barrier to my confidence, my gateway of uncertainty crumbled into a pile of afterthoughts.

"Thanks," I said.

She smiled.

The rest of the trip rolled through with a hush, everyone bracing themselves for yet another unknown jammed into our journey, another obstacle obstructing our view of the peak.

In time, however, the speakers electrified to life.

"Now arriving in the vicinity of Moon Titan!" they announced. "ETA: two minutes!"

I glanced out the front window, where my eyes met a compact globe of misty orange.

"Not as scary at Xerges," Ruby offered.

"But still scary in its own right," I argued.

Breaking through the atmosphere, our shuttle soared across canyon-like structures, their edges pointed as shallow puddles of water pooled at the bottom. No clouds in sight; just a solid field of bronze mixed with a boisterous sun. Oh, and the smog, swishing through like an ocean gasified.

"It's no jungle," Luna said.

"Again," Ruby slid in, "still scary in its own right."

The shuttle glided along to the side of a stubby mountain, landing upon a natural platform, flat as it overlooked the rocky plains.

"We have now arrived at Moon Titan!" the speakers announced.

"Was this the right landing spot?" Ruby asked.

"Sentinel Jax gave the coordinates," Luna noted. "He wanted us to be here."

Our wits locked and loaded, we exited the shuttle, stomping past the double doors to be hit briskly with the scent of sawdust. A zephyr kissed our skin, pleasant in temperature.

Our feet whined *kwish! kwish! kwish!* as our heels ground against the surprisingly squishy earth.

"*This* is where they chose to have their Selectors ascend?" Ruby asked, genuinely surprised.

"It would appear they possess the same mindset as Mr. Giles," Faith assumed. "Keep the profile low and no one can come to disturb the process."

. . . *Fair enough.*

"So, where's the temple?" Ruby asked.

"Should be around here somewhere," Luna guessed. "Look around."

So, I did, coming across a cave-like entrance carved into the side of the mountain.

"Would this be it?" I called out to the others.

They looked at me like I snorted crack.

"My boi," Ruby said, "is the heat getting to you?"

"What?" I asked.

"Jeremy," Luna said, "that's just a wall."

"No, it's not. This is a cave." I waved my hand through the entrance. "See?"

Now they thought *they* were snorting crack.

"H-His hand just went through that wall." Ruby cringed. "His hand just went through that wall, right?"

My Guardians came to my side, and Luna tested the theory herself, pushing her fingers into the entrance of the cavern as if the laws of the logic went haywire.

"Camouflage," Faith explained. "Perhaps only he can see it because he is a Selector."

Predicting right, they ambled through what they thought was a shield of rocks, to which I joined them.

"You're right," Ruby said, amazed. "Maybe the Sentinels aren't too shabby, after all."

Well, one of them is the owner of all wisdom, or so I hear.

Together, we carried ourselves through the narrow tunnel presented, lit up by flames swaying within glass lamps implanted into the sides.

Eventually, we made it to the end, rewarded with a structure that could've been plucked straight from mythology. A pyramid, it appeared as, no larger than my apartment, the pristine bricks black as a cat as solid gold streamed through the in-between. At each corner, a pillar of similar design stood, their tops accompanied by hovering prisms of soul-like energy.

"That is intense," Ruby whispered. "It really does look like the final boss arena."

I split from the pack, approaching the plaque engraved with violet letters embedded into the front face.

"Question is, how do we open it?" Luna asked.

I gave it a read:

*Only those who understand
the ceiling of their limits
may overcome what reality
refuses to define.*

Aside it, a circular formation of indented dots offered themselves.

"Any clues?" Luna asked the girls.
"None that I can forge," Faith said.
"It's a no-go from me," Ruby submitted.

I wonder . . .

Curious, I pressed my fingers against the indents, and like a stack of blocks tumbling, portions of brick crumbled inward and out, creating a gaping hole in the face of the pyramid. What smirked on the other side: pure darkness.

Not too shabby, Jeremy.

I swiveled my body around, catching two of my Guardians painting me in the light of shock and awe.

"Are you a wizard?" Ruby asked.

I just gave them an odd look as I returned to the pack.

"Good job, Jeremy," Luna praised. "Now, we can move on to the next step."

I regretted the assumption before I even thought of it.

"I'm going in there, aren't I?" I guessed.

"Alone," she added.

"Of course."

"But, if you're gonna do that, first, you're gonna need this."

The cherry blossom held her palm out facing up, and much like how she summoned her blade, my Tool digitized into her grasp.

"My wrench," I uttered as she handed it to me.

"I was wondering why you didn't have it when you left," she explained, "so I searched around and found it underneath your bed."

"I spaced about it."

Luna wagged her finger playfully. "You better not forget it again, mister!"

I smiled, whereas she giggled, and like a sister, Luna lunged forward to wrap her arms lovingly around me.

"Stay safe, okay?" she said softly.

I hugged her right back. "I'll try my best."

Once finished, the girl of the cherry blossoms backed away, jubilant, letting the girl of the cherries step up to bat.

"So," I said, "got any last-minute, breathtaking advice?"

She grinned. "Make sure you get at least one thing to explode. It'll add to the effect."

I chuckled. "I'll be sure to do that."

Her affection fanned out like the most pleasant of breezes.

"Hey," she whispered, pressing her fist against my chest, "I believe in ya. I mean, if you can save a trainwreck like me, you can do anything."

Letting my awkwardness just flow, I bumped my fist against hers, top to bottom to side.

"You're not a trainwreck," I told her.

"I was before I met you."

Ruby shuffled away.

As for Faith, she chilled against a rock, her nose buried in her book.

Should've expected that.

I made my way towards the temple's entrance, just as her voice called out to me.

"Jeremy."

My eyes went wide.

That's the first time she's ever said my name.

The greater surprise: as I looked to her, the blank-faced archer blessed me with a sweet smile.

"You better come back," she warned.

My lips had never curved so pleasantly.

"You got it."

Her sweetness still glowing, Faith turned back to her book, ushering me to finally face the cage of my worst nightmares.

I gave one final glance back to spot Luna and Ruby wave at me.

My smile solid, I nodded.

Then, with my heart of a budding lion, I stepped into the battlefield.

The Guardians watched as their little duckling advanced deeper into the blackness, until the wall of the pyramid reassembled back to its original state.

"He's gone," Luna said.

"He'll be back," Ruby promised. "That's just the kind of guy he is."

Nothing to my left.

Nothing to my right.

Nothing at all.

I marched through the unending fields, blind as a bat, certain that in here, illumination could be nothing more than a distant myth. Was I moving forward? Was I walking in place? I couldn't tell.

Then came the drop in temperature, my mouth spurting visible clouds, my veins shivering as if ice pierced my blood cells.

What happened?

"*You* happened."

A mysterious messenger, blending into the shadows.

I studied the space top to bottom but found no target.

"Looking for me?"

Suddenly, a glorious ray of light beamed down from the heavens, powerful enough that I had to shield my eyes with my arms.

When the dimness crawled back, though, I sent my focus to my front, coming face to face with none other than . . . me.

Definitely me.

Same physique.

Same skin tone.

Same hair.

Same age.

Only a few discrepancies could be accounted for: his hoodie, black rather than red, same as his shorts; and his eyes, the whites dark as night as the pupils and irises sneered a sinister crimson.

Upon the throne of bones, he sat, his interest towards me limitless.

"Hello there, Jeremy," he said. "So nice to see you."

"W-Who are you?" I asked.

"Who am I? Isn't it obvious?" He pointed at me. "I'm *you.*"

But as his twistedness scraped against my skin, I believed otherwise.

"No," I said. "You're not me."

"Oh, come on," the boy pleaded. "Don't say that, Jeremy. So what if our clothes are a little different? We're still the same on the inside."

Hell no.

He raised his hands in defeat. "Okay, okay. Maybe we're not identical. I mean, how boring would that be, right? To be the exact same as someone else? That's just ludicrous." He shook his head. "No, no, there is a difference between the two of us, Jeremy. Do you wanna know what it is?"

His lips went crooked. "I'm actually honest."

I forged a glare. "What does that mean?"

"I mean exactly what I said. You see, I know who I am, what I'm made of. But you . . . You, Jeremy, are just a ginormous heap of doubts and denials. You walk around, grumbling that you despise being social, but it's not the talking that you hate—it's the rejection. You can't handle not being accepted. You can't handle having people look at you with disgust. So, what do you do? You reject them first. All those people who are nice to you, all those people that try to bring light to your eyes, you push them aside. Can't hurt if they don't get close, right?"

No answer.

"I'd like to think that I'm right on point," the boy gloated. "If that's the case, then I am sure as hell glad that you came here. Because now, I can get you to see: you *are* alone, Jeremy. Those Guardians of yours, they're not your friends. Never were. They don't care about you. They're just looking out for you because it's their job."

That's not true.

"That Sentinel—Jax—he doesn't think you're actually special. He just chose you because he decided to have a few that night. The universe doesn't give a *shit* about you."

You're . . . You're lying.

"And Avella! Your best friend in the whole wide world! You think she likes you, but she just feels sorry for you. You're a pitiful excuse for a human being, and she knows it. The quicker you bite the dust, the quicker she can peel off that dead weight."

I clenched my teeth, fighting back the tears.

"You're wrong," I whispered.

"Am I, though?" the boy challenged. "I don't think you're getting the big picture here, Jeremy! We're nothing, you and me. Our existence doesn't mean jack shit. We have nothing to contribute, nothing to strive for. We're just puppets, tangled in these fuckin' strings of insanity! *Hahahaha!*"

Done.

Back to the straight lips.

"But I guess you just can't get that through your thick-ass skull. So, allow me to help ya out, from one loser to the other."

He rose from his throne, and holding out his hand, a silver chain materialized into his grasp, one end leading into the darkness. In a rhythm, the metal rattled, until what crept from the other end crawled into the scene.

My heart sank.

The beast of no face and a bloody jaw, its whispers still carved into my brain matter.

The boy sneered. "I'm sure you remember this guy. He's been missing you a lot since your last get-together, so be sure to treat him nice!"

I readied my wrench.

He released the chain.

"It's go time."

The Violet Reaper

"That was a great movie!" Veronica cheered.

She strolled down the sidewalk alongside her companions Jennifer and Amy, soaking in the sun's pleasant rays as the clouds rolled calmly through the sky of baby blue. On either side stood business complexes large and small, their faces stacked with windows as their bricks and cement chipped away.

"No kidding!" Amy remarked. "Even the second time around was killer!"

"You're telling me," Jennifer added. "I found so many easter eggs!"

"Right!? The directors were really going for the gold with this one!"

Across the street, a businessman dropped his ice cream cone.

"Maybe we should try inviting Jeremy next time," Veronica suggested.

"I'd love to," Amy said, "but do you even know where he is? I haven't seen him since that fiasco in the cafeteria."

"Now that you mention it, I haven't seen him either," Jennifer pointed out. "Maybe he's been staying home?"

"I only saw him when Ms. Diamond was yelling at him," Veronica said. "But over the past week, he hasn't been in class."

Amy and Jennifer glanced at one another, the full picture pixelated in their museum of knowledge.

"Gosh, I just wish I could've seen what went down," Veronica complained. "That is why I hate second lunch."

The others giggled, just as a sudden cry rang from nearby, sinking itself into their attention.

The girl of thunder-yellow hair halted, urging the others to do the same.

"You hear that?" she asked.

"Hear what?"

"That noise?"

"What noise?"

"Listen . . ."

Again, it scurried through, itching their backs.

The girls turned their heads to the alleyway they had just passed.

"I think it's coming from there," Veronica guessed.

They retraced their steps, stationing themselves before the alleyway's entrance. Deeper in, an ominous feel latched onto the space, the dimness threatening to swallow them whole.

"Hello?" Veronica called out. "Is anyone there?"

A third ring, only this time, the sound heightened in definition.

A whimper.

"Could be a dog?" Jennifer predicted.

"Wouldn't a dog come to us, though?" Amy countered. "Or just run away altogether?"

Straying from her string of theories, Veronica advanced into the eeriness, her reluctance zero.

Compelled, her companions tailed her.

As they drew closer, the whimpers echoed like starving wolves, the light of the sun abandoning them out of its own fear.

And once at the back wall, actuality mutilated their curiosity, deforming it into unadulterated perturbation.

"Oh, my . . ." Amy whispered, cupping her hand over her mouth.

A delicate figure wept towards the back wall, its shrunken frame wrapped in a ragged cloak as it hugged its knees close to its chest. With each cry, its limbs quivered something fierce.

"It's a kid," Jennifer whispered.

"You think they're homeless?" Amy wondered.

Veronica spent no time on the questions, tiptoeing her way to the broken child.

"Hello, there," she said softly. "Are you okay?" Once close enough, she knelt. "Are you lost?"

The weeping withered away; the child nodded.

"Did you lose your mommy and daddy?" Veronica asked.

Another nod.

"I'm sorry to hear that. But you don't have to be afraid." She grinned. "We'll help you look for them!"

"For sure!" Jennifer said.

"You can count on us!" Amy added.

Veronica reached for the little one. "So, you don't have to—"

Click!

Click! Click!

Slowly, oh so slowly, the cloak motioned, the child within turning to face the girls.

"Th-That's right," Veronica said, cautious of the odd noises. "You can look at us."

Click!

Click!

Click!

The head swiveled ninety degrees.

The head didn't stop.

Click!

Click!
Click!

From the girl of thunder-yellow hair, a stomach riled as the child's head twisted completely around, gazing upon the girls with a face of metal and jaws that unhinged like a broken puppet.

Veronica backed away. "W-What . . . ?"

Click!

Like a busted toy, the being's head snapped off the neck, rolling onto the cement.

The air around them went heavy.

"Kindness may heal the pack."

Klank!
Klank!

"However, kindness will never *lead* the pack."

Jittery, the three girls set their stares to the alley's entrance, and it was there that the towering metal man tainted their presence.

Veronica lost her breath, whereas Amy and Jennifer planted themselves at her front, their glares hardened.

"Easier than I expected," the being said. "Then again, the right human hearts will never disappoint."

"If you're here for your kid," Jennifer hissed, "then you're a little late on the draw."

"No." He pointed at the girl of thunder yellow. "I'm here for *you*."

Veronica swallowed hard the lump in her throat, her mouth dryer than cotton.

"He must be the one Sentinel Gideon warned us about," Amy whispered.

"Then we can't make any mistakes," Jennifer replied.

The metal man stood tall. "The universe requires correcting, and it will be I, Dirodotus, who lays the foundation for true harmony." He extended his hand. "Hand me the Gemini Fragment, and I will make your deaths as quick and as painless as possible."

"And if we don't?" Amy asked.

Dirodotus clenched his fist, his aura thickening with unadulterated viciousness.

"Then I will bring your spines to Zekra myself."

Tension, suffocating the trio like poison, their windows narrow as they pondered rapidly upon which one to leap through.

Amy gave her hand ample room to breathe.

"I don't quite like the sound of that," she growled.

"What a coincidence," Jennifer said. "Neither do I."

"Then you will obey," Dirodotus commanded.

"Yeah . . . How 'bout not?"

Her speed light-like, Amy summoned a kunai knife to hurl at the man of metal.

Voom!

In a flash, she vanished from existence, only to reappear where her blade had flown, right behind the menace.

She plopped herself onto his shoulder, then thrust her kunai into his throat, praying that she could pierce.

"Go!" she cried to the others. "I'll hold him!"

No time to waste, Jennifer dragged Veronica to a nearby door, and with the strength of a giant, she kicked down the obstacle, ripping it off the hinges.

She then led the girl of thunder yellow inside, entering the bottom floor of a parking garage.

Dirodotus gave little struggle, viewing the girl's attack as nothing more than a nuisance.

"Pointless," he growled.

A brute, he snatched Amy's forearm, squeezing it enough to crack the bone as he hurled her through the wall.

"Amy!" Veronica cried as she watched her friend crash into the building, her body joined by chunks of rubble and puffs of dust.

Amy rolled towards the others.

Klank!

Klank!

His crimson glow dispersing through the particles, Dirodotus stomped into the scene, unfazed.

"I have no time to waste," he said. "I'll be taking that Fragment now."

"Are you okay, Amy?" Veronica asked.

"Y-Yeah," Amy answered, rising once more. "Just a little scratch."

Jennifer bit her lip. "This is not gonna be easy."

"We didn't sign up for 'easy.'"

"Fair enough." Jennifer gave her own hands room, and like companions, a silver handgun digitized into either of her palms.

"Resistance is futile," Dirodotus warned. "You can't possibly hope of defeating me."

Amy stepped forward. "Jennifer, you take Veronica and head to the STS. I'll hold him off."

"I'm not leaving you," Veronica argued.

The girl of the kunai smiled. "But it's my job."

Jennifer joined her side.

"You can't hold him off," she said. "At least, not on your own. Not saying you're weak, but he already has a Fragment with him. That puts him on the same level as the Sentinels."

"It's not like we can send Veronica off on her own."

From the girl of the handguns, consideration.

"Not like we have much of a choice." She turned to face the thunder-yellow girl. "Veronica, get to the roof and call the STS, just like we showed you. You gotta get out of here."

Veronica shook her head, her eyes glassy.

"No," she whispered. "I'm not leaving you two."

Freeing one of her hands, Jennifer curled her fingers around her friend's.

"Hey," she said, "don't worry about us. Amy and I, we've been training our whole lives for a fight like this. We're not gonna go down easy. Besides, we just have to make sure we get you to the Sentinels in one piece. You have to go."

A noose, Veronica's hesitation strangled her, locked her legs.

Jennifer sent her fingers upward, caressing the frightened girl's cheek.

"Trust us, okay?" she begged. "We'll be right behind you."

Entangled in that sincerity, Veronica held her companion's fingers, embracing her warmth.

"I trust you," she whispered. "Both of you. If I didn't, I couldn't call you my best friends."

Jennifer giggled.

"Friends to the end," Amy sang.

Veronica wiped her eyes with her sleeve.

"Win," she told her Guardians.

A grin. "Always."

With that, although her body begged to play spectator, Veronica pushed herself away from the area, towards the ascending ramp in the distance.

Jennifer kept her lips curved for one last moment, her joy alive for one last beat, before joining Amy to face the man of metal.

"You're wasting your final moments," Dirodotus said. "No matter what you do, the outcome will remain: your ends are now, Guardians.

"I promised you mercy at the exchange of the Fragment, but you have disregarded my offer. So, now . . ."

He grimaced.

". . . I'm gonna drag your corpses to your precious Selector."

From the Guardians, no responses; only watchful glares.

"This is gonna be a tough one," Jennifer said to Amy.

"Yeah . . . When aren't they?"

Brisk as a bolt, she hurled her kunai past her enemy's skull.

Voom!

The vanish, then the follow through; as the Guardian reappeared before Dirodotus, she launched her fist with ferocity.

Easy.

Bored, the man of metal deflected the blow, snatching Amy's wrist to break her movements.

"I don't think so!" she howled.

As flexible as a ballerina, Amy twisted her body around, slamming her heel into her foe's shoulder blade.

With a heart of gold, Jennifer sprinted around Dirodotus, and after taking aim with her pistols, she mercilessly pulled the triggers.

Pop! Pop! Pop! Pop!

Embers burst from the muzzles as iron bullets zoomed out, hungry for the android's shell. But as they connected, they merely ricocheted off, the impact offering nothing more than bundles of thin sparks.

Still, the dual-wielder persisted.

"Enough!"

With tremendous force, Dirodotus flung Amy across the room, then aimed his palm at her torso.

Reeeeem! his hand cried as the center spat a trio of scarlet laser beams.

"Crap!"

Wham!

A sudden hit, as Jennifer tackled her comrade away from the attack, absorbing the assault herself. What felt like lava coated her bicep, searing her flesh to give off the odor of burnt meat.

"Jennifer!" Amy cried.

"I'm fine!" Jennifer barked. "Just worry about—"

Wham!

Like a raging bull, Dirodotus thrust forward, ramming his knuckles into the gunwoman's jaw, shooting her into one of the cement pillars.

"Damn you!" Amy hissed, flinging her kunai to his backside.

Voom!

Wham!

Predicted.

Right as Amy returned to reality, she received a blow of metal to the chin, courtesy of the self-proclaimed savior.

Wincing, she glided up into the air.

Dirodotus readied his lasers.

"One to go," he said.

Pop! Pop! Pop! Pop!

Just as he could deliver the blow, bullets ricocheted off his shell, disturbing his aim.

"I'm not done yet!" Jennifer barked.

"You should be."

The man of metal fired his lasers at the gunwoman, hopeful he could burn away her drumming heart.

Like a cheetah, Jennifer bounced around the space, dodging the heat that could melt her very bones.

Wham!

Her strength firm, Amy bashed her fist into the menace's jaw, disrupting his attack. Then, before he could bounce back, she dragged her blade across his chest, forging a jagged scratch mark.

Pop! Pop! Pop!

For her part, Jennifer unloaded her magazines, even as she bolted towards him.

Irritated, Dirodotus bashed away Amy, then tried his luck with the gunwoman.

No dice.

With pristine agility, Jennifer dodged her enemy's attack, countering with a mean roundhouse kick right to his jaw.

The metal man jerked.

Not finished.

Calculated, the gunwoman leapt onto Dirodotus's back and flipped gracefully into the air, where she unloaded even more ammunition into his castle-like armor.

Meanwhile, Amy flung her kunai to his abdomen, teleporting to deliver her own devastating strikes.

Like electricity, a crimson field of energy surged around Dirodotus's body.

"Know your place!"

Suddenly, a field of red burst in every direction, sending the Guardians flying as damage gnawed away at their innards.

Still airborne, Jennifer tried to fix her awareness, but the metal man had other plans: his viciousness unmatched, he boosted upward to punch the gunwoman in the gut, forcing her to gasp as she spit up blood and saliva. He then snatched her hair and hurled her downward, her body screaming as she crashed into the side of a van.

From there on, Jennifer matched Amy; neither could find the will to stand.

"Enough with the antics," Dirodotus implored. "You're merely delaying the inevitable."

"Anything can happen . . ." Amy choked, quivering. ". . . so long as you can get back up."

The metal man grimaced.

"Then I'll make sure you don't have that option."

Breaths raspy.

Lungs trembling.

Legs, raring to press onward.

Veronica had just passed the fifth or sixth ramp, her confidence dwindling as the distance between them seemed to lengthen and lengthen.

Down below, the chaos vibrated like distant roars of war.

Please be okay, she thought. *No, I can't think like that. I* know *they're okay. I just have to make it to the roof. They'll meet me there. I know they will.*

The ground rumbled, light.

Then, not so light.

Then, as heavy as a tank rolling through.

Then,

Cruck!

Suddenly, the cement before Veronica exploded, chunks flying left and right, and like a demon ascending, Dirodotus rose into view, hovering as his feet ejected waves of heat.

"We meet again, Veronica," he said, unimpressed.

Her fear sliced into her heels as she met that menacing crimson gaze.

Klank!

"Did you really think you could get away from me?" the android asked.

If you're here . . .

"Amy . . ." Veronica whispered. "Jennifer . . ."

"Your Guardians have failed you," Dirodotus said. "They were too weak to accept the truth, so I ended their delusions. Soon enough, you'll meet the same fate, as soon as you hand me my Fragment."

He stepped forward.

But with each advancement, Veronica countered, backing away.

"Don't make this harder than it has to be," Dirodotus said. "This is all for the sake of a brighter tomorrow."

"You're a psychopath . . ."

"No. I'm the savior these galaxies deserve."

Nowhere to run, Veronica pinned her back against a pillar.

"The end has come, Selector," said the metal man.

The girl of thunder yellow clenched her teeth—her frustration, her despair, culminating into something conflagrant, something that would have even the gods considering to kneel.

I won't let you have your way.

Veronica pushed her hand out.

"I'm not going down that easy!" she bellowed.

A star's birth, violet light surfaced upon the girl's palm, shaping into pixels that enlarged with each passing moment. Then came the outline, the frame, until the entire entity materialized, fitting snugly between the Selector's fingers.

The Reaper's tool, she brandished, simple in design yet more threatening than any horde of demons. The base shaped itself as a basic black pole, while the blade of the scythe gleamed with sharpened zikranium. Near the top, the violet, triangular gem embedded itself within the metal, and acting as the epicenter, it delivered purple cracks throughout the blade.

"I would expect nothing less," Dirodotus said, studying the instrument. "However, the story does not change. Whether I get it freely or I have to rip it out of your Tool, I will be collecting your Fragment."

"Prove it."

As brisk as a bullet, Veronica zoomed towards the metal man, and once his bubble had been pierced, she swung her scythe, scraping it against his limb.

Unfazed, Dirodotus swung his fist; however, he made no connection, for the Selector had already dodged, swiping her Tool again to deal damage. A vicious dove, she was, leaping gracefully through the air, her agility marvelous as she evaded and struck, evaded and struck. No heavy hits, but just enough that Dirodotus could feel his armor being worn down, his gears gaping with concern.

Veronica went for another connection.

Klink!

The cry of two forces as the girl's blade collided with her foe's knuckles.

"Commendable," Dirodotus praised.

"Save it!" Veronica retracted her Tool to swing once more.

Easy.

With little effort, the android grabbed her weapon by the base, then yanked it forward, bringing the girl in close.

Wham! his knuckles hissed as they dug into Veronica's cheek, popping her jaw.

Dirodotus then caught the girl by her hoodie's collar and hurled her across the room.

Veronica ground her scythe against the floor, smoothing her halt, just as Dirodotus fired his trio of laser beams her way.

A quick fix, the Selector spun her weapon before her like a shield, deflecting the attack.

I need to turn things around, she thought.

Wham!

As sudden as a lightning strike, the man of metal appeared before the girl, smashing her chest with his fist, sending her crashing into a car's side.

And before she could even think of recovering, he trained his arm on her, where barrels of guns ejected from the limb like hidden compartments.

Pop!Pop!Pop!Pop!Pop!Pop!Pop!Pop!Pop!Pop!

The muzzles flashed as the bullets zipped out, racing towards the young girl.

Not yet!

Her will strong, Veronica sprung to her feet and bolted around the arena, the ammunition chewing away at her heels.

But still, it wasn't enough, for not long after did Dirodotus zoom to her backside and jab roughly the back of her head, stirring her brain matter.

Veronica rolled across the floor, her vision blurry as a stream of red dribbled down her forehead.

"I give you full marks," Dirodotus commended. "You have exceeded my expectations. I assumed you would be on the same level as Jeremy Mitchell."

What does Jeremy have to do with this?

She lifted herself weakly to her feet.

"There's no need to resist any longer," Dirodotus said. "You and I both know that this battle is over."

"It's not over," Veronica groaned. "Not until I can't move anymore."

"Is that so?" The metal man readied his lasers. "Then I'll just have to melt your legs off."

The young girl braced herself.

From the hole in the ground, it spiraled upward, unbeknownst to the occupants of the space, and right when it aligned with the android's temple . . .

Voom!

WHAM!

They snapped into reality, those righteous Guardians, and with the force of a wrecking ball, Amy slammed her fists into the metal man's cranium.

"*Get away from her!*" she roared.

Cruck! the ground whined as Dirodotus plummeted through.

Cruck! from the floor below that.

Cruck! from the floor below that.

Before long, Dirodotus's presence dissipated to the down below.

Nonetheless, the Guardians refused to let their urgency unravel.

"Guys . . ." Veronica said, her joy boundless.

Amy grabbed her hand and told her, "We have to go."

Thus, the trio rushed to the rooftops, praying with each floor passed that their peace would lose no pieces.

"Sorry," Amy said as they jogged. "You shouldn't have had to pull out your Tool."

Veronica shook her head, her lips curving warmly.

"I'm just glad you guys are okay."

"Likewise," Jennifer said.

Eventually, after busting down the final door, the girls found themselves back in the blessing of nature's light, the bustling of panicked civilians rumbling down in the streets.

"Over there," Amy said, pointing to the hovering subway car parked near the rooftop's edge.

But as they approached, their path weakened, courtesy of the metal man's reappearance.

"I don't think so," he growled, aiming his fist at the shuttle, firing at it a miniature missile.

"No, *I* don't think so!"

Calm, Jennifer waved her hand to the side, ordering the STS to glide away.

Kaboom!

The shrieks of terror amplified as a billow of flames swallowed a chunk of the neighboring structure, blasting away debris like rain.

"We have to jump!" Jennifer cried as they approached the wide gap between rooftops.

Their bravery bold, the three girls bit the bullet and leapt from the edge, soaring across the abyss-like drop.

The gunwoman cleared it.

The reaper cleared it.

But she of the kunai struggled, barely hooking herself onto the edge.

"Amy!" Veronica cried, rushing to help.

His patience empty, Dirodotus ran the assault once more, launching a pack of missiles from his backsides to obliterate the girls where they stood.

Jennifer grit her teeth.

"It's now or never," she whispered.

Click! her pistols chimed as she flicked the switches attached to the handles.

She took aim.

Pop!Pop!Pop!Pop!Pop!Pop!Pop!Pop!Pop!Pop!

Still handguns, yet more ferocious than any model of assault rifle. She merely held onto the triggers, letting the vicious brass butterflies zoom through the skies.

Boom!

Boom!

Boom!

One by one, the missiles exploded midair, destroying nothing but the molecules of wind.

Veronica hoisted Amy to her feet.

"Thanks," her Guardian said.

"Come on!" the Selector bellowed, already bolting towards the STS's new parking spot.

Sensing their arrival, the shuttle's double doors slid open, and with clumsy movement, the three girls fumbled into the ship, just as the metal man darted through the wall of fire.

Amy rushed to the front console.

"Amy, get this thing going!" Jennifer screamed, firing her ammunition.

They stayed in place.

"Amy!"

The fiend didn't slow.

"*Amy!*"

A miracle, the doors slammed shut, and the STS thrust into motion.

Refusing to surrender, Dirodotus gave chase, gaining distance on the shuttle with each second passed.

"He just doesn't give up!" Jennifer growled.

"We'll make him, then!"

Determined, Amy pulled open the shuttle doors, then tossed herself out, right towards the android. And when she reached, she smashed her feet against his body, blasting him back with every ounce of her strength.

Then, just before she could plummet, she hurled her kunai back to the others.

Voom!

A moment in flight.

Then, the catch, as Veronica grabbed Amy's hand and pulled her back into the shuttle.

Their path clear, the girls breathed sighs of relief as they boosted through the wormhole and away from the battlefield.

Dirodotus merely scowled as he hovered in place.

"Run all you want," he said. "The end is near, no matter how much you fight it.

"Besides . . . I already know where the other one is."

A Certain Memory

Through the darkness, I ran, my veins frozen as frost as I struggled to maintain my hold on my wrench.

All around, the scurrying threatened me, like rats grinding their teeth against the walls.

Here?

No.

Here!

A hunter unleashed, the beast of a bloodied jaw lunged from the shadows, its claws starving for my flesh.

My strength solid, I bashed its head with my Tool, forcing the beast back into the wild.

The steadiness of my breaths flickered, the fatigue splitting holes in my nerves.

I have a few seconds, I concluded. *I can—*

"*Graaaaahhhhh!*"

Back for more, the creature leapt onto my back, and after cocking its head back, it sunk its teeth deep into my shoulder.

I wailed in pain, blood oozing from my body as those sharpened edges shredded my flesh.

"Get off of me!" I screamed.

Wham!

Wham!

Wham!

Savage-like, my hits were, my wrench busting apart the creature's skull like some f*cked up piñata.

By the grace of God, the beast released me, tossing itself back into the unknown.

I ran my fingers along my wound, my hoodie damp with my scarlet.

"Oooh~," I heard the twisted boy say. "That looks painful. I'd hate to be you right now."

I'm holding on just fine.

He giggled.

"That's what we all like to think," he noted. "But I'll admit, we could use some *flavor* in this show; some *épice*. What do ya think?"

I don't care.

"That's the spirit!"

The boy clapped his hands together, and like a painting melting, the blackness around me morphed away, transforming into cool shades and textures. A moment later and the new scene presented itself—a space that strung along my uneasiness, cracked open my box of nightmares.

A hallway.

The hallway.

The rubble lying across the tiled floor, right alongside the lockers splattered with blood. The glow of the moon, swirling through the gaping hole in the ceiling, offering a full view of the army of stars.

"No . . ." I whispered. "Not here . . ."

"You said you didn't care." I could hear his lips twist into a devilish smirk. "Time to put your money where your mouth is."

Just then, a soft whimpering caressed my attention, the source planted just a little ways down the hall; a little boy, sat against the wall as he hugged his knees close to his chest. Skin, like mine. Hair, like mine. Figure, a smaller version. He even wore the outfit that revealed all, those crimson lines stretching across his flesh.

Carefully, I approached him.

"Hey," I said. "You okay?"

He kept his head buried in his legs.

"Help me . . ." he wept. "Help me . . ."

I crouched down beside him.

"It's gonna be okay. You're gonna be okay."

"But . . . But . . ."

His muscles tightened.

"I just wanna be normal."

I went to stroke his shoulder.

And like an animal gone mad, the boy shot his head up, revealing his bloodshot eyes and bloodied, shark-like teeth.

"Why can't I be normal!?" he screamed as he leapt onto me, pinning me to the floor. "I just wanna be normal!"

I choked beneath his rancid breath, struggling to keep my jugular safe from his jaws.

"Let me be normal! Let me be normal!"

We can't always get what we want.

With a heavy heart, I heaved the boy off of me, and before he could recover, I bashed his head in with my wrench, over and over and over again, splashing his red across my hoodie with each meaty thud.

Once finished, once his still corpse tumbled to the ground, I collected myself.

"Jeremy?"

Far from over.

A gentle voice, sprouting from the other side of the hall, sprouting from the little girl adorning the silver necklace, her pink, heart-shaped gem flooding me with a bevy of emotions. She wore what she had on that fateful night—the blouse with the polka dots, the dress shoes. And as she gazed with her rich blue eyes, her innocence shimmered like a divine presence.

"Avella?" I whispered.

"Why . . . ?" she asked softly. "Why did you run away?" She scrunched her face, tears rolling down her cheeks. "Why did you leave me all alone?"

"No," I told her, my sanity crumbling. "It wasn't like that. Please, listen to me."

"I felt so alone. I thought you hated me. You never came to help me."

The pink of her necklace clouded itself in black.

"Aren't we supposed to be best friends?"

"We are."

But my mind could only shatter more as her life stumbled into danger, as the beast of the bloodied jaw emerged behind her, its sinistry ready.

"No!" I cried, sprinting to my soulmate. "You get away from her!"

We can't always get what we want.

With boundless viciousness, the creature slashed its claws against the front of Avella's dress, tearing away her precious skin. The beast then unhinged its jaw, ready to devour.

"Get the hell away!" I screamed, swinging my wrench like a baseball bat.

Wham!

My metal sunk into the creature's skull, forcing it to wince as it retreated from the hallway.

I then put away my Tool and held onto Avella, trying my damndest to fight back the tears as her mangled body etched itself into my memory bank.

"Why, Jeremy . . . ?" she asked, blood leaking from the corners of her mouth. "Why did you do this to me?"

She rubbed her hand against my cheek, smearing me with her carmine.

"Why didn't you love me?"

I hugged her.

"I always will."

A new level, as the world around me shifted once more, scrapping the hallway for the more eerie bubble of a forest at night. Bushes and trees, dead leaves down like fallen soldiers. A breeze blew against my skin, erasing my beloved from my fingertips.

I grieved my grievance.

"I'm waitin' for ya," the boy told me.

I stood tall amongst the blades of grass, soaking in the serenity, however slim.

Then, my chin held high, I pressed onward.

Again, he lay upon the operating table, the mechanical arms tinkering with his metallic shell. This time, however, he clung to consciousness, calculating.

And when his servants had finished, he rose.

"Fools," he spat, carrying himself to the hallway. "They can only see what is, *not* what can be."

Soon enough, the android arrived at a hexagonal door, and after it had slid open, he ambled through. Beyond that, he approached a balcony that overlooked an abyss of nothingness.

"But no matter," Dirodotus said. "In the end, only I will be alive to tell the tale."

He ran his fingers across the control pad nearby, and like ominous fireflies, swarms of blue eyes began to stare back at him from the abyss.

"*That* is a promise."

△18△
Assault on the Empire

Through the subway station, desolation resided, pardoning only the pillars of smooth stone that connected the cement flooring to the curved ceiling. Upon the walls of bronze bricks hung lamps, brilliant as they showered the area in golden luminance. A little lower and a series of rails stretched through the unending tunnel, fading out of view when continuing either way.

Idleness.

Then, a spectacle: a duo of headlights peeking through one end of the tunnel, widening and widening with each passing moment, until into view rushed the pristine subway car.

It gave a smooth glide before halting beside the platform.

And as the double doors slid apart, the violet reaper and her Guardians stumbled through, unarmed, still shaken up by what they'd just trudged through.

"Let's go," Jennifer said, already jogging towards the dual staircase close by. "We need to get to Sentinel Gideon."

Concurring, the other two followed, ascending towards the shroud of light swirling past the topmost step.

Beyond that, the streets of the empire welcomed them, drumming into their ears the jovial chitter chatter of the elegant civilians. They showed themselves as all walks of life, the melting pot defining every aspect of the crowds. Like industrial mountains, structures of all shapes and sizes surrounded the girls, their walls supported by coffee-colored bricks and lightly stained glass. Beneath their feet, a ground of pristine golden glass supported their weight, simple in appearance yet more dense than the purest of zikranium. As for the up above, a sky of night relished in the waves of eager stars.

Veronica couldn't get enough.

"So, this is Zekra," she said.

"That's right," Amy noted. "This is your first time being here."

"Mm-hm! And I have to say, it looks really beautiful."

"We'll have to show you around," Jennifer offered. "You know, when the universe isn't on the verge of being erased."

Suddenly, a young boy bumped into the Selector, halting her flow.

"Ow," the boy whimpered, rubbing his head. Then, to Veronica: "Sorry, ma'am. I should've watched where I was going."

A second later and a young woman came scrambling to the group.

"Thaddeus," she said, grabbing the boy's hand, "what did I tell you about running?"

The little one frowned. "Sorry, Mother."

"I'm terribly sorry," the mother said to the girls. "My Thaddeus, here, was quite rude."

"It's no problem," Veronica assured, smiling. "I was like that when I was a kid too. Lots of energy, huh?"

The boy grinned. "You betcha!"

"Thank you," the woman said, and with a bow of respect, she led the boy away. "You three have a nice day!"

The little one waved at them. "See ya later, sisters!"

The reaper mimicked the gesture.

"You too!" Amy replied.

The rhythm's return, the three continued on their journey, their strolls brisk in pace.

"This place sure is big," Veronica remarked. "How do you not get lost?"

"We have maps you can buy," Jennifer explained. "Amy and I, though, we had to memorize the entire layout for the Academy."

The girl of the kunai sighed. "Not my cleanest test."

"So, where are we headed now?" Veronica asked.

"Council Hall," Jennifer answered. "Hopefully, Sentinel Gideon will be there. We have to tell him about what just happened."

"Shouldn't he already know, though? I mean, isn't he always watching over me?"

"He should be, but it's been a while since we've had a threat like this, so the Sentinels are a bit scattered right now."

"A while?" Veronica asked. "Has something like this happened before?"

"Only once." Gravity sunk into Amy's vocal cords. "And it was the worst thing that ever happened to this universe."

The Selector nearly refused to ask, "What happened?"

"We'll tell you some other time," Jennifer said. "We're here."

Now before them, a building shaped like an octagon rested between the intersection of eight roads, its frame sturdy as silver ran along the in-between of the coal-colored bricks. At the top, a dome curved outward, protruding a needle-like element that yearned to pierce the heavens. At the structure's front, a pair of double doors greeted them, composed of solid gold as exotic carvings etched themselves into the surface.

"I'm telling you," the flame-haired girl said, "if he was intelligent, he'd attack here first." She leaned against her golden chair, inspecting the mechanics of her rifle. "The quickest way to kill a legend is to wipe out the heart."

"But no legend has ever been faced with equal matching," Reaver argued, studying the holographic map floating amidst the center of the room. "Surely, he'll gather forces before he arrives here. It should be easy for him to assimilate whatever these galaxies have to offer into his own."

Beside him were Jax and Athello.

"Tetra," he of the trench coat said, "make sure those HOMEs are ready to fly."

"Haiii~," sang the girl of many petals, tinkering with a control panel close to the sniper. "Do you wanna help, Persephone?"

Nearby, the young woman shook her head, saddened.

"No shifts yet," Jax noted. "All quadrants are running business as usual."

"It's only a matter of time," Reaver said.

"Yeah, before we're all stabbed in the back," Codex hissed.

Klunk! the doors groaned as they swung open, letting the trio of girls waltz in.

They marched across the tiled floor, all focus latching to them like glue.

"Veronica?" the Selector heard from her Sentinel—the chiseled man who rested upon his golden seat, indulging in a book.

The girl of thunder yellow rushed to him as he stood, embracing him tightly.

"Thank goodness you're all here," Jennifer said. "I didn't know what we'd do otherwise."

"Why are you all here?" Gideon asked. "What happened?"

"We were attacked," Amy explained. "By that robot."

The hairs on the supreme's necks stiffened.

"Dirodotus," Athello growled.

"Looks like he may be diverting from both of our expectations," Reaver said to Codex.

"He was crazy strong," Amy recounted. "That Gemini Fragment is no joke."

"I even had to use my Tool," Veronica said.

"Did he have a Gemini Tool?" Jax asked the girls. "How did he use the Fragment?"

"I think . . . I think it was *in* him," Jennifer answered shakily. "He had power that made him seem like a Sentinel."

The severity dug itself in to forge a home.

"It would seem he has integrated with the Fragment," Gideon uttered.

"Now he's *really* a threat," Codex said. "Thing is a literal walking Gemini Tool now."

"Then he shouldn't have comrades," Reaver added. "Why have teammates when your strength is so monstrous?"

"That is what a normal man would think," Jax argued. "That is what even Veltrix would think. But Dirodotus is no mere mortal. He is a machine—an entity that can overcome the limits we have placed on ourselves. He can evolve beyond our imagination. In a sense, he is stronger than any of us could hope to be."

From soul to soul, the reality of the situation fractured their morale.

And the nightmare only deepened as the Devil's voice rang from outside.

"People of Zekra . . ."

Slowly, every pair of eyes turned to the golden doors.

"Is that . . . ?" Veronica choked, unwilling to complete the thought.

All breaths held.

All hearts pounding against the chest.

With Athello at the lead, everyone tiptoed to the entrance, their bones stiffening as their nervousness branched across their flesh like new veins.

He opened the doors.

And as the pack poured from the building, their gazes joined the rest of the Zekrians, beholding the man of metal who levitated near the skies.

"He certainly looks . . . *different* from when we last saw him," Jax noted.

Dirodotus projected his voice across the entire empire.

"You may be wondering who I am," he said, surveying the miscreants. "You may be wondering why I have appeared before you, why I have thrown this wrench into your meaningless lives. Well, the answer is simple: I am Dirodotus, savior of this universe, he who will bring about harmony to these starways.

"I have watched you roam, and while the minority of you truly have tried to bolster peace, it is the greater whole that defines our actuality. You do nothing but shed war and violence, extinguishing lives left and right, all for the sake of personal gain and satisfaction. You indulge in the cycle of suffering eon after eon after eon, convinced that you will survive because of your victorious battles. But battles are futile in the face of war. And in this war for stability, you march towards a peak that will never be reached."

He pointed to the pack of Sentinels.

"Your Sentinels have failed to uphold their duties. They preach of protecting the galaxies, yet watch with ease as the rivers run red with your blood. They are unfit to lead.

"But fear not, because I have taken the duty from them, and *I* will do you the justice you truly deserve. *I* will correct that which has fragmented."

The man of metal raised his hands in a holy gesture.

"Today marks the end of the Zekrian Empire, as well as all life that claims existence. As of this moment, the commencement of your extinction unravels itself. When all is finished, when the dust has settled, the only living thing . . . will be *me*."

BANG!

Its roar thunderous, the barrel of Codex's rifle quivered as a flash of azure popped from the barrel.

"Shut up already," the Sentinel hissed, her finger still itching the trigger.

The android jerked back.

The android recovered, unfazed and unharmed as a layer of red energy coated his body.

"Foolish girl," he chastised. "As my body is now, not even the bullets of your Infinity Weapon may harm me."

Codex sucked her teeth, frustrated.

Dirodotus narrowed his eyes.

"Now then . . . Let us begin the evolution."

They descended in unison, those masses of blue light that had abandoned the stars. Closer and closer and closer, until the droves of metal men lashed out on the empire. Some donned Dirodotus's original body—the sturdy, slender build— while others basked in the physique of iron giants, their heads domed as their bulky limbs hissed with machine gun turrets and rocket launcher barrels.

They invaded from both ends—raining down from the skies and digging up through the ground—and like a swarm of yellow jackets, the bots wreaked their havoc, firing their missiles and bullets into the crowds of innocent Zekrians. Explosions boomed. Fires spread. Debris plummeted like mad as skyscraper walls broke apart. Chaos quickly choked the empire by the throat, the screams of children dancing like butterflies with torn wings.

Dirodotus merely watched, satisfied.

"The time has come!" Athello announced to his fellow Sentinels. "We will now prove that pile of scraps wrong! We will show that we *can* protect!"

His comrades nodded.

"Persephone," Athello said, "I want you and Tetra to escort our people to the HOMEs. Save as many as you can from this invasion."

"Understood." The young woman gestured for the girl of many petals to follow. "Come along, Tetra."

"Yay!" the girl cheered as the two levitated away.

Athello continued. "Codex, you work on dwindling their numbers. Take out as many as you can."

"Not a problem," the flame-haired girl said. Rifle in hand, she took off, sprinting up the side of a skyscraper.

"I'll head over to the Academy," Reaver suggested. "The older students are probably dying for a chance to ditch the books."

"I like the sound of that," Athello concurred, ushering Reaver to disappear into the battlefield.

"What about us?" Jax asked.

"We can fight!" Veronica assured.

"No," Athello said. "I want the rest of you to remain here at Council Hall. Keep the Selector safe, whatever it takes."

"But I can hold my own!"

"I understand that, but we cannot risk having you captured. In all this chaos, Dirodotus may use the chance to kill you and take your Fragment. If he does, then he truly will be unstoppable."

Although her spirit quaked for the good fight, Veronica understood beyond the battlefield and accepted her role.

"Copy that," she said, deflated.

Gideon lovingly stroked her shoulder.

"But, Athello," Jax said, "what will you do?"

"Me?" The lead Sentinel hooked his glare into the main metal fiend. "I'm going to take care of that scrap heap personally."

With no parting message, he floated off the ground to make his way towards his enemy.

And after he had blended into the distance, the remaining figures began their journey back into their shelter.

"Keep your chin high," Gideon told his depressed Selector. "Your time will come."

Veronica kept her frown.

"I hope so."

Athello halted meters away from Dirodotus, his rage seething.

"Your efforts will be for naught," the metal man said. "There's no stopping the evolution, even with someone of your caliber, Athello."

"I hold authority over this reality," the Sentinel hissed, "and I will see to it that I exclude you from the vision."

"You're welcome to try."

Quickdraw, as Dirodotus fired his crimson beams, right as Athello charged forward.

Man versus machine.

Calculation versus hope.

Ideal versus truth.

Against the wall, Faith relaxed, her mind warping itself into the crisp pages of her book.

Thus, she barely noticed when the girl of cherry hair approached her.

"Hey, Faith," Ruby said. "Mind if I sit here?"

"Help yourself," the bibliophile replied.

And Ruby did, blushing as she plopped herself down.

Silence.

Awkward silence.

Like a child, Ruby fidgeted, twirling her thumbs every which way.

"H-Hey, Faith . . ." she managed to utter.

"Hm?"

"Do you . . . Do you think we can talk for a minute?"

The archer glanced up, and noticing the vulnerability of her companion's character, she decided to stray from her printed text.

"About what?" Faith asked.

Ruby shut her eyes and breathed in deep, sorting out the jumbled mess swirling in her head.

Then, in a soft tone: "I just wanna say, I'm sorry about what happened on Gridlock. I was just so confused about everything. I had all this anger pent up and I didn't know what to do with it. I did what I thought would help, which is why I said those awful things to you and Jeremy. Not an excuse, of course, but yeah."

She sighed. "I dunno. I'm pretty weird; that won't ever change. But I just wanted to let you know, Faith, that all the things I said didn't come from my heart; they came from my anger, my frustration. I didn't mean any of those words.

"You're an amazing person, Faith, and I'd kill to be as smart and as beautiful as you."

Down the Rose's face, a single teardrop streamed down.

Flustered, the girl of no emotions stared dumbly at her legs.

"I, too, must apologize," she whispered. "The words I spoke were far from what my true feelings are towards you. I envy your charisma and ability to uplift the emotions of others. The luminosity of your soul is unlike anything I have ever witnessed."

Their eyes met.

"You inspire me to be the best I can be," Faith said. "Thank you, Ruby."

The girl of cherries merely cried more, her storm of emotions finally figuring out what belonged where.

Faith gestured to her read. "This novel had informed me that to strengthen a friendship, you must brutally highlight the flaws, even if it hurts that other person. It would seem that they are incorrect."

The cover: *How to Be a Good Friend.*

Excited, the Rose lunged forward to hug her companion, her lips curving into that bright knucklehead grin.

"Oh, Faith!" she sang. "You're the bestest friend in the whole universe! I'm so glad I have you, Luna, and Jeremy!"

By perhaps an iota, the lid of that bottle twisted off, letting the many, many flavors commence their escape.

Faith smiled, returning the embrace.

"I am delighted to have met you three as well."

Outside the cave, the girl of cherry blossoms stood guard, her sword at her side as she surveyed the earthy contours in the distance.

But even if she couldn't locate a signal threat, her body couldn't shake off this restlessness.

Something's not right.

She turned to head back to the others, but once she had reached the cave's entrance, she paused, distracted by the pieces of rock that tumbled near her head.

Luna looked up.

The servant of metal looked back.

Like a ragdoll, the girl of cherry blossoms rolled messily into the scene, right as Ruby and Faith wrapped up their conversation.

"Luna!" the girl of cherries cried.

She and the archer equipped themselves with their weapons and rose to their feet, just as a cluster of robots stomped towards them from outside.

"It would appear we've been discovered," Faith noted, loading her bow.

Ruby readied her spear. "No kidding."

Eating the pain, Luna recovered to a fighting position, joining the others to clog up the narrow pathway.

"You okay, Luna?" Ruby asked.

"Yeah," the leader assured. "More importantly, we have to stop these guys." She aimed her blade at the invaders. "No one gets to Jeremy!"

"Right!"

Two Sides of
the Same Coin

I just kept on going and going and going and going and going. The forest refused to submit its end, stacking and stacking the towers of raw wood like a reality endlessly crafting itself. Hours devoured the minutes; eons, the hours. Fatigue lacerated my body, my fingers struggling to stay pressed against my wrench. One of my lungs had already deflated, the other well on the way.

But maybe, just maybe, I had been following fate's design, for as my hopes of collapsing drew near, a new scenery engulfed my existence, wiping away the oak monotony.

Now, I stood at the edge of the grassy plain, the trees now volunteering as the walls to the circular space.

This place again, I thought, unsure of what emotion to pull from the bag.

In the center, as calm as the storm's eye, waited the boy of a twisted vision, seated upon a wooden chair.

I stepped closer.

He grinned.

"Hey," he said softly. "You made it. Welcome to where you're going."

A few feet away, I halted.

Nothing slid past my lips.

"Man," the boy said, looking me over, "you look. Like. Shit. Not a great night, I'm guessing?"

"Bite me," I barked.

"Ooh, look at you, getting all feisty. What? You think you're hard now just because you bashed a little kid's head in?

You're not that cool. I will admit, though, watching all that blood splatter against the wall." He blew a chef's kiss. "*Merveilleux!*"

I had never felt more sick.

"And you think we're the same . . ." I whispered.

"Do *I* think that?" the boy asked. "No. I *know* that. Did you think I didn't feel anything when I watched you hold Avella? I was hurt, just like you."

"Don't you dare say her name."

He leaned back in his chair. "Why's that? I know all about her, just like you. I know her favorite color. I know her favorite book. I know her dreams. I know her nightmares. But, unlike you, I also know her truths. I know that she's just damn tired of you. She's tired of having to deal with your pathetic life. She's tired of listening to someone who will *never* be able to move forward. Once at the bottom, always at the bottom, Jeremy."

"That's not true."

"*Yes, it is!*" the boy screamed, flinging his chair to the side. "*It will always be true, you fuckin' idiot!* You're *nothing*, Jeremy Mitchell. You will always be nothing. You're worthless. You're a waste of space. You do not deserve to live because you are the epitome of patheticness."

His tone softened. "I just want you to see that for yourself. I want you to understand that all those suspicions you had were correct. Don't trust the ones that are kind to you, because they're only doing it out of pity. Be ashamed to be alive, because you offer nothing to the table. Never reach for the sky, because you know full well that you'll never make it. Just give in, Jeremy. Accept the fact that you will die alone, as you are destined to. You'll only have your thoughts to hold, and they will become your best friends."

But even as his words pierced my flesh like arrows, my soul remained animated, my resolve more potent than any venom.

"You're not gonna budge, are you?" the boy asked, irritated.

Not an inch.

He grimaced. "Then I'll *make* you understand. This path here, it's the only one we've got."

A hint of sorrow wisped across his visage.

"It's the only one where we'll be safe."

The boy slid his fingers to his mouth, then blew, shooting out a resonant whistle that echoed across the forest.

At first, nothing.

Then, the growls, scurrying through the bushes to burrow their way directly into my eardrums.

"Last chance," the boy told me. "Tell me you're going to fall, Jeremy."

At first, the growls.

Then, the stomps, the dirt flying into the air as their claws dug into the ground.

"Not on your life," I spat, readying my wrench.

"Fine." The boy hardened his glare. "Then you can die here like the failure you are."

At first, the stomps.

Then, nothing.

Nothing.

Nothing.

Something.

Like rabid coyotes, the beasts of bloodied jaws erupted from the tree line, their viciousness oozing as viscous as the scarlet dribbling down their teeth. Four in total, each just as hungry as the last.

"Get him, lads!" the boy ordered.

No amusement this time.

Following their masters, the creatures all rushed to me, clawing at my flesh as soon as they drew near.

I swung my wrench wildly, bashing the metal into the monsters' skulls. Yet, they absorbed the impact, ignoring their own damage for the sake of inflicting mine. Of course, history always had a way of repeating itself, and just like with those bots at Mr. Rikaden's, I found myself cornered, my placidity deteriorating as my body collapsed upon more and more abuse.

A claw to my shoulder.

A slash into my calf.

A bite into my side.

I flailed and flailed, only to be punished thoroughly, from my limbs being torn to my nostrils suffocating beneath their rancid breath.

Ultimately, the pain tied me up in its puppet strings, ordering me to collapse to the ground. And even then, the beasts didn't let up, enjoying every inch of the feast before their eyes.

"You see!?" I heard the boy cry out. "You can't fight it! Just accept it, Jeremy! Accept that you're nothing!"

Is this it? I wondered. *Is this where it ends?*

My willpower had already begun deforming, the destroyed portions fading into fine ash.

For sixteen years, I had these things in my head. For sixteen years, I had this weight on my shoulders, forcing me to the ground, never giving me the time to even imagine a way up. All I ever knew were

> *my doubts,*
> *my faults,*
> *my mistakes,*
> *my loneliness.*

But the chance is here now.

Now, I can finally look my monsters right in the eyes. Now, I can bark at them all I want for all the hell they put me through. As I am now, I'll only be proving the point that I belong down here. I have so many people counting on me. They want me to strive. They want me to go where even imagination cannot define.

> *They want me to be happy.*
> *I have to fight back.*

I have to be in control.
I have to take a stand!
"Enough!"

A roar that I never would've thought would explode past my lips, one that made every atom present quiver.

As if a gust shoved them, the beasts gnawing at my bones soared back, rolling clumsily along the grass.

"What the hell . . . ?" the boy uttered, displeased as he watched me rise to a battle stance. "Why won't you just stay down!?"

"That's all I've been doing," I said. "It's time for me to get off my ass and do something about all of you."

I pointed my wrench at my foe.

"You made me want to blow my brains out from the moment I could think. Not anymore. This is where I take my life back. This is where I can start being glad that I'm alive! You won't take this from me!"

"Why won't you understand!?" the boy screamed. *"Kill him, you dirty mutts!"*

Onto round two as the creatures recovered to charge at me once more;

only this time, I had Lord Valor right here to guide me.

I carried myself back to that dojo beneath the bar, back to the bots that annihilated me, and like the notes of my favorite song, Luna's voice spun in my head.

"Remember to breathe."
Inhale.
Exhale.
"Always be aware of what's going on."
Four total.
One in each direction.
"Believe in yourself!"
I can do this!

They closed in, those foul creatures, slashing their way through my personal bubble.

This won't be like last time.

A promise I fulfilled as I swiped with my wrench, cracking the metal against one of their skulls.

Believing in the window, another beast lunged forward, its jaw unhinged to snap onto my neck.

Too slow!

I jerked my body to the side, then bashed the monster against the chin, rattling its brain matter as it collapsed to the grass. To ease my certainty, I smashed its head in, popping the skull like a busted melon.

One down.

"No! No!" the boy cried as he witnessed my valiance. "This isn't right!"

A dual strike, as one beast sank its teeth into my calf, just as the other thrashed into my forearm similar treatment.

I winced at the radiating pain.

"That's right!" the boy bellowed. "Get him! Teach him!"

The third beast bolted to my front, determined to rip out my jugular.

"Compared to what I've already been through"—I tore the creatures off my body, hurling one of them towards the third—"*the pain I'm feeling now is nothing!*"

All three beasts crumbled to the ground, dazed, and before any of them could recover, I dashed to the nearest and attacked with my Tool, splitting apart the jaw as the fallen teeth tumbled down its throat.

That's two.

I glared at my remaining foes, balanced.

The creatures still standing hesitated to approach me, whimpering like frightened pups.

The boy refused to meet my eyes, his head tilted to the ground.

"Why?" he whispered. "Why won't you understand? This is the only way."

When he looked back up, I expected rage to sear his being. However, the only sensations I could discover were misery and anguish.

"I'm trying to help you," he said. "I just need you to see. *Why won't you see!?*"

His voice thunderous, the sound blasted through the battleground, reducing the ferocious creatures into piles of ash in an instant.

If only by a little, I lowered my guard, especially as I watched the tears trickle down his face.

"Why can't you understand?" he choked. "Why can't you see that this is the only way for you? For us."

Despite the malice he lashed against me, my pity poured through my veins.

"Hey," I said, "are you okay?"

"Shut up. I'm fine."

"But you look—"

"*I said shut up!*"

Another deafening cry, this one summoning another pack of those filthy beasts, much more than I had just faced.

They charged ahead, ready to drive the nail in the coffin. But just before they could reach, before I could even brace myself, they vanished into ash. Gone as quick as they came.

The boy wiped his eyes.

"We're worthless," he whispered. "Nobody should give a damn about us. We can't do anything about what we are."

There it was again, that fuzziness encapsulating my heart's chambers. It came to me only once before, when the Rose spilled her faded petals upon my lap—petals which had scribed within them an inviting familiarity.

And as I gazed at the broken boy before me, I began to understand the clearer picture.

You are *me, down to a T.*

My voice.

My heart.

My soul.

They're all just like yours.

But I should've realized it sooner: because you're me, you must've felt it too—that loneliness, that doubt, that suspicion that you'll never be good enough. You're in pain, just like me; only difference is, you've accepted that pain. You've accepted how unworthy we think we are.

You don't believe we deserve to be happy.

Am I right?

He gave it his all to hold back his sobs, to continue playing the villain; however, his facade had already shattered, the true blue of his soul bleeding into the wind.

I stepped forward.

"Get away from me," he cried.

Don't worry. I'm here for you.

Closer.

"Get . . . Get away."

Closer.

"Please . . ."

Here,

my warmth blending with his as I hugged him as close as I could.

"I'm sorry," I told him. "I should've realized sooner. It hurts, doesn't it?"

He hesitated, but only for a moment, returning the gesture.

"It's always hurt," he told me. "From the time I could think."

"I know. I know. But I think we can finally make it stop hurting."

"How? All we ever do is make mistakes. All we ever do is disappoint them. How could it ever stop hurting when we're just plain failures?"

"Because"—a tighter hold—"we're *not* failures. Not completely. We will make mistakes. We will disappoint. But we weren't made to be perfect. We were made to be us. We were made to try our hardest to be the best we could be."

"What if . . . What if it isn't enough?"

"It will be."

They flashed into my thoughts, those caring smiles that wanted nothing but the very best for me.

"They'll accept us for who we are. They'll never throw us away. They'll always be by our side. If everyone else can love us, isn't it about time we started loving ourselves?"

His tears soaked into my shoulder.

"Can we?" he asked, earnest.

"We can," I told him. "We're allowed to appreciate ourselves. We're allowed to not be alone. Not anymore."

Little by little, his own hope rebuilt itself, from a dying ember to a lively sun.

"I'll trust you," he told me. "Just promise me it'll be okay."

"It will. It always will."

Acceptance,

as my other became incorporeal, disintegrating into fine grains of white sand.

His last words bloomed faintly into my ears, just as the sand swirled into my body like a piece I'd been missing. And with the transfer, I swore his smile had been etched into my wall of accomplishments.

"Thank you."

A nightmare closing, the forest around me melted away, placing me back in the unending planes of darkness. But now, I had nothing to fear, my suffering poured out in favor of the stability of my me.

No more wondering if my step was correct.

No more crying beneath my incompetence.

Only Jeremy Mitchell, gazing forward as I tried my best.

And to the right people, that was all they truly cared for.

In the distance, a globe of light appeared, and, my wrench right at my side, I sprinted towards it.

20

Into the Chaos

"They just keep comin'!" Ruby roared, thrusting her spear.

"Don't let up!" Luna ordered, slashing away with her own blade.

The trio of Guardians defended the entrance to the temple, beating and bashing every robot that cursed their presence. But with every scrap of metal vanquished, two more would offer replacement, clogging up the cavern with iron both living and not.

We can't a single one pass, Luna thought. *Not until Jeremy is finished.*

Reload.

Reload.

Reload.

Faith delivered her arrows to her foes' necks, erasing their lives as the fiends closed the gap.

Reload.

Reload.

No time.

A bot at her twelve, the archer lunged her arrow from her hand, jamming it into the enemy's skull, bringing the fiend down.

With the current climate, the Guardians barely gripped the momentum; however, a single mistake would bury them, proven by Luna's own incompetence.

She went to slice, only to strike nothing but the air.

A costly mistake, as the robot snatched her by the throat, slamming her against the wall as her windpipe compressed shut.

"Luna!" Ruby cried. She went to aid her companion, only to be halted by the other metal men.

Her veins suffocating, the girl of cherry blossoms fought to raise her sword. But instead, she dropped it to the ground, her fingers loosened as her captor slugged her arm with a free fist.

Vision began to blur.

Lungs began to deflate.

Escape narrowed.

Piece by piece, her hope dwindled, until, as sudden as a thunderclap, the menace of metal released her, tackled to the ground by the boy of the monsters.

Delicious air poured down Luna's throat, her senses equalizing to what they once were.

She then took hold of her sword, just as her savior smashed his wrench against the enemy's head, caving it in.

Kill confirmed, he stood tall.

And as collected as a murder of crows, a pack of bots rushed forward to snatch him away.

Not on my watch.

Shing! Luna's sword howled as she delivered her swipe, beheading the foes with remarkable elegance.

She then curved her lips at the boy and whispered, "Jeremy."

"Yo," I said. "I'm back."

"Took ya long enough!" Ruby bellowed, doing some major damage. "I was startin' to think you'd bit the dust!"

"Sorry. I had some things to take care of." I carved my attention into the here and now. "I see you guys have been busy."

"I suppose," Faith noted, launching her ammunition.

I readied my own wrench.

"Let me join in."

As unified as a platoon, my Guardians and I wreaked havoc on our invaders, eliminating them one by one as our synergy expanded to heights never dreamt of. Sparks flew as robotic limbs crumbled, as live wires flailed through the open air.

Only after the final foe had lost the lights of its eyes did the placidity return, our fatigue as apparent as a runner who'd just slayed a marathon.

Luna leaned against the wall.

"Give . . . Give me a minute," she begged, panting.

"I shall also take that minute," Ruby said. "Maybe two." To me: "Seriously, though, what the heck, Jeremy? The minute you show up, we start wiping the floor with those guys. You're like an SSR or somethin'."

I don't know what that means, and, quite frankly, I'm too exhausted to ask.

"It's not over yet, though," Luna noted, straightening herself. "Now that Jeremy's finished, we gotta head out."

"Heh~?" Ruby whined. "You're not gonna let me pass out?"

I don't think that'd be good for any of us.

Despite the protests of the valiant Rose, we strolled to the cavern's exit, weaving past the clusters of robotic corpses. And as our sights feasted upon the virtually untouched STS, we let loose sighs of relief.

"Still in one piece," our leader said.

We carried ourselves through the sliding double doors, taking our place on the benches as Luna entered the info on the front console.

"Where are we going?" Ruby asked.

"Home," Luna answered. "Our home. I don't know why, but I've been getting bad vibes ever since we came here."

"As have I," Faith said. "Something is happening, and those metal assailants confirm it."

After doing what she had to do, Luna took her seat, and like clockwork, the shuttle's thrusters boomed with life, lifting us off to boost us away from Titan and back into the vastness of space.

I sank into my bench.

Just five minutes. That's all I need. Just five minutes.

"Hey, Jeremy," Ruby said.

"Yeah?"

"You okay?"

"I think so. Why do you ask?"

"'Cause you're bleeding everywhere."

I studied the wounds I'd received in the temple. The pain had thankfully subsided, but I guess the physical marks had no intention of going away.

My Guardians (two of them) stared at me with worry.

"Don't worry," I urged them. "Just went through some things when I was in there. Doesn't hurt anymore."

Nonetheless, Ruby kept on staring, her pupils glistering as if she were analyzing the components of my very soul.

"I can't quite put my finger on it," she said, "but, ignoring all the scratches and stuff, you look different."

"In a good way?" I asked.

She grinned. "In a good way."

I relished the compliment, now convinced that my clash with my monsters was more than a mere dream, more than a longing thriving in fiction.

I did it, I thought. *I really did it. It took me sixteen years, but now, I can finally make my way past the starting line.*

The rest of the trip followed through with this atmosphere, my Guardians and I hoping to recover every ounce of strength possible.

But once the shuttle speakers gave their announcement, once I peered out that front windshield, the realization dawned on me: no amount of rest could prepare us for what came next.

A floating city, connected to a plain of golden glass, more opulent than a dazzling Eden, more massive than an entire galaxy. However, the serenity had been mutilated. Iron soldiers mountainous and slender glided across the skies, unloading their ammunition to forge monumental destruction. Hives of flames ate away at the skyscrapers like infestations, spitting plumes of smoke every which way, debris showering down as swift as icy raindrops.

"*That's* your empire?" I asked, devastated.

We barely had the details of the metropolis defined, and still, I could imagine the screams breaking though.

"I knew it," Luna growled, pissed off. "Dirodotus put all his chips on the table."

"As should've been expected," Faith noted. "Slay the head of the pride and the rest will follow."

Ruby stretched. "Looks like we're at the last level."

The STS slid into a dim tunnel situated beneath the city, the luminance of the hung lamps shimmering off the railroad tracks.

"Almost to the platform," Luna said. "Once we get into the city, we make a beeline for Council Hall. Ignore all the—"

Boom!

Suddenly, the shuttle quivered, the backside damaged as an explosion detonated.

"What was that!?" Ruby cried.

Digging deeper, we found a pair of robots soaring towards us, their arms morphed into slim cannons.

"You gotta be kidding—"

Boom!

Another strike, shattering the back windshield.

Our archer took aim with her bow, only to be stopped as the STS rumbled.

"I can't get a clear shot," she said.

Pop!Pop!Pop!Pop!Pop!Pop!

From cannons to machine guns, the metal men opened fire, riddling the front console with bullet holes as we ducked to dodge.

Unfazed, Luna dragged herself to the double doors, wasting no time tearing them off the aircraft with the flat of her foot.

"Then we jump!" she bellowed.

"Jump?" I asked, timid.

"You heard me!"

Minding the bullets, our leader snuck a peek towards the front, then lowered herself again.

"Platform's coming up!" she told us. "On my mark!"

We crawled to her side.

I never get a break.

"On three!

"One . . .

"Two . . .

"Three!"

With nothing more than a wing and a prayer, I leapt out the STS, my Guardians right there with me. One moment, I was kissing the smoke-stained air; the next, I found myself rolling along the subway station platform.

Kaboom!

Right as we split from the shuttle, it collided with another already parked, resulting in a fiery explosion intertwined with chunks of scattered parts.

Fate on our side, a block of debris rammed into the robots who chased us, shattering their bodies into nothingness upon impact.

No time to rest.

"We have to go!" Luna cried, springing to her feet.

Ruby helped me to mine, and together, the four of us raced up the broad staircase and into the battlefield. As expected, the chaos flourished like a thunderstorm. Screams left and right, too many to count. Top to bottom, havoc played its ruthless course, from the citizens tumbling from bullet wounds to the soldiers of Zekra fending off the invaders across the rooftops.

"This way!" Luna said, gesturing forward.

She bolted off, the rest of us following.

Levitating midair, she surveyed the battlefield—the young woman whose irises roared with pinkness. Citizens of her empire scrambled for their lives, their young ones held tightly in their grasp.

"Keep calm, Zekrians," she urged. "We will protect you."

But she would have to pause that promise, for as she saw the boy of the wrench scuttling through the streets, she drifted over to where he would be.

But not for long; not after a little boy's whines crawled down my spine.

"No!" he wailed, shoving and shoving against a robot who choked a woman against the wall. "Leave her alone! Leave my mom alone!" Tears and snot raced down his face.

Not again, I decided. *Not for him too.*

On instinct, I threw myself into the scene, hurling my wrench into the metal man's head to knock it clean off.

The woman shrank down and coughed as her windpipe opened back up.

"Mommy!" her son cried as he wrapped his arms around her.

She returned the gesture.

"Thaddeus!"

Then, to me: "Thank you! Thank you so much!"

"Now's not the time," I told them. "You gotta get out of here!"

Just then, my cherry-haired Guardian emerged at my side.

"We gotta go, Jeremy!" she urged.

I nodded, and after waving goodbye to the duo, I continued with my companion on our journey. Along the way, various robotic fiends sprang into our bubble, thirsty for our blood. But so long as we kept our composure, we knocked them out with ease, squeezing through the calamity just barely, until our destination developed into sight.

"There it is!" Luna said, pointing to an octagonal building resting at the meeting point of eight roads.

We picked up pace, right as a colossal heap of fire zoomed past us, blitzing a nearby building into a mound of bricks and face-down bodies.

I stopped dead in my tracks, staring at the wreckage, finally absorbing just how f*cked up everything turned out to be. The scene around me slowed to a near still, the sounds muffled, leaving only my raging heartbeats to pound my senses.

Then, the return,

as my cherry-haired Guardian graciously grabbed my hand, pulling me forward as she blessed me with that sweet, sweet smile.

From then on, the devastation softened, and I could study only her, her loving voice acting as her embrace.

"We can do this."

You're right.

We can.

We will.

A helping hand that went a long way.

Literally.

Faith and Luna at the front, they crashed their shoulders through the building's golden doors, splitting them open, allowing the four of us to flee from the battleground.

It felt as though I'd gone through a portal: the chaos, the death, the devastation, now all gone, replaced by a pleasing hush and home-like scent.

Ruby let me go, and I hunched over atop the tiled flooring, panting like a tired dog.

"That . . . That sucked," Ruby groaned.

"I agree," I said. "I . . . I agree."

"Jeremy?"

A call from a familiar voice; a collection of vocal cords ripe with kindheartedness.

I looked up, my surprise leaping across planets as the girl of thunder-yellow hair stood before me.

"V-Veronica?" I uttered.

She took a step forward. "Is that really you, Jeremy?"

"Th-That's what I should be asking."

"Well, shoot."

More surprises, as both Amy and Jennifer popped into the picture.

"I guess the secret's out now," Amy said, shrugging.

"You guys too?" I asked.

Confusion resisted the glue of the puzzle pieces, but I managed, constructing the painting to be as clear as glass.

"Y-You're a Selector?" I asked Veronica.

She smiled shyly. "Since you know what that is, I'm guessing you're one too, huh?"

"I never would've guessed it."

Ruby folded her arms.

"You dunno how loud I wanted to scream when I saw y'all sitting together at lunch," she said. "I wanted to be like, 'She's one of your own, dude! She's one of your own!'"

"Good thing you didn't, though," Amy argued. "Otherwise, the Sentinels would've given us an earful."

I surveyed the space, spotting an aged, chiseled gentlemen and the one who had kept his promise.

Jax smiled. "You've gotten a lot taller since then."

We're basically the same height now.

He outstretched his hand. "We meet again, Jeremy."

I accepted it.

"We meet again."

That night from nine years ago sprouted into my thoughts, lining up the syllables for three words:

A full circle.

"Sorry to interrupt," Luna said, "but I don't think now is the best time."

"She's right," Jax said, releasing his grip. "We'll catch up soon, though."

Another promise.

Back to the impending doom of our existence.

"What's the plan, Sentinel Jax?" Ruby asked. "Whose butt are we kicking?"

"Well, originally, Sentinel Athello wanted us to stay in here with the Selectors."

"Which I think is pretty dumb," Veronica argued.

Wait a second.

Aren't there supposed to be three of us?

"Veronica," the chiseled man said, "we talked about this."

"I know, Gideon, but even you gotta admit that we should be out there fighting!" My fellow Selector summoned forth a fierce scythe embedded with a violet gem. "We can hold our own."

Where's the third one at?

"That psychopath has a Gemini Fragment," Veronica continued, "and from what I've seen, he's not afraid to use it. Jeremy and I are on equal footing with Dirodotus, just like the Sentinels."

Even if they don't have their Fragment anymore, they should still be here with us.

"She has a point, Gideon," Jax said. "It really is a waste that the two of them are in here when they could very well turn the tides of the battles. They've shown that they are capable of holding their own."

"And we'll be right there beside them," Jennifer added. "With all of us, we'll be unstoppable."

Realization.

The chiseled man rubbed his chin, his expression loosening.

"With all due respect," Luna said, "I believe it is a risk worth taking."

"It's a gamble," the Sentinel argued. "A very big gamble. But even so"—he grinned—"I believe that we'll win such a wager."

Everyone else flaunted their cheers, ready to dominate the battlefield.

Not me.

Not one bit.

"Who was it?" I asked Jax, straight faced.

"I'm sorry?" Jax asked back.

"Who's the other Selector?"

Luna raised an eyebrow. "Jeremy, what are you talking about?"

"I was told there are three Selectors," I said. "I was also told that I know who they are. Veronica and I are standing right here with our Fragments, and Dirodotus is out there with the third one, so who the hell is the other Selector and why aren't they here with us?"

Silence.

Averting eyes.

"Who was it?" I barked at Jax. "Who the hell was it?"

"It's all right. I'll handle this."

From the background emerged a young woman who more or less appeared as an older version of Luna. Only difference: this newcomer had been sobbing for what seemed like eons.

"Persephone," Jax said, surprised. "What are you doing here?"

"I came as soon as I saw the boy traveling here," she answered. "I was certain that he would draw the conclusion, and seeing as how she was my responsibility, it is only right that I tell him."

The young woman approached me, her sorrow bleeding into my garden of emotions.

"The reason there is no third Selector," she said, "is because she was killed by Dirodotus and his master. Neither her nor her Guardians survived the attack."

Even as she gave a weak smile, she wept.

"I know she fought her hardest. I know that had the circumstances been different, she would still be with us today. I'm . . . I'm so proud of her, regardless of the outcome. There will never be another quite like her."

She caressed my cheek.

"There will never be another Avella Summers."

21
My Light, Diminished

"What?" I whispered.

I must've misheard. It happens from time to time.

The young woman rubbed my cheek with her thumb.

"I'm sorry, love," she said softly. "She was my responsibility, and I let her down. I have no right calling myself a Sentinel."

I backed away from her, the eyes of everyone glued to me.

"She's not serious, right?" I asked the group. "This is just me being dumb, right? This is a different Avella. It has to be."

No one said a thing.

"Tell me I'm right."

No one said a damn thing.

"Please . . . I'm begging you . . . Tell me she's still here."

"I'm truly sorry," the woman offered. "I'm . . ." Her sobs fluttered like blue butterflies as she covered her mouth with her hand.

My vision blurred as my eyes grew moist, as I held onto every single sensation that invaded my heart.

But then came that gentle voice, its tone just right to mend my shattered soul; or perhaps, to allow my aura to be reshaped into something worth carrying.

The message spoken lasted only a few syllables, yet I couldn't find more value in a billion words.

It's okay not to be okay.

So, I let go.

I screamed in anguish, dropping my wrench to the ground as I collapsed to my knees. Every bone quivered. Every finger twitched beneath the overwhelming weight piling on like darkened clouds. I wept as if the world had faded to black and gray, as if my dreams had fallen into a coffin, as if not a single inch of this reality held meaning.

As if I strolled through an art gallery, images of my beloved played through my mind, fully defined, down to the vibrancy howling in her demeanor.

Her smile.

Her waves.

Her kindness.

"I'll see you again tomorrow, okay?"

"All you had to do was protect her," I said. "All you had to do was give her a tomorrow. It didn't matter what happened to me. All we had to do was make her happy! *Damn it!*"

I slammed my fist against the ground, once, twice, thrice. My tears rolled off the lens of my glasses.

"Avella . . ."

"Jeremy . . ." Ruby said softly, her own despair unwinding along with the others.

Only one being took action as the grief froze the bodies of those present: a petite little girl, around the age of six or seven, arriving onto the scene from behind one of the golden chairs. Her skin fair, she had hair hued like ravens plummeting to her shoulders, complementing the redness of her irises, purer than the most valiant of tanagers. Elegance intertwined with the threads of her clothing, from her black sundress with white polka dots to her ankle-high socks to her dress shoes.

The others watched with curiosity as the little one approached the broken boy.

Luna leaned towards Jax and asked, "Who is that?"

"Miss Avella's younger sister," he answered. "She had been living with Avella when the attack happened, but by the grace of Zekrac, she survived. To keep her safe, we've had her stay here for a while."

I was at the top. I was right there. And just when I thought I could go even further, I ended up back at the bottom.
Snot dribbled out my nostrils, splashing to the tiles alongside my tears.
I wanted to show you what I'd become. I wanted to show you that I was worth loving.
A sister's touch, as the other half of the Summer girls hugged me close, stroking my hair tenderly as she offered a warm smile.
"It's okay," she told me. "It's okay."
My sobs only intensified.
"It's okay," she said. "I miss her too."
I returned the embrace, appreciating the warmth of her being.
"Rosaria . . ." I choked.
She soon pressed my head back to lay her hands on my cheeks.
"It'll be okay," she said. "We just need to stay strong. For her. Big Sis believed in you right to the end, and I'll do the same."
I wiped the mucus away as Rosaria fished out a folded piece of paper from her pocket.
"This is for you," she said, offering the gift. "It's from Avella. I've seen her write this over and over again, throwing away so many pieces. She could never find the right words, and even with this one, I don't know if she nailed it. But she wanted you to read this. I know because she wouldn't want it perfect for anyone else."

I accepted the note, handling it as a sacred document. And after unfolding it, I let myself be taken away in the lines of ink.

"Dear Jeremy,

"I'm writing this to let you know how sorry I am. Ever since I moved, I feel like our connection has been slowly dwindling away. Heck, we don't talk nearly as much as we used to. I miss that.

"I know it must seem like I'm neglecting you, but I just have so many things going on right now; my head is practically spinning. And I'd love to tell you all about it, but I just can't. Not that I don't trust you, because you're one of the very few people I can actually open my heart to.

"It's just complicated.

"You're probably annoyed by this point and have most likely stopped reading. But if you're still with me, then I want you to know, Jeremy, that I love you very much. That time that we spend on the computer together, I cherish every second of it. Every word you speak, every smile you give, it gives me the strength to keep pushing forward.

"I promise, when this is all over, I'm going to move back to New Haven. I don't know how, but I'm going to do it. Then the two of us can be together, just like old times. Then I can give you all hugs I owe you for your past birthdays.

"We can be Avella and Jeremy again.

"All I ask is that you wait for me.

"Love, Avella.

"P.S. I'm sorry I never saw your monsters."

This is her—her thoughts, her feelings, her reality—all bundled up just for me.

Till the very end, she really did care about me.

Another piece of evidence, as Rosaria wrapped around my neck a simple silver chain with a pink, heart-shaped gem hanging from the middle.

I was speechless.

"There we go," she said, smiling. "Fits perfect."

Escaping from the gem, the memories flooded in: all the happiness, all the hope I had ever experienced, centralized around that glorious human being.

* * *

"Come back soon, okay?"

"I promise I'll be back. Don't forget about me when I'm gone!"

"Psh! I'll never forget about you! Let's talk every day! My mom's gonna buy me a new computer soon!"

"Okay! I'll ask my dad to set up a program for us! We'll talk all day and all night!"

"I like the sound of that!"

The boy fired his wave,

while the girl boarded the plane.

* * *

Suddenly, a pair of robots crashed through the ceiling, their weapons ready.

"We've got company!" Jax said, unsheathing his sword.

Anger.

Fear.

Sadness.

Confusion.

Guilt.

Shame.

Insanity.

"Ahhhhh!"

My emotions pulling the strings, I grabbed my wrench and smashed it against the ground, summoning twin bolts of lightning that raced to the rude newcomers.

It took only an instance for the metal men to perish into piles of ash.

Dumbfoundedness encased those around me.

I, however, simply stood tall, wiping my eyes with my sleeve.

One more second, I begged. *Let me be sad for one more second.*

And once that second had passed, my grief, my agony, evolved, shapeshifting into feathers of pure wrath.

I leaned my Tool against my shoulder, my glare hardened.

"Let's go," I hissed, stomping towards the exit.

In all the time we had spent watching over him, and all the time we had spent by his side, I had never seen such a look on his face. He was focused. Driven. Brave. But beneath those traits of the lion's heart lay something so cruel, so spiteful, that even Death himself would not dare interfere.

Nonetheless, I stuck close to him. After all, with everything he'd done for me, I'd follow Jeremy anywhere.

The Hero
vs The Savior

Back to the war-torn battlefield, where the clash between mortals and inhumans rained down like condensed droplets.

I surveyed the skies, noticing every single shift of atoms, until a peculiar set snatched my attention: the android of the gears, his body decorated with a crimson glow as he faced off against a warrior in a trench coat.

"Is that Dirodotus?" I asked.

"The one and only," Jax told me. "Athello is dealing with him at the moment, so we should focus on destroying—"

"I need a favor."

The group lent me their curiosity.

"I need one of you," I said, "to throw me at him."

"Have you lost your mind, Jeremy?" Jax asked, astonished. "You're not ready to face him. He's giving even Athello a run for his money."

The veins of my heart refused to soften.

"I don't care. He killed my best friend."

My Sentinel went to argue even further, but the chiseled man stopped him.

"He'll go regardless of what we tell him," he said. "Better to have him go through the air than through the streets."

You're damn right.

Despite the words he still wished to deliver, Jax bit his tongue.

Ruby stepped to my side.

"You sure about this?" she asked.

"One hundred percent."

"Then, I got you."

My Guardian dug her fingers into the back of my hoodie, lifting me up with her monstrous strength.

"One Jeremy cannonball, ready to fire!"

She cocked me back.

"Go get 'em, buckaroo!"

The launch, my body zooming through the wind like an arrow as Ruby hurled me forward.

As clear as day, my path connected to the root of my despair, and I just couldn't wait to get my hands on him.

The pack watched the Selector, Jax's hesitance still written across his face.

"Don't fret," Gideon told him. "Believe in your successor."

"I do," Jax said. "I always will. But even I must remember that emotions do not make us invincible."

"What's done is done. The only thing we can do now is save our home."

"I know."

The Sentinel of Light readied his weapon, as did the others, and like tigers protecting their den, the warriors split off to defend their empire.

Pop!Pop!Pop!Pop!Pop!Pop!

Through the turrets in his arm, Dirodotus unloaded his stream of bullets, aiming straight for the Sentinel before him.

A counter, Athello zipped through the air, evading every piece of brass that hungered for his arteries.

"Resistance is futile," the android said. "In the end, your time will come to pass."

"Only I am the ruler of my fate!" the Sentinel bellowed. He outstretched his hand, summoning a circular field of energy, and as the bullets made contact, they disintegrated into fine particles of dust.

Now on the offensive, Athello played with his creation, morphing the waves of specks into narrow stone spikes, which he shot directly at his foe.

Dirodotus quit his fire to copy the Sentinel's defense, soaring through the air to evade. However, Athello's projectiles would not give up so easily, and like mad hounds, they chased after the metal man.

"Not good enough," he said.

From his palms, Dirodotus fired off his laser beams, erasing the spikes into mere nothingness.

He then thrust towards the Sentinel, his fist ready to feast.

"Too slow!" Athello roared, transforming the nearby rubble into vines that then wrapped around the android, killing his movements.

Dirodotus appeared unimpressed.

"I can't tell whether you're trying to test me or not," he said.

He collected the scarlet glow within, then let it howl, unleashing a bubble of menacing light that burned the vines to a crisp.

"I was right not to underestimate you," Athello commended.

"Is that so?" Dirodotus asked. "Because from what I've gathered, I must admit that you're performing below my expectations."

"Let's just say, I haven't gotten serious yet."

The metal man prepared his weaponry.

"I must implore you to change your strategy," he said. "Otherwise, you won't make it."

Wham!

A clean connection, right against the menace's forearm he had raised in defense.

From the impact, I could tell that I had landed a solid hit, my satisfaction barely clicking as I rolled upon the nearest rooftop.

No time to waste, I recovered to my feet, then locked my sights onto the bastard who hovered up above.

"*You,*" he growled, glaring.

I did the same damn thing.

"Selector!" the man in the trench coat exclaimed. "What are you doing here? You should be in Council Hall!"

I ignored him.

"Select—"

Before the man could argue any further, the resonant screams of his citizens burrowed into the atmosphere.

"I suggest you tend to that, Sentinel Athello," Dirodotus said. "Otherwise, you won't have anything left to protect."

Despite his spirit begging him to stay, the man in the trench coat knelt to his duties, fleeing the scene to aid his fellow Zekrians.

His final message to me:

"Don't you die, Selector."

Not planning on it.

At least, not alone.

Like a corrupted angel, the metal fiend lowered himself onto the other side of the rooftop, his heels clanking against the landing.

We stared at one another.

Tension,

dense enough to sink my teeth into.

"We meet again, Jeremy Mitchell," he said. "I must say, something about you has changed."

"Shut the hell up," I hissed. "I'm not here to talk."

"Eager. I find that intriguing. After all, I assumed that out of everyone here, you would be the one to cower in the corner."

"I got rid of the voices in my head, so I'm okay with myself. And you took away the one thing I was afraid to lose. What could possibly scare me now?"

"Isn't it obvious?" His glare darkened. "There's *me.*"

I squeezed my wrench.

"We'll see about that."

Ruby thrust her spear into the robot's chest, tossing the menace over her shoulder, forcing it to burst apart as it crashed against the ground.

Thirsty for vengeance, a second invader lunged towards the Guardian; however, just before its fingertips could reach, an arrow went drilling into the being's skull, shutting away its life.

Ruby looked to Faith, who already had another piece of ammunition loaded.

"Thank ya!" she said.

The archer nodded, already searching for her next target.

Luna slashed through the limbs of iron, decorating the ground with frayed wires and bantam sparks of electricity. Not a single hand could touch her; not a single bullet could graze her skin. Her movements barely passed the first benchmark, her limit nowhere to be seen.

Calm.

Steady.

Merciless.

The Violet Reaper twirled elegantly through the air, slicing off the heads of any bots who dared pierce her midst. With each kill, her scythe grew more and more ecstatic.

Pop! Pop! Pop!

The robot's body jittered as the bullets spiraled through its armor, disabling it. But just before the enemy could tumble, Jennifer leapt off its chest, using the time airborne to fire even more shots into a bevy of inhuman skulls.

Once back on the ground, she reloaded.

Her might relentless, Amy fired a smooth uppercut into a robot's chin, shooting it into the air.

She then threw her kunai to its position, teleporting above her foe to bash her fists into the top of its head.

A hard crash, the robot's body exploding into bits and pieces upon impact.

Once back down, the Guardian noticed the pack of metal men headed her way.

Her placidity never betrayed her.

A calculated flick of the wrist and her kunai went sailing through the horde, all the way to the back.

Voom!

The young girl teleported.

And when she opened her eyes, the group of invaders exploded into piles of scrap.

"I suggest you stand down," Dirodotus told me. "You have no chance of stopping me."

Shut your damn mouth.

I sprinted to the menace, my Tool cocked back, and when I reached, I swung, desperate to bash his head in.

No such luck.

Dirodotus merely deflected my strike with his forearm, then countered, cracking his knuckles against my chest.

Wham!

I flew back, rolling across the rooftop; but in no time did I recover, charging towards my foe once again.

Similar results,

over and over again.

No matter how many times I attacked, he would simply deflect and retaliate, hammering his fist into my body, torturing me with radiating pain.

Eventually, he altered the cycle, firing at me a trio of scorching laser beams.

Not yet!

My teeth clenched, I jerked my body to the side, dodging.

Whoosh!

Like a hawk, the metal man thrust forward, penetrating my space to deliver a monstrous punch to my cheek.

My jaw popped as I stumbled back.

"You are nothing more than a hatchling in this paradigm," Dirodotus said. "Meanwhile, I have already spread my wings. I have already soared to galaxies undefined. Compared to me, you are worthless."

"Worthless, huh?" I wiped the blood dribbling down my chin. "I've heard that enough times"—I dashed forward—"to know it's not true!"

Another go with my wrench, my strength begging to be unleashed.

"Futile," my foe warned.

He went to repeat history.

Not this time.

Right before he could defend, I swiveled like a tornado, bashing my Tool into his ribs, marring the surface.

"Anything's possible," I said. "All you have to do is take the damn step!"

From me, another strike,

only to be halted as Dirodotus grabbed my Tool mid-swing.

"Not all dreams can be turned into reality," he said.

With his free fist, he clobbered my cheek, forcing me to spit up scarlet as he then tossed me high into the air.

Dirodotus took aim with his arm.

"Hope can only take you so far."

From the top of his fist, a single rocket spiraled forth, jetting right for my chest.

My medal of valor glinted in the starlight.

"Hope is what saved my life!" I roared.

With flawless timing, I swung my wrench at the missile.

Kaboom! the projectile cried as billows of flames erupted inches from me, licking my skin with tremendous heat. Still, my damage taken remained minimal.

Like an anvil dropping, I descended back to the terrain, right as the mastermind thrust towards me once again, his knuckles cocked back.

As swift as lightning, I lifted my Tool, both hands on the job.

Klank!

Dirodotus's fist whined against my wrench's body, and we glared at one another, as still as statues.

"And you," I growled. "You took that hope away from me."

"This way, everyone!" Sentinel Tetra said, directing the semi-calm citizens into a tunnel that led underground. "No shoving, please!"

In spite of the ravage strangling the empire, the young girl kept with her jolliness, her lips curved into a warm smile.

Her attention only slipped from the crowds once she noticed a quartet of robots flying towards her, their cannons ready to draw blood.

"Sorry, mister bots," she said. "There's no room for you here."

She aimed her palms, forging bubbles of bright purple energy to encase the invaders, pausing them in their place.

"Goodbye now."

Cheery, she was, as the Sentinel squeezed her hands, as she erased the metal men completely from existence.

Now, back to her constituents.

"It'll be okay! We'll make it through this!"

BANG! BANG! BANG!

One by one, Codex sniped at the invaders, penetrating their torsos with her ammo to send them crashing down.

Before long, a murder of metal men came boosting to her backside, determined to end her reign.

Naïve.

Codex widened her eyes, and as if her soul brightened, a crimson glow gleamed within her irises.

In unison, the ambushers froze in place, their realities paused in all regards.

The Sentinel then retrieved her sidearm—a handgun— and unloaded the magazine, one casing for each temple.

Once finished, she released the light of her gaze, causing the robots' time to return, just as they plummeted lifelessly to the streets below.

Back to the rifle.

Codex scanned the area, searching for more targets, until her focus latched onto the clash between the alpha android and the little Selector.

"Where the hell is Athello?" she spat. "That boy is biting off way more than he can chew."

The Sentinel stored away her weapons, then leapt rooftop to rooftop, towards the most pivotal battle.

Wham!

His strength boundless, Dirodotus rammed his fist into my cheek, shooting me back.

But rather than stumbling, I threw myself back to him, bashing my wrench into his thigh.

Little damage, as usual.

But still damage, nonetheless.

In retaliation, the android punched me once more, this time sinking his fist right into my gut.

A familiar sight.

"Your movements are sloppy," Dirodotus chastised, unimpressed. "Your strategies are limited. At this point, you're no better than a monkey with a stick."

Blood and saliva coated my lips.

"I'm not—"

Wham!

Another hit, directly on the top of my head, stirring my brain as I dropped to my knees.

Wham!

This time, my temple, knocking my glasses clean off my face as my blood splattered onto the concrete.

"Give it up," Dirodotus told me. "Your time is finished."

Fighting my blurred vision, I swiveled my body, landing another swipe with my Tool.

In return, my foe shot me away with a blast of scorching wind, forcing me to roll across the rooftop, my skin blistered.

"I will commend you where it is deserved," Dirodotus said. "Your vitality is much more than I had anticipated."

"I'm not here . . . for your filthy compliments."

Fatigue peeled away at my body from head to toe, and I found myself wavering as I struggled back to my feet.

Conveniently, I had landed next to my glasses, and as I put them back on, the cracked lens reeled my attention.

"You'll still rise?" the android asked.

"You can knock me down as much as you'd like," I said. "Until I see you dead at my feet, I'm not backing down."

"Then you will die unfulfilled, because as it stands now, you are nothing more than a thorn in my side."

I pointed my wrench at him. "Even a thorn can cut as deep as a sword. You just have to keep trying."

Dirodotus analyzed me.

"Naïve," he said. "No matter what you do, the outcome will not change. We are merely following in fate's design, and in this paradigm, you are destined to perish along with the rest of the riffraff, just like that little girl back in Golden Gate."

Nerves, snapped.

Like a statue decaying, my inner-peace disintegrated into fragments of pure hatred.

"What did you just say?"

His response: a volley of missiles launched from his back, all curving to eradicate my being.

My teeth clenched, I darted to the side, narrowly dodging the projectiles as they exploded against the nearby structures.

Not over yet.

With pristine speed, Dirodotus dashed to my backside, grabbing my hoodie to hurl me across the rooftop. My bones crunched against the hard landing.

"She was just like you," he said. "No matter what I did, she would rise once more. Her eyes were just like yours: full of hope and resolve." His visage brewed disgust. "She refused to know her place. So, I made sure she learned. First, I broke her leg. And when she kept shooting, I broke her arm. And even then, she refused to back down." His eyes darkened. "So, I snapped her neck."

I pictured it: my beacon of hope, lying still on the carpet, blood pooling around her as the isolation crept near from all sides.

"And the Sentinels had the audacity to gift her a Fragment?" Dirodotus asked. "Avella Summers—a Selector? I had never met a more pathetic being."

There it went, the remaining scraps of my reasoning.

All the morality I had been building up, all the energy that had seeped into my heroic integrity, now washed away, replaced by the monster I didn't know thrived in the closet.

What is this feeling?

I've never had something like this before.

Back then, I was just pissed off. But now . . .

Something ominous, something gruesome, scurried out from the deepest chambers of my being, lurking between the veins like a poison—a toxin I somehow craved for the more I stared at that bastard in front of me.

. . . more than anything, I want to break him.

Dirodotus's curiosity spun as he watched the strands of electricity flicker around the boy's Gemini Tool.

"Avella was anything but pathetic," I said. "She was kind. She was loving. She accepted me for the mess that I was. Because of her, I didn't end up six feet below by my own hands. So, if you think I'm just gonna let you get away with what you said"—my rage roared—"*you got another thing coming!*"

I smashed my Tool against the ground, summoning a bloodthirsty bolt of lightning from my Fragment, and like a wild beast, the attack zoomed to the metal menace, burning away the armor of his arm.

Barely scathed.

But before Dirodotus could make his move, I dashed forward, my wrench growling as lines of electricity brushed against its entirety.

"Your emotions won't save you," he said.

Wham! his fist groaned, connecting well with my brow.

Barely scathed.

My hatred salivating, I swiveled my body like a hurricane, bashing my Tool against his ribs, chipping away the plating.

The metal man flinched.

"You took away someone who gave us all hope," I barked, "and now, you're gonna pay for it!"

Back and forth, the two of us went, trading blows like boxers in the ring.

Blood for blood.

Bone for bone.

Pain for pain.

Unlike before, I devoured the aches carved into my muscles, my yearning overpowering all—my drive to drill this villain right into the dirt.

Eventually, Dirodotus broke the cycle, forcing me back with his blast of sizzling air.

"Your words mean little to me," he said. "When the bottom of the trash bin praises a fellow member, there's nothing to be impressed by."

"I may be at the bottom," I said, "but I'll still take you down!"

Once more, I clobbered the ground with my wrench, releasing twin bolts of lightning that slithered violently to their prey.

To defend, Dirodotus fired off his laser beams, deflecting my electricity with his own force.

"Enough," he ordered.

After clearing the battlefield, he shot another laser right at my chest.

I ducked, barely avoiding my skull being singed.

"You're powerless," Dirodotus said. "Just like that girl—"

"*Just shut the hell up!*"

My power oozing, I ground my wrench against the rooftop, unleashing a quartet of monstrous lightning streaks.

Even my foe appeared surprised.

Zap! ZapZap! Zap!

One by one, the bolts lashed against his limbs, fused with his gears, forcing his body to jerk wildly as the electricity surged through his innards.

Weakened, Dirodotus collapsed onto his knee.

"Impossible . . ." he growled, unable to budge an inch. "How could this be . . . ?"

With my saliva pouring, I charged toward the android, my finishing blow begging to be let loose.

One problem after another.

Hurdle after hurdle.

I just could never get a break.

Always, my life was a slope, going further and further down.

My mistakes.

My shortcomings.

My fear to march onward.

All of that has led me to horrors no one could ever dream of. But because of those horrors, I was forced to finally do something about being pathetic. I was teased with the future where I could be happy, never knowing that such a smile could truly exist.

Until now.

I've already overcome one mountain. And while this next one wasn't what I was expecting, I'll clear it all the same. I won't stay in one spot anymore. I'll keep rising and rising, until I become for someone else what Avella was—is—to me.

And you can be damn sure I'll make you remember her too.

"You're finished!" I roared.

He didn't even flinch.

"Likewise."

Like a vulture, one of his minions swooped down to suddenly hoist me into the air, wrapping its arms around my neck.

My Tool cried as it tumbled onto the rooftop, away from my grasp.

Collected, Dirodotus straightened himself, his injuries still less than par.

"I told you when we first began," he said, "and I will say it again: You are but a hatchling in this paradigm. Your moves are sloppy. Your strategies are weak. And above all else, you are unable to look past the glimmer. The moment you saw even a speck of victory, you chased after it like a dog."

A grimness cast over him like the Reaper's cloak.

"And dogs are easy to trap."

I struggled to free myself but to no avail.

"I hit you, dammit," I said. "Why the hell aren't you hurt!?"

"I can assure you: my injuries exist. However, they aren't as fatal as you had hoped. Thankfully, I was able to prepare myself for that lightning of yours."

"There's no way you could've seen it coming! Unless . . ."

Recollection, back to my emotional outburst in that room.

"You understand now, don't you?" Dirodotus asked. "What you're fighting is not the core of the hive mind but the collective whole itself. With every second, I learn of my enemies so that when the time comes, I'll know just how to end them. Through death comes wisdom."

He pointed his palm at me.

"I'm going to kill you now, Jeremy Mitchell. Rejoice, for you will be one of the first to experience this universe's rebirth."

It can't end like this. I refuse to let it end like this!

But effort could only get me so far, the iron arms around my throat refusing to budge.

Until I avenge her . . . Until I make you remember the name Avella Summers, I'm not going down!

Dirodotus's hand heated up.

I still have my fight!

Fate agreed.

BANG!

A shot heard 'round the galaxies.

Instantly, the robot behind me had its head blown off, loosening its grip to release me back to the ground.

Next thing I knew, someone carried me to a safe distance away from Dirodotus, along with giving me back my wrench.

From me, confusion at first, until I looked ahead to spot a flame-haired girl with a sniper rifle guarding my twelve.

"R-Ruby?" I asked.

"You're the Selector?" she countered, her tone stern. "Looks like you still have much growing to do."

You look as old as me, though.

"Sentinel Codex," Dirodotus announced, unperturbed by the newcomer. "What a pleasant surprise."

"Sentinel"? Then she's . . .

"Tell me," the android said, "what brings you to our little clash?"

"Had to change up the rhythm of the fight," Codex answered. "Otherwise, I would've went braindead taking out your men all night."

"From my calculations, you have, indeed, been active. But with each one of my soldiers destroyed, I only gain the stronger hand against you. You can stop my time all you'd like; it won't help you."

"Is that so?" The Sentinel smirked. "Wanna test that theory?"

"Hang on," I said, barely able to get off the ground. "He's mine."

"You can barely stand," Codex pointed out. "The best you can do right now is just sit there and rest. If it wasn't for me, you'd be dead already."

"I don't give a—"

"*Silence!*"

A voice lined with thorns.

"This is no time to be naïve," she said. "One misstep and the battle's over. Be smart about this. Otherwise, you'll just be putting the Selector name to shame."

As much as I wanted to argue, I couldn't deny the logic; that, and my HP bar, if I had one, was teetering on zero.

"I . . . I understand," I admitted.

Codex nodded, then shifted to a battle-ready stance.

"Don't fear, Selector," she told me. "I *will* protect you."

Dirodotus curled his fingers.

"We'll see about that."

"Run, you guys!"

A trio of child scrambled through the chaos, the talons of Death scraping against the flesh all around them.

But children could only make it so far.

The one furthest back jammed her toes against a jagged brick, causing her to topple onto the ground.

The other two stopped.

"Hotaru!" one of them cried.

Just then, an iron juggernaut plummeted to the children, its missiles peeking through its turrets.

The little girl quivered.

"Mama . . . Papa . . ."

The invader took aim.

Shing!

A single swipe of the blade, and like a sheet of paper, the robot's body split in half, the corpse falling down.

And through the area's clearance came Sentinel Jax, who helped the girl to her feet.

"Take the alleyways, children," he instructed them. "As soon as you find the crowd, follow. It'll lead you to the HOMEs."

The little ones nodded, and after the girl had hugged her savior, they fled the scene to find safety.

Jax glanced around at the battlefield.

"Hopefully, this ends soon." A worrisome expression. "Hopefully, you're holding up, Jeremy."

BANG!

Codex took the shot, her aim steady.

His reflexes hasty, Dirodotus caught the bullet, a layer of red energy coating his hand. And as he squeezed, particles of the otherworldly ammunition sprinkled to his feet.

Quickly, the Sentinel played her next card.

She widened her eyes to the size of quarters, triggering the crimson glow of her irises, and like a newborn statue, Dirodotus's body froze in place.

Codex then dashed forward to deliver a roundhouse kick straight to the metal man's waist.

A firm hit; however, no damage given, Dirodotus's armor protected by scarlet energy that soaked in the attack.

The sniper sucked her teeth, annoyed.

In no time, the fiend broke through his cage, his movements returned to blast Codex away with his gust of boiling air.

She flew back but was quick to recover.

"You're all identical," Dirodotus said. "You follow the same passage, hoping that a difference will come. You can't expect another ending if you never stray from the beginning."

"Don't mind me," said Codex. "I'm just testing my theories."

From his backside, the metal man unloaded his volley of missiles.

"For a Sentinel, you are disappointing."

Codex whipped out her handgun.

"I'm just getting started!"

Pop! Pop! Pop! Pop!

With deadly precision, she knocked the rockets out of the air, forging jagged clouds of fire to pop off like fireworks.

And it was through the blistering flames that the android darted, his fists joined together to hammer down on the girl.

A narrow escape.

Codex lurched to the side, the gust of Dirodotus's miss toying with her hair, then pointed her handgun at the fiend's neck.

Pop!

Pop!

Pop!

Pop!

Pop!

The bullets whined delicately as they bounced off the zikranium.

Dirodotus glared,

an expression that Codex gladly returned.

I observed the battle closely, understanding just how different the Sentinel's level was from my own.

Maybe it was good that she benched me, I thought. *I'd only be holding her back. Besides, I needed to cool my head. As much as I hate the platinum bastard, I have to admit that he's right: emotions alone won't get me far.*

I clenched my teeth at the frustration taunting me.

There has to be something *I can do. I doubt I'll be able to throw those lightning bolts like earlier, but even so, I'm not just gonna sit here doing nothing.*

I watched and watched and watched;

watched as the bullets boosted like furious bumblebees;

watched as Codex landed her hits perfectly;

watched as that red glow protected Dirodotus.

Was that there when I fought him?

The moments flashed by like snapshots.

No. They weren't. Every time I hit him, I'd manage to break off some armor. It was only a little bit, but still. In that case, why can't she . . . ?

My gaze drifted to my Tool—to the Gemini Fragment that rang.

What aren't you telling me?

Another memory, fresh off the island:

"Veronica and I are standing right here with our Fragments, and Dirodotus is out there with the third one . . ."

Then, the prediction, uncoiling like a prey clawing out the spider's cocoon.

Maybe I am the only one who can do it.

Codex rolled clumsily to my position, just as I began to lift myself up.

"What do you think you're doing?" she asked me.

"Getting off the bench," I said. "I'd rather not keep the seat warm all night."

"Don't think that your resolve will get you far. As you are now, you'll only be holding me back."

"Right, right." The stale lecture didn't impress me. "Don't worry. I'm not fighting just on what I'm feeling. Not anymore. Besides, if we wanna win, you're gonna need me."

"Hoh~?" Codex raised an eyebrow. "Do tell, Selector."

Dirodotus dined upon his curiosity as he watched the pair converse in secrecy.

"No matter what plan you come up with, it won't make a difference," he told them. "Either way, you're finished."

They ignored him, engulfed in their own bubble.

"You're sure about this?" Codex asked. "Because if you're wrong, you're done for."

"I'm sure," I said. "Never been more sure in my life."

I'm not gonna doubt.

Not anymore.

My partner cocked her rifle.

"I thought you were wet behind the ears," she said, "but maybe Jax didn't waste his pick on you." She then sent her hardened focus to the enemy. "Let's do this, Selector!"

"Right!"

With firm confidence, I charged ahead, my wrench in my hand.

"They never learn," Dirodotus lamented.

He delivered his laser beams.

But before my bones could be pierced, I dodged, my sprint never faltering.

"It will be the same every time, Jeremy Mitchell!" the metal man growled. "Whether you're close or at a distance, you'll never overcome me! You're merely too small!"

Maybe I am too small.

But that's what helping hands are for—to give you that boost!

I shuffled to the side, giving Codex a clear view of our opponent.

"Ma'am!"

"No need to tell me!"

The Sentinel crafted that glow of her irises, forcing all manners of time to halt within Dirodotus.

The opening now clear, I rushed to his front, and with the might of a thousand rams, I bashed my Tool into his chest, damaging the armor.

His Fragment didn't absorb the impact.

I knew it.

BANG!

Codex let fly her rifle's bullet, connecting it to the android's fresh wound, and like a cannonball, the ammunition ripped clean through his body.

It worked! I thought, ecstatic.

Dirodotus's reality returned to normal, just in time for him to quiver against the breaking of his armor.

"What . . . ?" he uttered, confused.

"I thought it was odd," I said. "Sentinel Codex couldn't make a scratch, even though she was way more experienced than me. Was it dumb luck that I managed to hurt you?

"No. It was fate."

I pointed my Tool at him.

"We're connected, you and I, and I intend to make full use of that fact."

"So, you've found a hole in my shield," Dirodotus said. "Don't think for a second that you've gained the upper hand. Sentinel Codex can only stop time in intervals. In that case, the solution is simple."

He armed himself with his machine gun barrels.

"I'll just kill you before she can stop me again!"

The muzzles flashed as his firearms vibrated, the bullets salivating for my blood.

I sprinted around the rooftop's edge, praying and praying that I could outspeed.

In came the lesser robots, gliding downward to swoop me up once again.

BANG!

BANG!

Easy kills,

Codex's rifle roaring as it took down my pursuers.

"I'll cover you in the meantime!" she bellowed. "Just try to stay alive!"

My determination swelled. "Right!"

"Why won't you understand?" Dirodotus boosted to my side. "You're inferior!"

He went to knee my guts, only to be blocked as I brought up my wrench.

"We can change," I said. "That's what life's all about!"

"Nonsense!"

Wham!

My chin ached as he cracked his knuckles against it.

"You can't control destiny!"

The metal man went to fire his lasers.

He froze in place.

"Now, Selector!" Codex roared.

As swift as a hawk, I dashed to Dirodotus's backside, slamming my Tool against his thigh.

BANG!

Another perfect shot, mutilating the zikranium of his leg.

The fiend returned to normal with a slight limp.

One more!

I went to strike again, only to soar back as Dirodotus hammered his fist into the ground, releasing a wave of scarlet energy.

"Try all you want," he said. "Destroy every single one of my circuits. You can't stop the revolution."

"We can, and we will!" Codex declared, pulling the trigger.

BANG!

As expected, this shot shredded nothing.

"What?" Dirodotus asked. "Giving up that strategy already?"

"No." The Sentinel grinned. "Just enhancing it."

My strength unmatched, I hurled my Tool into the back of Dirotodus's skull, forcing his head to lurch forward.

A counter, he swiped with his arm, only to miss as I ducked.

I then bashed his knee in.

Enraged, the android grabbed me by the hoodie and flung me away, nearly tossing me off the rooftop.

But before he could go on the offensive, his movements paused.

"This is it!" Codex bellowed. "Go for a vital spot and we win!"

She already had her pupil glued to her rifle's scope.

Obeying, I cocked back my wrench and charged ahead.

This ends now, I thought. *Nowhere left for you to run!*

Fate disagreed.

In one smooth motion, Dirodotus broke free of his imprisonment, leaping high into the air, over my head.

And like a sun withering into nothing, my certainty of a brighter tomorrow vanished without trace.

Y-You're kidding . . .

Again?

"You faltered, Sentinel Codex," the man of metal said. "And because of your weakness, this boy will die."

Codex grimaced.

Dirodotus aimed his palm.

"Don't do it!" the Sentinel cried.

No hesitation.

Pew!

Next, a hot, hot pain, as if puddles of lava coursed through my chest, stripping away my power to even breathe.

Weakly, I fell to my knees, and as I brushed my fingers against my wound, I found a warm, liquidy substance stick to my skin.

Blood.

A lot of blood.

I gave the Sentinel one last confused look before crumpling onto my face.

Beyond that, only blackness.

"Selector!"

Destiny's Outlier

Her pupils quivered.

Her breaths staggered.

A million thoughts raced through her mind, all centered around the lifeless boy lying in a pool of his blood.

Klank! the metal man's feet howled as he landed back on the rooftop.

"Bottom of the trash," he said. "Now, you're where you belong."

Enmity exploded from the Sentinel.

"*You bastard!*" Codex roared.

But before she could aim her rifle, Dirodotus's minions flanked her on either side, holding her in place.

"Get off of me!"

She went to freeze their time.

No luck, the back of her eyes squealing as a sharp pain pierced through.

So instead, she went to speak with the core of the hive mind.

"How did you escape my time lock?" Codex asked. "I don't care if you have a Gemini Fragment; you shouldn't have been able to break free that easily."

"I'll tell you what I told that now-dead boy," Dirodotus said. "With death comes wisdom. Every time you killed one of my soldiers, I noticed how much weaker your ability became. First, ten seconds. Then, nine and a half. Then nine. You're not capable of being consistent. You may be a Sentinel, but you're still eons behind your predecessors. And because of that incompetence, you killed the only hope you had."

Codex scrunched her face, frustrated.

Dirodotus approached the corpse, eyeing the hole in the chest as his soles dipped into the viscous carmine.

"You're worthless, Jeremy Mitchell," he said. "If you had just listened to me, you wouldn't have died as a failure. Instead, you starved yourself to move forward, only to find out that not everyone can afford to take the next step."

The android bent over and picked up the Gemini Tool.

"But fear not, for through your death, I will ensure that harmony flourishes through the starways. No more wars. No more suffering. Only peace."

The wrench in his grasp, Dirodotus strolled to the edge of the skyscraper, where he then lifted the Tool. And like a ripple in the sea, a ring of violet pulsated from his hand, stretching out to the corners of the empire.

Instantly, his minions halted their actions, setting their gazes upon his divinity.

Soon after and the people of Zekra did the same, causing everything—the chaos, the despair—to wilt away, leaving only a stillness that burrowed into the battlefield.

All focus paid respect to the supposed savior.

Dirodotus studied his audience.

"Zekra . . . is finished. Your hero is dead."

The majority of the masses basked in the confusion; however, a select few understood the message full and well, understood the meaning behind the bloodstained wrench.

Luna covered her mouth in horror, whereas Jax furrowed his brow.

"I taught him, as I will teach all of you," Dirodotus said, "that you cannot change what destiny has already laid before us. As it stands now, the universe is a miserable heap of needless suffering. Wars left and right. Blood shed at the cost of egotistical ideals. But I will end such trivialness, for fate wills it so. I will reset reality and bring harmony to all."

His gaze darkened.

"I'm going to kill all of you."

Some raised their weapons in protest, but Dirodotus implored them to stand down.

"I am now in possession of two Gemini Fragments," he said. "This alone makes me stronger than any Sentinel standing. I suggest you surrender now and accept your deaths. Otherwise, you'll end up a failure just like Jeremy Mitchell."

A poison, uncertainty spread through the Zekrian forces—doubt that that promised tomorrow could still shine upon them, fueling their smiles.

But not all were affected.

"You're wrong," she whispered. A little louder. "You're wrong!"

The attention spun to the girl of strawberry hair, her eyes glassy.

"Wrong?" Dirodotus asked. "In what regard?"

"Jeremy's not dead," she assured. "Just you wait. He's gonna get you right now. It'll be the comeback of the century! The perfect hero move!"

They waited.

Nothing.

"Come on, Jeremy!" Ruby said. "What are you waiting for? Take him out!"

Still, nothing.

"No one's coming, little girl," Dirodotus said. "I watched the light leave his eyes as I punched a hole through his spine. There are no heroes; only the strong who strive and those foolish enough to oppose them."

Ruby broke into a sob.

"But . . . he can't be gone . . ." she wept. "Please, get him, Jeremy. I'm begging you! Don't leave us!"

Luna held her companion close, fighting back her own tears.

And just like that, hope became nothing more than a feeble concept.

"Jeremy. Jeremy. Jeremy!"

He lay on the bed of grass, among the plethora of lilies, his eyes shut as he breathed as gently as a sleeping cub.

"Looks like you're not waking up," she said. "Even so, I hope you can hear me. I'm happy that I get to see you again, but you shouldn't be here. Not yet. You still have so many things to do, so many lives to help. You're just getting started, and I know that you'll be able to accomplish so much, Jeremy. You'll make the world a better place for everyone, friend and foe."

She brushed her fingers against his face.

"I'll help you out a little. I'll give you what I've learned. That way, you won't have to feel alone in this fight. Then again, you haven't been alone for a while now, have you? You've met so many amazing people, and I'm sure that you've helped each one of them, whether you realized it or not."

She smiled.

"So, get back up. Go back to them, because right now, they need you more than ever. Give them the hope they need, just like how you did for me."

A kiss on the cheek.

"Be the hero I know you to be.

"Be the man I fell in love with."

Whoosh!

A fracture in actuality.

A sneer of disobedience to the so-called Ruler of Destiny.

Awe glazed over Sentinel Codex as she witnessed the phenomenon, as the trails of azure light glistened over the fallen Selector, swirling around his body like a whirlpool of luminance.

Dirodotus, too, shifted his attention, steering away from his declaration of victory.

Bit by bit, the gape in the boy's chest closed, the flesh returning as the blood soaked back into his veins. Then came his irises, tossing away that hue of ash for the lively ink they were known for.

Before long, motion returned to his body, his fingers curling like a newborn's.

Take it easy.
Take it nice and slow.

Slowly, my senses came back to me, as if I had just awoken from a thousand-year slumber.

Touch—the cool rooftop pressing against my cheek.

Sound—a placidity too warped with anticipation.

Smell—the wisps of war-torn smoke mixed with the family members forcibly taken.

I was . . . here.

I sat myself up, examining my torso.

"Huh?" I asked myself. "But didn't I . . . ?"

Nearby, the Sentinel of Time smiled.

"Selector," she said, "you're something else."

The metal man, on the other hand, grimaced.

"What are you, Jeremy Mitchell?" he growled. "You're no mere human. No matter what I do, you just refuse to get out of my way. Why go so far for this sorry excuse for a universe?"

I didn't flinch.

"Because this is home, to me and to the people I care about. And I'll be damned if I'm gonna let you take that away because of your ideals."

Ruby grinned. "That's what I'm talking about! You kick his ass, Jeremy!"

The others shared similar sentiments.

"Your enthusiasm is misplaced." Dirodotus waved around my wrench. "So long as I have this, I *am* the strongest in existence. No one can stop me now."

Codex sucked in a hefty breath.

This isn't the time to wait for a miracle, she thought. *If I can't turn the tide of the battle, then I have no room being a Sentinel!*

Despite the pain gnawing the back of her eyeballs, she triggered the crimson glow of her irises, freezing the android in his place.

"Go, Selector!" she roared, blood dripping down her sockets like tears. "Take back what's yours!"

I'm on it!

My steps steady, I dashed to the metal man, ripping my Tool out of his grasp.

At my touch, the Fragment hummed, now back home.

Then, with fear that even an atom could overshadow, I leapt off the rooftop, gliding through the air.

Why did I jump? I wondered. *If this was the past me, I would've been terrified to even grab my wrench, let alone throw myself off a building.*

Well, the answer's simple:

With the speed of a liger, my Guardian of cherry hair boosted through the wind to catch me.

I have people to back me up!

In her arms, I went, until Ruby dropped me off at a nearby rooftop. After releasing me did she wipe her eyes.

"You're a jerkface," she joked, "making a girl worried."

I smiled.

Before long, the rest of my comrades—no, my friends—joined me, all ready to rain hell on the army of bots.

"You never cease to surprise me," Jax said, grinning.

Veronica perched her scythe on her shoulder. "I didn't know you were so wild, Jeremy."

We faced forward, and I glared at Dirodotus, who had returned to his normal state.

"This is where we belong," I told him, "and I refuse to give that up!"

My friends buzzed with their defiance.

"That hope of yours . . ." A madman, Dirodotus thrust towards me, yanking me away by the collar of my hoodie. ". . . it's bothering me."

"Jeremy!" Luna howled.

"Luna," Jax said, "don't worry about him." Not a shred of doubt lingered in his character. "He'll win."

Of course, the cherry blossom accepted such hope, brandishing her blade to dart back into the raging battlefield.

Again with the rooftop, Dirodotus tossing me to the other end.

"Your persistence is irritating," he growled. "Why do you insist on protecting this reality? You understand its imperfections. You know how unjust so many lives have it. Why promote the cycle?"

"Because the cycle can change," I answered.

Ruby flung her spear, piercing the skull of multiple bots.

However, just before the weapon could lose momentum, Amy appeared beside it via kunai, grabbing the gold to toss back to the warrior of cherry hair.

"No, the universe isn't perfect, and I don't think it'll ever be. That harmony that you want so bad, it'll never come; at least, not for a *very* long time."

With the flat of her foot, Veronica kicked an iron soldier high into the air, where an arrow went drilling into its temple, extinguishing its life.

"But the universe wasn't meant to be perfect, because perfect never lasts. Instead, it was meant to change. Evolve."

Luna thrust her sword into the ground, letting Jennifer fire her bullets into the steel, ricocheting them into the torsos of the metal puppets.

"The universe is going in the right direction, and while it may take a thousand lifetimes to get where it needs to be, I'll stand by it. Always."

For the first time, Dirodotus's anger surpassed a subtle hint, his rage rattling the space around us.

"Jeremy Mitchell . . ." he whispered. "*You couldn't be more naïve!* The galaxies are a disgrace, and I refuse to let those like my master suffer any longer!"

The energy of his Fragment sizzled around him like a vapor, filling the gaps where he had taken damage.

Dirodotus joined his hands together, fusing them to forge an intricate cannon.

"I'm going to end this silly fantasy of yours!" he howled.

Particles of scarlet gathered around his new weapon until, as fierce as a beast of myth, a massive beam of energy burst forth, determined to morph me into a pile of ash.

I shot my wrench to my front, holding back the attack as a layer of lightning poured from my own Fragment. My arms quivered as I tried to fend off what felt like a wildebeest.

That's right.

The way things are now, not everything will go the right way. But if we can take even one step towards the light, then nothing can defeat us!

I'm the same.

Little by little, I'm starting to realize just how much you all have helped shape me.

The Cherry Blossom, proving that with a fine heart, I, too, could protect.

The Rose, patting me on the back as she let me know there were more of my kind.

The man of the heavens, admiring my potential before I ever knew I had any.

And above all else, my own light, guiding me before she even dared guide herself.

You all did so much for me.

You saw my worth when I couldn't bring myself to look for it.

So, allow me to return the favor.

Allow me to assure you that you didn't waste your time on me!

Suddenly, a ghost-like hand laid itself on my own, and as I looked, I found none other than my light drifting beside me. She spoke not a single word, but her smile offered more than a thousand syllables:

"You're not alone. Not anymore."

I'll always have you all right beside me.

"Surrender, Jeremy Mitchell!" Dirodotus ordered. "Know your place!"

"I do know my place," I barked back. "That's why I'm standing here!"

My power bottomless, I flicked my wrench upward, deflecting the scarlet ray into the night sky.

"I'm going to end you, Jeremy!"

"That's my line!"

My Fragment howled with valiance, ringing through the battleground, and like a beast tearing through the boundaries of its legend, my ultimate weapon came to fruition: Atom by atom, the crimson of Dirodotus's attack morphed into traces of sapphire, strands of electricity snapping excitedly throughout.

Then arrived the final form, magnificence blessing the entirety of the empire.

In the midst of the anarchy, in the midst of blood spilling onto the ground of glass, the warriors found themselves lost, if only for a moment, gazing at—admiring—the spectacle lustering at the center of their empire:

A ferocious, wingless dragon, soaring into the heavens, grander than any planet, livelier than any army. The body danced with fresh lightning as the orb-like eyes basked in magenta. Its rumbles forced the debris to tremble, tested the structures still standing. Respect, the beast demanded, growling into the core of their conceivable actuality.

Ruby smiled at the creation.

"Told ya: the perfect hero move."

The metal man gaped.

"Impossible . . ." he whispered. "You're nothing . .
. You're supposed to be *nothing!*"

"Just because I'm nothing"—I swung down my
wrench—"doesn't mean I can't become something!"

Raaaaaaah!

On my command, the dragon nosedived to my enemy,
and with a valiant roar, it unhinged its jaw wide, already tasting
the android in his entirety.

Zaaaap!

Dirodotus wailed in pain as the mounds of lightning
piled atop him, scorching his being from surface to heart. The
zikranium burned white hot, peeling off to melt in the endless
shreds of electricity. Next went his arm, disintegrating into the
sapphire void. Then went his leg, vanishing to leave only
pieces of circuitry behind.

Finally, his chest burst open, and like a lone sunbird,
the scarlet Gemini Fragment erupted free, withstanding the
pressure of my ultimate move to tumble the metal man's front.

Once the beast had its fill, the dragon dissipated,
already waiting for its future summon.

One by one, right in the heat of battle, the iron minions
dropped to the arena's floor, their eyes dulling to gray as
lifelessness clung to their figures.

At first, the Zekrians didn't know what to make of the
change.

But as they realized the placidity slowly forming, the
quietness that their empire craved to enjoy, they rejoiced, their
victory casting proudly over their heads.

Ruby hugged her fellow Guardians close.

"We did it!" she cheered, beaming.

And they smiled back, thankful that they would get to
appreciate their home for another day.

It's . . . over? I asked. *We won?*

Not quite,

as I noticed the slightest movements from Dirodotus's battered body.

With one arm still intact, he struggled to curl his fingers around the scarlet Fragment nearby. But no matter hard he pushed, he could never reach.

I approached him, retrieving the gemstone to slip into my own pocket.

Our eyes then met, his flickering with hues of soft white.

"It's over, Dirodotus," I said. "You lose."

The android chuckled weakly.

"It's not over," he promised. "It will never be over. So long as the universe remains as it is, there will always be another Dirodotus—another visionary. The ideals may differ, but the core of the argument will not falter: not everyone deserves to live, Jeremy Mitchell.

"You may have won today, but this was merely a stepping stone in the grander scheme. You won't always be on top—fate wills it so."

"Then I'll just have to deny fate, because as long as I'm around, I'll protect everyone who deserves help."

The metal man analyzed the boy's gaze, finding not a single shred of fiction, not a single shred of distance strolled into a pipe dream.

Another chuckle.

"I'd like to see just how far you make it, Jeremy Mitchell," Dirodotus admitted. "Because in the end, you will lose. In the end—"

Wham!

No more patience.

My mercy hollow, I smashed my wrench into the side of his skull, tearing the android's head clean off his body.

His remains went still.

That . . . was for Avella.

24

The Father I
Never Acknowledged

Several hours later . . .

Calmness.
Stillness.
A certain kind of serenity, flourishing across the empire like roses budding in the meadow. The flames still loose quit with their monstrous outbursts, instead murmuring their inviting crackles that, to the surviving citizens, couldn't have been a more pleasing melody. The remaining Zekrians roamed the streets, analyzing the demise that the iron invaders had crafted:

homes with nothing more than the back door;
hospitals littered with lifeless bodies;
that stench of death, tainting the air like an abusive
lover.

But as grim as the nightmare seemed, the Zekrians never lowered their chins. Rather than wallowing in the pain of today, they looked forward to the doors of tomorrow, where joy would be sure to bless their actuality.

Among the ruins ambled Codex, displeased by the outcome.

We should've been better, she thought. *Protectors of the universe? We could barely even protect our own home.*

But before she could drown in the guilt, a boat drifted over to save her, its form that of her brilliant younger sister.

"Big sis!" Tetra sang from behind, squeezing Codex with the warmest of hugs.

The elder sister returned the gesture. "Tetra."

Once they let go of one another, Codex studied her little sis from head to toe.

"You're not hurt, are you?" she asked, worried. She noticed the cut marks on Tetra's shins. "Ah! Your legs!"

"It's no big deal, big sis," Tetra assured. "Just some mean robots was all."

"No big deal? You're gonna start bleeding again. Medkits. We need medkits! We need—"

A hush, as the girl of the petals embraced her loved one once more.

"I'll be okay, sister," she promised. "Besides, if I was really hurt"—she squeezed with every ounce of her affection—"I couldn't hug you this hard!"

Although still hesitant, Codex caved in, patting her dear sister kindly on the head.

"I really do love you," she said.

"That makes two of us!" Tetra replied, grinning.

Tired.

What I'd give for a nap right now.

I relaxed atop the rooftop's edge, my mind shuffling through the million and one thoughts as the limitless night sky called to me with her dress of stars.

I sure am a long way from finishing that worksheet.

"Mind if I have a seat?"

The new arrival, my Sentinel waited patiently beside me, his expression hinting he hadn't slept in several centuries.

"Go for it," I told him.

"Thanks."

Jax plopped himself down, joining me in admiring the heavens.

"So," he said, "how are you feeling?"

"I'm starving," I answered. "Apparently, making a dragon really works up an appetite."

"You really surprised me, there. I don't think even I could've made something like that when I was your age. I suppose you were more than ready for this life. Sorry for doubting you."

"Eh, I don't blame you. I mean, I used to be that kid who'd pee his pants just from *thinking* about talking to strangers. Heck, part of me still has that mentality."

I encased myself in a blanket of melancholy.

"This world—or rather, these worlds—can be terrifying. One minute, you're chatting it up with your best friend; the next, you're wondering when you'll be visiting her grave."

"I'm sorry, Jeremy," Jax said softly. "She was a good person. Always tenacious. Always aspiring for greater heights. Whenever she'd come here to train, she'd never back down. Had Avella survived, she would've made for a fine Sentinel."

"No point talking about the *if*s. We'd just be wasting our time."

"Okay. Then I'll share with you a certainty. Would you like to know what Avella talked about whenever I saw her?"

"What? How she was born for this?" I guessed.

"No." Jax smiled. "She talked about *you*, Jeremy. She would beg Persephone to let her tell you that she was a Selector, and whenever she was on the brink of defeat, she would remind herself that everything she did was for you, for Rosaria. She cared about all of you. She loved all of you, whether or not you realized it."

I realized it, I admitted. *I just didn't think it could be real enough to exist.*

A sigh slipped past my lips.

Oh, to not be confident. Really does bite you in the butt, doesn't it?

To my gloom, Jax brandished his sincerity.

"Jeremy," he said, "I've been watching over you for a long time now, and I understand that life hasn't been easy for you.

"I know how hard it's been since your parents passed away, and if I may . . . I'm sorry we couldn't pull them out of the car in time. Luna, Ruby, and Faith, they were so young, so inexperienced. Saving you was their top priority.

"So, please, don't blame them for the death of your mother and father. If you must blame someone, then blame me."

His guilt stripped the shades of his face.

"If only I had trained them better . . . If only I had taught them how to be stronger . . . I truly am sorry, Jeremy."

"I don't blame them for my parents' deaths," I explained. "I don't blame you either, Jax."

"Then, who do you blame?" my Sentinel asked, surprised.

"Myself. Er, I used to. Not anymore, though."

For the first time, I let the ink of my soul spell out the words.

"I used to think that bad things happened because God wanted to punish me. I thought so lowly of myself that I genuinely believed that even He hated me, that even He wanted to give me pain.

"But now I realize that I was never being punished for being me. On the contrary, I think that I was supposed to learn. Isn't that what life is all about? Taking the lessons given so that you become a better you every single day?"

"And what did you learn, Jeremy?" Jax asked.

"That life is hard," I told him. "That the path we're given will never be clean; there'll always be the bumps, the craters. There will be loss. There will be pain. There will be tears. But that's okay, because with each hill we climb, we get just a little bit stronger. Being rough around the edges is nothing to be ashamed of; however, staying rough is. We have to keep moving forward; that way, we can prove to the ones we lost along the way that they didn't waste their time on us."

The Sentinel merely gazed at his successor, appreciating the wings that had sprouted from his back—the wings that he had visualized since that fateful night.

"Is that so?" Jax asked.

The boy nodded.

"You really have changed since our first meeting, Jeremy Mitchell."

"That reminds me," I said, "I have a question for you."

"Go for it."

"Why did you choose me as your Selector? Your element is Light, right? I don't know if you'd noticed, but until today, I was anything but that. My biggest dream was to blow my brains out, for Pete's sake."

"A simple answer." My Sentinel smiled. "Because you're a cupcake."

I chuckled. "A cupcake?"

"Hear me out. Think of a cupcake filled with cream. You have the outer layer, which can be rather thin, right? But then you have the cream, which is so potent and rich that you can't help but remember it.

"You're the same, Jeremy. Your outer layer is nothing but darkness, yes; but beneath those shadows lie light of such vigor that logic may not recognize it."

My awe glimmered.

"I'm . . . that amazing?"

"Indeed, you are," Jax said. "That is why I chose you, Jeremy Mitchell, to take my place once the time comes. There is not a shred of doubt in my mind that with you as the new

Sentinel of Light, we may bring to fruition that future of harmony that Dirodotus longed for."

I think I should go about this slowly. I'm just now beginning to find my own peace, after all.

"Plus," Jax said, "I have to make sure I teach you well. Otherwise, Athello won't let me hear the end of it."

"The Reality one, right?" I asked.

"The very one. He's also someone who wanted you as a Selector.

That's news to me.

"I'm sure you've already noticed," Jax said, "but your connection to reality is different from most. You can bring what your mind conjures into our objective universe. You are only the second person to possess more than one element of the universe. Impressive, indeed."

I could already feel the headache coming.

"I think I'm just gonna stick with the one element for now," I said.

My Sentinel chuckled.

"Fine by me."

Then came the end of our melody, signaled by the Time girl appearing behind us.

"Selector," she said, "the STS is ready. It's time to go."

"Already?" Jax asked.

"Time sure does fly," I said.

"Was that a pun?"

"You tell me."

My Sentinel grinned. "Either way, I'm glad I got to talk with you, Jeremy."

"Likewise," I said, lifting myself up.

He did the same.

"The guy who got rid of my monsters." I outstretched my fist. "I won't be forgetting you, Jax."

"I didn't do anything, Jeremy." He tapped his knuckles against mine. "I merely gave you the path. *You're* the one who followed."

We smiled.

"Be seeing you, Jax."

"Be seeing you, Jeremy. Take care."

With that, I parted ways with the man from the heavens and followed Codex, passing through the empire's streets to end up back in the subway station.

On the railway, the shuttle housed my Guardians, along with Veronica and her own.

Through the window, Ruby beamed at me, waving.

I waved back.

Also present were Persephone and Avella's little sister, Rosaria.

As I approached, Persephone wrapped her arms around me.

"We can't thank you enough," she said.

"D-Don't mention it," I uttered, nervous as could be.

Baby steps.

The young woman brought her lips to my ear and whispered, "I can see why she adored you."

I blushed.

Really tiny baby steps.

The focus then latched onto the little one.

"What'll happen to her?" I asked.

"She was the only survivor of Veltrix's attack," Codex explained. "Unfortunately, we can't find any other members of her family. More than likely, we'll have to send her to an orphanage on Earth. I doubt any Zekrian would accept her given they don't know much of you humans."

Rosaria accepted this fate, silent. But I could see it in her demeanor—that hope that a better road would clear before her, that the light at the end of the tunnel would become so radiant it'd be blinding.

I'll give you that light, just like your sister did for me.

"Could she live with me?" I asked.

Rosaria's happiness slid to her sleeve.

"I don't see why not," Codex said. "But will that be okay?"

"Yeah. My aunt and uncle are always nagging me to spend more money, anyway."

Except for that door fiasco.

I crouched down to match Rosaria's height.

"How 'bout it? I'm not the most social guy, but I'll try my best!"

Her answer: a warm hug.

"Thank you," she said.

"Don't mention it."

And so, after bidding the Sentinels farewell, I led Rosaria by the hand into the STS, where the greetings piled on like mountains of lilies.

"The hero of the universe has arrived!" Ruby cheered.

"I don't think I'm all that," I said.

Nonetheless, Luna played along as she approached the front console.

"Where to, hero?" she asked.

I smiled.

"Home."

The New Usual

Four months later . . .

Eyelids, heavy.
Motivation, groggy.
Fatigue, more clingy than a one-night stand.
I awoke atop my couch, the cushions dragging me down as if I sunk through quick sand. Nearby, the blinds of my living room greeted me, waving in the rays of the sun that begged to lend me a hug.
Past my lips, a yawn slipped by.
That seals that deal, I thought. *Sleeping is overrated. I went to bed early, so why . . .* Another yawn. *Why am I so tired?*
I pushed my blanket off, then sat up to do some light stretches.
Well, either way, I feel refreshed. Gonna make finishing that worksheet easy as cake.
That's a saying.
. . . I think.
The routine called to me, and I answered:
First, the bathroom, where I washed my face and brushed my teeth; and as I gazed back at my reflection, at those lively ink-black irises, I couldn't help but smile.
Today'll be a good one.

However, Lady Life apparently wanted to test me, for as I moved on to the next area—the kitchen—I reached an impasse: an empty fridge.

"No milk, huh?" I said. "Good chance to get some groceries while we're at it."

Then, another thought:

I wonder if she'll want to come with.

Through the hallway, I strolled, opening the door into my (now old) bedroom.

On the other side, the sweet little girl had already begun her morning, buried in her blanket as she read from the pages of a novel.

Upon my entrance, however, her focus shifted, followed smoothly by a smile.

"Jeremy," she said.

"Good morning, Rosaria," I replied. "Already awake, huh?"

"Mm." She gestured to her read. "I started this last night but couldn't wait to finish it."

"The total opposite of your sister. She'd stay up till the sun came back."

The little Summer smirked, smug.

"A mission I shall gladly partake in."

"Let's . . . Let's not do that," I suggested. "Before she lectures me in my dreams."

Rosaria giggled.

Back to the topic.

"So," I said, "wanna come with me to the store? Gotta get some groceries."

My roommate shut the covers of her novel.

"I'd love to."

* * *

Hmm . . .

Hmmmm . . .

Hmmmmmm . . .

"Jeremy . . ." Rosaria said beside me. "I don't think it's that serious."

I studied the cartons of milk in my hands, analyzing them closer than an officer would analyze a crime scene.

"I humbly disagree," I argued. "This just doesn't make sense."

Both appeared identical, yet the one on the right cost a dollar more.

"What . . . Just what am I missing?"

"Did you read the nutrition thing?" Rosaria asked.

"I skimmed. And before you ask: no, that was not a pun."

My partner in crime chuckled.

"Jeremy?"

I sliced my theories short as I found the girl of thunder yellow approaching us.

"Veronica," I said.

"Hello~," she sang back. Next, a wave to the little Summer. "Hi, Rosaria!"

Rosaria bowed. "Hello."

"What brings you here?" I asked the newcomer.

"Mom's having a picnic today," Veronica answered. "Gonna go watch the cherry blossoms."

"Ah, that's right. They're supposed to be pretty in bloom right now."

"I've been wanting to watch them for a while. If you want, you can join us. You can even invite Luna and the others."

I sighed. "I'd love to, but if I don't finish that packet for Ms. Diamond, she's gonna kill me."

"You didn't strike me as someone who procrastinates."

"Jeremy got a new game," Rosaria explained. "He's been glued to the TV for days."

"Time well spent," I tried to argue. "Those achievements aren't gonna pop themselves."

"Well, good luck with that," Veronica said. "Who knows? I might even snag that number one spot from you this time around."

I grinned. "Bring it on. I ain't afraid."

* * *

"It's not a date."

"It's a date."

"It's not a date."

"It's a date."

We faced our reflection in the bathroom mirror, my fingers struggling to adjust my tie as Rosaria gave her brilliant insight.

"We're just hanging out," I told her.

"That's what they all say," she pointed out. "Face it, mister: you're going on a date! And I must say, I approve!"

"Why, thank you very much, Miss Rosaria," I said. "It's not a date in the slightest, but I appreciate the support."

My roommate didn't let up.

"You'll see," she said. "You'll be getting the butterflies in no time."

Highly doubtful considering who it is I'm going out with.

Right on cue, a series of knocks erupted from the front door.

"She's here," I announced.

Together, Rosaria and I headed to the entrance, and upon pulling the door open, all reason fled from my mind like a flock of doves, leaving behind only a single word in its nest—beautiful.

Adorable, she was, that teenage girl of cherry-red hair dressed in her usual outfit, with the addition of cat-like traits—painted-on whiskers, a dot on her nose, and fluffy ears clipped onto her head. The strawberry on top: a lovely rose pinned to her hair.

I blushed. "H-Hi."

Rosaria smirked.

Our visitor beamed. "Yo-ho!"

Instantly, my awe settled down.

Right.

This is not a normal girl.

"Hey, Ruby," I tried again.

"How goes it?" she asked. "Hiya, Rosaria!"

My roommate bowed her head. "Good evening."

Back to me: "Ya ready, Jeremy?"

"Yeah." I joined Ruby on the porch, turning to face Rosaria. "I'll be back by ten. Don't stay up too late reading."

"Gotcha," she replied.

"Still need something to eat?"

"We just had dinner."

"Okay. What about—"

"Just get going!" Rosaria already started to close the door. "Enjoy your date!"

"I told you, it's not a—"

My message split apart as I noticed the girl of the cherries blushing, causing my own cheeks to heat up.

My roommate snickered.

"Have fun, you two!" she told us. "I'll be fine."

I nodded, my confidence brewing.

"You got it."

With that, Rosaria shut the door, leaving my Guardian and I stranded on the front porch.

"So," I said, "got any ideas on where we should go?"

Ruby rubbed her chin, before the epiphany struck down like lightning.

"Ah!" she rang. "How 'bout the park?"

The night sky glistened from every inch, the stars dazzling as happily as diamonds as Ruby and I strolled through the serene park grounds. No other occupants took up space, as if the two of us had entered our own planet.

"Mind if I ask you something?" I poked.

"Shoot," Ruby encouraged.

"How come you look like a cat?"

"Oh, this?" She gestured towards her furry ears and whiskers. "Apparently, boys find it erotic when they see cosplay like this, or so I hear." She nudged my shoulder and winked. "So, how 'bout it? Have the hormones started kicking in? Wanna 'accidentally' tackle me onto the grass?"

When will the blushing stop?

"No!" I protested. "No, I don't want to do that!"

Ruby snickered.

"I'll admit, though," I said, "you do look cute."

Her joy soared to the ceiling of the galaxy.

"Oh, you~!" she sang. "Quite the charmer!"

"Just speaking the truth."

We took a couple more steps.

"Mind if I ask *you* something?" she poked.

"Go for it."

"How do you feel? Er, how have you been feeling? Ya know, after saving the universe and all?"

"I don't think I saved the *universe*," I argued. "You're giving me too much credit."

"You kiddin' me? Those robots were gonna wipe us all out. Good thing we had your super dragon on our side."

I smiled shyly.

Still don't know how I managed that one.

I then set my gaze on my hand.

"I guess I feel . . . different."

"Wow~," Ruby said. "Thanks, Mr. Descriptive. Really got me there."

"Let me elaborate."

The record of my life spun.

"I never really felt anything before I met you guys," I admitted. "I just went with life, went with the flow. Nothing really excited me. Aside from Avella, nothing really made me wanna stay alive.

"But now, I have this purpose. I know what I wanna do, where I wanna be. There's finally something I can strive towards."

My happiness hugged me close.

"I like this feeling."

And I like watching you have that feeling.

"Ruby?" I asked, curious of her gaze.

"Oh, nothing! Nothing!" she said. "I was just thinking that there was another feeling you could have."

I raised an eyebrow.

"Apparently," she explained, "if you close your eyes and think *really* hard, you can bring yourself to your heart. There, even your happiness can't compete."

"Really?" I shut my eyes. "I wouldn't mind trying that!"

Again, she stared, this sensation in her chest refusing to calm.

"Just like that," Ruby said. "You just gotta concentrate."

Her cheeks red, she brought her lips close to the boy's cheek.

"How long should I do it for?" he asked.

"Just a little longer," she whispered.

Choo~

A soft caress, right on my cheek.

I flinched.

And as I reopened my eyes, as I studied my Guardian, she couldn't have been more embarrassed.

"R-Ruby?" I stuttered.

"Thank you," she said softly, "for saving me."

I rubbed my face.

"I couldn't have beaten Scar without you," I guessed.

"That's not what I'm talking about."

Before we could nudge this conversation along, though, Ruby shut her eyes and leaned forward, puckering her lips.

"Ruby? What are you doing?"

"I saw it in a movie," she told me. "This is the part where you push your lips against mine."

Kissing, I was not prepared for.

Not. In. The. Slightest.

"How about next time?" I suggested.

"It has to be this time," Ruby insisted.

"I promise, Ruby, I'll give you a kiss next time."

My Guardian grimaced. "Jeremy, I want my kiss *now*."

"B-But . . . we have a bunch of time to do it."

She pushed her hand to the side, summoning her beloved spear.

"Ruby? What are you gonna do with that?"

"Give me my kiss *now,* Jeremy!" she growled.

I took a step back.

Then another.

Then another.

Before I knew it, I was bolting in the opposite direction.

She chased me like a yandere.

"Jeremy Mitchell!" Ruby roared. "You give me my kiss!"

"We can talk about this, Ruby!" I begged.

"No talk! Only Do!"

"*Ruby!*"

I ran for my life, while undeniably having the time of my life.

I Am
Not Alone

Here, I have been, surpassing twenty eons, waiting and waiting for even the smallest glimmer to call to me.

Yet, nothing changes.

Or at least, nothing was supposed to.

The foundation remains—the narrow cliffside, feeble enough that a single syllable could shatter the whole; the abyss stretching onward, hissing its venom as those grotesque hands squirm out, begging to stroke my peace.

But I can see it: the ripples, spiraling through the nothing, mutilating the laws designed to cage my sanity.

No more cold, as if my assurance flooded my veins like fresh flames.

No more chains, as if the metal had rusted beneath the weight of my purpose.

No more shadows weaving through the in-between, tainting my reality. Up above, the pockets of luminance peek through, their edges softened yet defined, meager yet suffice. They whisper to me, urging me to grab on, to join them in the Wonderful World.

But the darkness hisses back, ordering me to stay put, assuring me that this place is my rightful spot. This realm of limited possibilities is my home, my salvation.

And yet . . .

And yet, I can't help but be drawn to those rays of light. I can't help but want to hunger for their warmth, march for their grip.

They seem . . . familiar, like a passion you ignored out of frustration, only to come right back, ready to pick up the pieces you yourself scattered.

The shadows say different, imploring that such brilliance is an illusion, a facade of Lady Fate.

But I know better, because if such spectacles were mere imaginings, I wouldn't be able to swallow their fervor. I wouldn't be able to smile beneath their weight as if my parents kissed me on the cheek.

No.

This light is real.

It always was.

I just chose to ignore it, because nothing terrified me more than the unknown. The darkness, the solitude, they kept me company. They let me feel something. But now I know that I don't deserve such a sensation—this belief that sent chills down my existence.

I'm more than what I've been told.

I'm more than a husk waiting to be devoured.

The radiance knew that, and all this time, it was trying to tell me so, promising that I could be more than what I was.

I think this time, I'll listen.

This time, I'll accept these hands that reach down, delighted to hoist me up to where the rainbow sings, to where the ravens glide until the moonlight tucks them in.

I'll grab on, leaving this domain of my doubts and demons, betraying the horrors of my imagination.

Instead, I'll tag along with a new companion, one who cares for my well-being, one who understands the limitlessness of my potential.

I'm in your hands, Madame Hope.

And for your first gift, I say thank you from the bottom of my heart.

Thank you for the gift that reshaped my universe.

Thank you for the gift that toppled my understanding of me.

Thank you for the gift of realization—the promise that I am not alone.

Epilogue

Two years later . . .

Quietude roamed across the forest floor, lending her guidance: how the berries tumbled off the bushes; how the leaves swayed against the alpine towers of wood; how the critters played in the orchestra—the tweets of the blue birds and pitter patter of the dainty bundles of adorableness.

Amidst Mother Nature's playground, She crafted a placid lake, the water fine like glass, capable of reflecting perfectly the azure sky and marshmallow clouds.

However, she was not the only admirer, for another rested upon the aqua's edge, atop the fine blades of grass. A teenage girl, she was, build thin but not scrawny, short but not microscopic. Parts of her glistened with royalty—the luscious, unkempt hair flowing to her waist, greener than the finest piece of leaf; the vividness of her anime-sized eyes, yellow like delicious honey; the delicacy of her lightened skin. However, other aspects clung to a peasant-like feel—the raggedness of her T-shirt and shorts; the blotches of dirt and grime scattered across her body.

She spoke no words, her bell of curiosity rung as she studied the glass case in her palm, the center majestic as the scarlet gemstone hummed.

She knew not what the item wanted from her; only that it did long for *something*.

Her success?

Her failure?

Her strength?

She rummaged through the possibilities, the map of her mind expanding past lengths beyond the conceivable galaxy.

"You know, you shouldn't hold it out in the open like that."

Her eyes widened, the girl turned her head to the newcomer behind her: a teenage boy, his skin brown like coffee as spectacles shielded his irises black like ink. Dark, curly hair spread across his head's top, the hue similar to the light stubble decorating the lower half of his face. He wore the outfit of an onyx hoodie with dark shorts and red sneakers.

The boy smiled, and from that gesture, the girl's skin tingled with his immovable confidence.

"Not a lot of nice people in the universe," he told her.

He approached her side.

"Mind if I have a seat?"

The girl shook her head, allowing the boy to settle down beside her.

Soon enough, the girl's attention slid to the wrench buried in the loop of his shorts. A sapphire gem hummed in the metal, shining more brilliance than the most eager of suns.

"What's your name?" the boy asked.

"Pendra," the girl answered softly. "Pendra Unix."

"Pendra, huh? That's a pretty name." The boy held out his hand. "Nice to meet you, Pendra. I'm Jeremy."

The girl knew nothing of this visitor, nothing at all, and yet, she felt drawn to him, as if his very presence could erase the doubts and struggles of her inner-planets.

She shook his hand.

"So," the boy said, "what brings you out here, Pendra?"

"I like to come here and think," the girl said.

She gestured to her gem, her curiosity and confusion nowhere near empty.

"Yeah? Well, that's fine and all, but be careful about who you show that to. A lot of bad people would love to get their hands on that."

"What is it?"

"Sorry, but it's not my place to tell you. I'm still new at this myself, after all."

The girl raised an eyebrow.

"New at what?" she asked.

The boy grinned.

"You'll find out eventually. When the time is right."

Although not the answer she had hoped for, the girl accepted it nonetheless, sending her gaze back to the lake.

Silence.

Then, the beginning of the next chapter.

"So, Pendra . . ."

The girl turned once again to find the boy holding out his fist, his lips curled into a knucklehead smile.

". . . would you like to be friends?"